SPIDERWEB TRAIL

When Steve Ware came home to Verde County, proud of his new rank as a Ranger, Verde greybeards refused to treat him as anything but the cowboy who had worked on their outfits. As a Ranger, Ware couldn't fight back against their insults as he could have if he were still a cowboy; he could only wait for a chance to prove himself. The chance came unexpectedly soon, when Fyeback, the storekeeper, was mysteriously murdered. At the same time, Black Alec Pryde's highline gang was raiding, and Steve wondered if the murder and Black Alec's blows were connected. The trail was "tangled as a spiderweb", leading Ware and his fellow Ranger, "Bar Nothing Red" Ames, far from Verde County. It was a trail to make brave men hesitate, but Ware followed it . . .

SPIDERWEB TRAIL

Eugene Cunningham

GUNSMOKE

First published in the UK by Collins

This hardback edition 2008
by BBC Audiobooks Ltd
by arrangement with
Golden West Literary Agency

ISBN 978 1 405 68219 0

British Library Cataloguing in Publication Data available.

Printed and bound in Great Britain by
CPI Antony Rowe, Chippenham, Wiltshire

TO

MILDRED

In memory of Cap'n Tom Hickman's Guns

CONTENTS

I. 'Don't hurrah a Ranger'

FYEBACK's old store was almost crowded. Young Steve Ware looked grimly at the familiar faces about Sheriff Loren opposite him. At his elbow, working with pencil and tattered ledger, Fyeback kept his white head down and seemed not to hear Loren's lazy drawl. But the other men of Verde were grinning, or laughing outright. Ware was almost the only one in the place who found nothing funny in the sheriff's remarks. But, then, they were aimed at him.

'What've you done about Black Alec Pryde and his bunch?' Ware interrupted Loren. 'Of course, I've been away. But we did hear—I heard Captain Durell mention it in camp—that Black Alec's highliners rode right through Verde County. I'd call that downright impolite, Sheriff. But, of course, you're aiming to make Alec curse the day?'

Loren only grinned at the thrust. So did some of the others, ranchers, townsmen. It was no audience for a youngster, particularly one like Steve Ware, who as orphaned son of a one-cow nester had ridden for many of them. These graybeards saw him as the boy he had been in Verde County, not as an ambitious young Ranger private.

'You working the Pryde case?' Loren demanded anxiously. 'I mean, you aim to stick in our middlest and hang and rattle till you cuff that miscreant, Black Alec, and the last murdering man of his awful bunch? And does the State pay your board, or will you have to pay Mis' Flaherty's annual-per year rates out of your own pocket?'

The listeners laughed outright at that. Fyeback's round, pink face came up from the ledger. He caught

1

Ware's eye and slightly shook his head. Ware held his temper in check.

'I'm not on the Pryde gang,' he said evenly. 'There's a little bunch of fence-cutting trouble at Wind Mountain. Happened I had to come through Verde on the way.'

'Well, now, I am glad to hear that! You do' no' how you relieve my mind, Stephen F. Austin! I was scared the Governor had decided to suspend the *habeas corpus* and put in a Ranger to run the county. And I'd hate to have to give up the jail keys and my gun and badge and all, right now. I have got an important case just about worked up. I wouldn't want to mention it where a word'd get back to him, but Lige Fyeback has undoubtedly been selling crackers and cheese to minors. After hours, too. I'd hate to have you Rangers coming in and taking credit for all the work I done on that case.'

'Ah! Home with the lot of you!' Fyeback rumbled. 'And let Steve Ware alone, Dave. Don't hurrah a Ranger. Bad luck in Texas. They tell me that Steve's going to make one of the best, time he's seasoned. Give him time. He ain't been with Durell a year, yet. And reputations are built on luck, lots of cases.'

'Hurrah a—what?' Chick Graves drawled, from behind Loren.

He was a hulking, dark and sulky young man. Now, he stood with thumbs hooked in the belt of his leggings, looking contemptuously at Ware's Mexican *charro* outfit.

Ware sagged slightly on his box. One thing Captain Durell had impressed upon every man of X Company: A Ranger was not an ordinary man and could not act with the freedom of a cowboy—either for a friend or against an enemy. He must take risks and bear slurs as the common citizen need not, simply because he represented the whole Ranger Force. So, Ware kept his face blank and his green eyes narrow as he watched Chick Graves.

'A Ranger!' Chick grunted, then laughed. 'He goes down to roost in a Ranger camp and draw the best pay he ever seen in his life, for playing monte or stud with the rest of the loafing bunch. He collects him that Mex' rigout and fancy white-handled guns and a silver-trimmed saddle. Then he comes back here to strut and blow. But what's he done, this year he's been Ranger-ing? Anybody know? What's the whole Ranger Force done, for that matter? Alec Pryde and his bunch are still r:ding, I notice! Still cracking stores and banks and trains! Ranger! *Agghhh!*'

He turned and went lurching up the store. Fyeback shrugged, and even Sheriff Loren looked suddenly serious.

'Don't mind him,' the old storekeeper told Ware. 'He's soured on the world. Going to lose the G-Bar. What Old Chick got together, Young Chick couldn't keep. Outfit's plastered clean up the chimney. He can't borrow another dollar. And he always did hate your insides. You wouldn't knuckle to him just because he was rich and you wasn't.'

'That's right. Don't bother about Chick,' others of the men agreed, with real friendliness in their manner, now.

They began to go out. Ware looked at Fyeback and a corner of his hard mouth lifted.

'I know,' he said grimly. 'An officer can't hit the man he hates just because he hates him, the way a cowboy can. He has to lean clean backward to give that man a fair deal. But it's tough to do, sometimes. Well, how's everything? I certainly was glad to pick up that little reward for Joe Amargo and settle the last of what I owed you. And I'm glad to get back here, to say how much I appreciate that loan. If it hadn't been for you lending me the money for an outfit, I couldn't have got to Durell's camp in shape to enlist and——'

'Shoo!' Fyeback growled. 'Nothing a-tall. I don't make a slew of mistakes in my judgments. I knew your father. But I know his boy a sight better! And I'll tell you something right now, son: You've got it in you to be a great Ranger. Don't worry about climbing in the Force, or making a rep'. There's something in your head—I have noticed it working more than once!—different from what goes on in other folks' knots. Do'no' what you'd call it, exactly. But, seems like you see both ways from what you're looking at. As for nerve—well, you don't have to bother about owning that! Seems to run in the Ware blood not to worry about being hurt. Now——'

He halted in what was for him a tremendously long speech, to squint critically at the smallish, dark-tanned Ware.

'When you took Joe Amargo out of the middle of his whole tribe, was you scared a li'l' bit? Own up, if you was.'

'Why—I wondered if they'd make trouble. The bunch was yelling a lot and brandishing guns,' Ware said thoughtfully. 'I wondered if it would be common-sensible to wait and catch him where I could certainly pack him back to camp. But, I thought, that would look like the Rangers weakening, to the Amargos. Even if I got Joe, later, some of those boys would own notions; think that sometimes, anyway, they could buck a Ranger and make him take it. So I put the hooks to Rocket and he split the crowd and I rammed a gun against Joe's neck. I told 'em if they killed me it wouldn't take a posy off Joe's coffin.'

'But, was you scared?' Fyeback persisted, watching him.

'I never thought about it!' Ware confessed honestly. 'I was too busy in my one-track mind, worrying about the Amargos.'

'Well, run along! See you tomorrow. Don't bother about Chick, now. Not about Dave Loren, neither. Dave has got a sarcastic tongue and folks expect him to be a wit, and he knows it and don't disappoint 'em. But you know and I know that he's a fine officer, too. One day, he'll admit that you're a Ranger out of the old rock. He's just having fun with you, now.'

'I can stand him! Well, good night! And I don't have to tell you that, if ever I can do anything for you——'

'You don't,' Fyeback stopped him, slapping his shoulder.

Outside the store in moonless darkness, Ware moved on to the corner of the Gem Saloon, fifty yards upstreet from Fyeback's store. Men stood there in the dim light from the Gem. As Ware neared them, he heard Loren's complaining tone:

'So, peaceful as she's been, lately, I don't see what possessed the Governor and the Adjutant General to send Rangers into Verde. Tomorrow daylight I'm going to telegraph my protest, official. By Gemini! I do'no' but what I might vote Republican next election! It just makes my blood boil! Nothing to do here that'd justify taking a valuable, important man like Cap'n Ware off big jobs to send him to Verde!'

Ware grinned very slightly, knowing that Loren had seen him or heard him. But the few minutes of talk with wise, kindly old Fyeback had proofed him against Loren's tongue. Even against Chick Graves. He thought of the G-Bar, which in Old Chick Graves' efficient lifetime had been the finest ranch in all that great scope of country. He shook his head. If *he* had been left that outfit, there would be no mortgage on it today! Idly, he wondered who would take it over from the bank. Whoever got it would be a lucky man.

A thought came, pleasant, yet so funny that he laughed softly. All a young Ranger need do was spin a county loop and drop it over Black Alec Pryde; the rewards offered by banks and express companies and cities and counties would buy the G-Bar and allow running expenses for a half-dozen calamity-years! If that young Ranger could add Doggy Tibb and one or two others of the murdering, robbing gang to his bag——

He was within six feet of Loren and the others, now. Loren said indignantly:

'Nothing ever does happen, here in Verde, so——'

Ware spun like a cat, to face downstreet. He leaned

a little, poised on his toes, listening strainedly. But that hoarse, agonized cry did not come again, from the direction of Fyeback's.

He went forward like a cat. Unlike most cowboys, he could *run*! And now he covered the fifty yards to the store as if racing for a prize. Behind him, he could hear Loren and the others clattering on the plank sidewalk.

When he reached the shadow of the wooden awning of the store he paused automatically outside the shaft of light from the open door. Something moved at the corner of the building, a shadow among shadows. Ware's hand snapped up and under his *charro* jacket, came out with the Colt from left-hand holster. But the man whipped around the building and when Ware streaked to the corner and looked down the store wall, there was no sign of him. The hammering of feet on planks came closer. Ware turned and went to the door, to stare along the crowded length of the store, toward Fyeback's desk.

A foot, with a patch of gray pants-leg above it, showed on the floor by the desk. Ware slid inside with gun up and went noiselessly to look down upon his friend. Fyeback sprawled face down beside his chair. His buttonless vest was pulled half off. Projecting from his back was the staghorn handle of a hunting knife. Blood from the wound was beginning to make a puddle on the warped planks of the floor.

'What's it?' Sheriff Loren demanded from the door. Then, coming in and down the aisle to peer past Ware, he breathed harshly through his teeth. 'My—lord!'

Ware looked at the great iron safe beyond the desk. It was open. The cash drawer was pulled out—and empty.

II. *'He murdered Lige!'*

WARE shook his head impatiently when Sheriff Loren asked what he had heard to send him running here. He pushed through the gathering crowd and went outside to that corner around which the dark figure had jumped. The murderer? It must have been. But, even now, he could not see what else a man could have done, in the circumstances, but what he had done.

'Might have hit him, of course,' he told himself. 'But, not knowing that anything was wrong, I couldn't shoot him. But it's hell! Just hell.'

He squatted and flicked a match on his thumbnail, then leaned to look at the ground lighted by its tiny flame. There was a deep print where the man's left foot had struck, no heel showing. The right foot, also, had touched without more than smudging earth with the heel. Ware struck another match and worked along the store until those running prints disappeared in a jumble of tracks, of wagon tires, hoofs, boots.

Ware straightened and looked around. But the darkness had nothing to tell him where that man had gone. He went at his silent, catlike gait back to the front of the store. Loren and some others were in the door, silhouetted against the light.

'I reckon I saw the killer,' Ware told the Sheriff. 'As I ran up, somebody jumped around the corner. You can see his tracks going down the store, a yard between 'em. But the back is so cut up it'll take daylight to show where his horse was, or which way he headed out.'

'Uh-huh,' Loren answered absently. 'Well, you stick here a few minutes, will you, Ware? I'll be back right soon and—you stick around.'

He stepped out to the edge of the veranda and went off in the dark. Ware looked after him, then at the men

7

in the door. They let him pass, then followed him inside. Fyeback had been moved to the top of a cleared counter, covered with a new blanket from stock.

'Where's the knife?' Ware asked, looking around the quiet group. 'Loren take it out of him?'

'Uh—yeh,' McDonald of the Spade drawled. 'He's got it with him. It—well, it give him a notion, Steve.'

He looked Ware in the eye and very slightly shook his gray head. To Ware, it seemed that he was warning against more talk of the knife. Ware shrugged his shoulders and began to poke about the store, looking at the drawers pulled out, the open safe, the rifled cash drawer, the floor about the desk. McDonald crowded up close to him and muttered in his ear:

'Just a few of us know; but that knife looked like one I watched Chick Graves dickering with Lige Fyeback about, today! Dave's gone quiet to see if Chick's still in town. Going to bring him here, if he is. But if the whole bunch took a notion it was Chick done this——'

He touched his neck significantly. Ware stiffened.

'I'd be the first to pull on the rope!' he said savagely. then caught himself. 'I mean, I'd feel like it.'

He pictured Chick Graves as he had known him for so many years, swaggering among poorer people because of Old Chick's money, unpopular except with certain cowboys and townsmen who borrowed from him and drank at his expense. He was still trying to see Chick slipping up the store to drive that hunting knife into Fyeback's heart, snatch the money from the safe, when Loren pushed Chick into the store and hustled him back.

'I tell you I don't know a thing about it!' Chick said angrily, but with a shaky note in his voice. 'I went up to Mis' Flaherty's and I was just going to bed when I heard somebody running outside, saying something about Fyeback's. I lay there a few minutes, but finally I got up and—and you met me.'

He looked around the intent faces, some grim, some

puzzled, until he found Ware. Then he took a quick step forward.

'I suppose this is some of your Rangering!' he snarled. 'All puffed up over that Mex' rigging and the name of Ranger! And you try to hang something like this on me and——'

Loren thrust out a big hand and jerked him back. Ware continued to stare blankly at him.

'Mac,' Loren called to the Spade owner, 'tell Chick howcome he's got some questions to answer. Remember, Chick, nobody's accused you of murder, yet. But you have got some talking to do. You better talk it straight and loud. Ne' mind all this being insulted account I'm telling you to talk. You know, this happens to be a case of murder. Low-down murder!'

'He was buying that bowie knife from Lige this morning. Before dinner, it was,' McDonald said quietly, staring at Chick. 'It's out of a new bunch Lige had just got in. Different in some ways from any others Lige had ever stocked. Chick talked awful anxious to get one. And—he hefted it and he kind of laughed and he asked Lige if it wouldn't kill a man!'

Something like a concerted gasp ran around the tense listeners. Loren looked at them, at Chick, then at McDonald. Quickly he snapped:

'Ne' mind that. Might mean something; might not mean a thing. I might've said as much if I'd picked up one. Question is——'

'I never bought it!' Chick cried harshly. 'I never bought it, at all. Lige wanted five dollars apiece for his knives and I couldn't—I wouldn't pay no such price for a bowie. He put it back in the case. I never bought it and I never killed him. Why would I want to kill him? I didn't like him special, but I never had a thing in the world against him.'

'Might've been three-four thousand, or more, in that safe,' the sheriff remarked grimly. 'Everybody knows how Lige banked for the whole town, the whole neighborhood. You been hubbing hell on the mortgage, Chick. Everybody knows that, too! Plenty reason for killing Lige, if he had to be killed to clean out the safe, no matter if you never had reason to kill him otherwise.'

Chick swore furiously, brokenly. Then he seemed to find Ware again by an accident of roving eyes.

'This is some of your damn Rangering!' he yelled. 'You——'

'Ah, shut up!' a rasping voice commanded from the watchers. 'No doubting you slunk in and up behind Lige and knifed him! Mac seen you buying the very knife—from the very man you damn well knowed you was going to murder with it!'

It was Blaser, stock-trader, a dark, hook-nosed man. All the Verde country knew his hair-trigger temper, Ware as well as any, because of an incident in his boyhood.

'He murdered Lige!' Blaser snarled to the other men. 'Hanging's too good for him! But it'll do! Hell with the courts——'

Ware moved as if a spring had been released in him. He covered the two yards between him and Blaser and had the trader by an arm before any other there had shifted position.

'Easy, Blaser,' he drawled. 'No wonder they call you "Half-Cock." Dave Loren hasn't finished his questions and it's impolite to break in like this. And I'm not even started asking a question or two I've got in mind. It would spoil my sleep if I didn't get a chance to ask 'em. I'm hell on my sleep, when I can get it. Take it easy, now. Don't fight the bits.'

Blaser jerked angrily at Ware's hand. Loren moved a little, taking Chick with him, so that they were backed into the alcove beside the desk. He looked steadily at the trader.

'That's awful good advice Steve's giving you. Lots of things have happened to me, in my time as sheriff. But nobody's ever got a prisoner off me, or beat a Verde

man out of his right to trial in court. I don't expect to
be alive after that does happen. Let him go, Steve. He's
thought it over—now.'

Ware stepped back, folding his arms. Under the
fringed, embroidered *charro* jacket twin Colts hung in
a skelton holster-vest. His hands were just over the
butts, ready for the cross-arm draw practiced for so
many hours in camp and on the trail. He watched the
hook-nosed Blaser closely, while speaking to Loren:

'If you can't think of anything else special,' he said,
'I'd like to take a look at the soles of Chick's boots. You
see, Lige's killer tramped in the blood on the floor
some when he was robbing the safe.'

'You certainly can't find blood on my boots,' Chick
growled. 'Because there never was none on 'em—no way
to get it on 'em. But if you think you can try a smart
trick——'

'It could have been walked off, if any was on 'em,'
Loren told Ware doubtfully. 'But we'll look. Let's see,
Chick.'

He and Ware and McDonald stared at the worn soles
of the boots turned up for inspection. Ware shrugged.

'No sign of it. Of course, it might have been walked
off. But dry leather soaks up blood like a sponge, Sheriff. I remember Cap' Durell took a boot that didn't
show a bit of blood, and he soaked it in water, and a
doctor found blood in the water. But I've got another
notion. You see, one time or another, I worked in the
store here a little bit, years back. I know Lige's ways.
Chick, have you been running a bill with Lige?'

'Not for a long time,' Chick answered sullenly, sus-
piciously. 'He cut me off six-eight months ago.'

'That's bad. For if he'd been carrying you, there'd
be a line in the book about you buying a knife, and no
entry would mean you hadn't bought a knife. I'd swear
to that! For if Lige ever forgot anything, I don't know
what it could have been. But cash—a sale for cash——'

He moved quickly to a counter and began to get out
of it a group of hunting knives. The men watched curi-

ously, Loren and Chick no less than the others, while he placed them on the glass top. He came back to the desk, then.

'Eleven of 'em, so he probably bought a dozen,' he said. 'I can find out, though, from his entries.'

He opened the old ledger in which Fyeback had kept his simple accounts, studied the later pages, and nodded.

'Dozen it was. They got here yesterday. One's gone, then.'

'You can't say from that, or anything else, that *I* bought it!' Chick snarled at him. 'You——'

Ware lifted a blank face from the book to look at Loren.

'You checked the knife that killed Lige against the knives yonder? It's the knife missing out of the dozen?'

'Yeh. Mac thought it was the one he'd seen Chick and Lige dickering on. So I looked and—yeh, it's the knife.'

'Then you won't have to soak Chick's boots, unless you just think they need the water. For Lige sold that knife, for cash, to a man riding a Plumb Bob horse.'

'I seen that horse!' a townsman cried, crowding forward. 'Just before supper tonight. Hitched back of the Gem. Heavy bay, it was, with one white stocking. I took a extry look account of the Plumb Bob being clean over in the Devil's River country and I wondered how he got to Verde.'

Loren came to look at the scrawl, the last entry on the page. He read it aloud:

'Knife, Lot 627, Traveler, Plumb Bob horse, $5.00 Cash.'

'You see!' Chick said shakily. 'I never bought the knife, like I told you! But you was hell on hanging this on me. You——'

Then he looked at Ware, swallowed, made an awkward shoulder movement. His face was red and embarrassed.

'Steve, I—I owe you for this. I reckon I've got kind of sour on the world and I ain't much on talking. But if there's ever a chance of doing something——'

'Shoo!' Ware drawled grinning. 'I have given a good deal of thought to your special insides, Chick. I have spent a good deal of time figuring out what's wrong with you. But somehow I couldn't see you, not offhand and easy, driving a knife into anybody's back. And, too, it's a Ranger's job to catch the right man, not just catch any man. Now, we've got work to do!'

III. *'I'm after wolf!'*

In the Gem the bartender gave them a description of the man who had ridden the Plumb Bob bay. But Ware scowled grimly and eyed Loren's impassive face.

'Thickset man,' he repeated. 'Yellowy hair; wasn't brown-eyed, so he must have had blue or gray eyes. Not tall, but not short, either! Old gray or light brown coat—hard to tell, account of the dust on it. No scars. Loren! I've seen that man! Yes, sir. I've seen him a hundred times in my life and I'll bet you he had a different name—his own real name, too—every time.'

'Saw him when you run up to the store—couple minutes after he murdered Lige,' the sheriff reminded him dryly. 'I ain't blaming you for not shooting, Steve, but it does look like, kind of, you could've grabbed him.'

'Would've been nice,' Ware admitted, with a calm that belied his feeling. 'But I don't shoot or grab at a man unless I know what I want him for. Suppose you'll be getting out a posse, soon as it's light?'

'Reckon. No use trying anything tonight. That Plumb Bob horse could've headed just about any old way.'

Ware nodded and went out of the Gem. His horse was in the stable behind Flaherty's hotel. He had nothing in the room hired the day before. His few possessions were in the *alforjas*, the carven leather saddle pockets. So he got his big black out of a stall, saddled quickly,

and pushed his sleek Winchester carbine into its scabbard. He swung into the saddle and turned Rocket out
of the yard, rode to the Gem, and drew in.

Men were still at the long bar, talking about the murder. He could see them by stooping slightly and looking under the wooden awning. Other men were in the
shadows of the saloon porch. Their talk, too, was of the
storekeeper's death. Some of it was loud, angry talk.
But as Ware looked for Sheriff Loren, listening for his
voice, a man moved under the awning. The yellow light
from the doorway silhouetted his gaunt shape and
hooked nose. He lurched out toward Ware—Blaser, the
trader.

'Now, I got something to say to you!' he snarled. 'I
don't take pawing and shoving off nobody, much less
off a smart Aleck kid that's swelled up account he
slipped into the Rangers. You——'

'Blaser,' Ware said drawlingly, 'once when I was about
eleven you took after me, because you claimed I scared
your team on purpose. You never hit me with that black-
snake whip of yours or, maybe, I'd have forgot to be
scared and just thought of how mad I was. But, tonight,
I'm not eleven; and I'm not a bit scared; and my word
to you is—don't crowd me!'

'Crowd you?' Blaser yelled furiously. 'I'll——'

He snatched at Ware's leg with long, steely hand,
dragging at him, grunting incoherently. Ware's knees
pressed Rocket's barrel and the big black spun around
the trader. Ware leaned and slid right arm around
Blaser's neck, hooked fingers in belt, and sent Rocket
surging forward. Blaser struck furiously at him, but the
clamping arm shut off his breath and only his toes
touched ground. Rocket swerved to left and right and
back again with touch of the reins upon his neck. Blaser's wild blows stopped; he clawed at Ware's arm and
gasped.

'There you go!' Ware told him at last. 'Now see how
you feel about preaching necktie parties—for the wrong
man!'

Rocket charged the veranda where men leaned to peer into the darkness; brought up short as Ware let Blaser go with a jerk that sent the trader reeling against the watchers' feet.

'What's the trouble?' Loren called sharply from behind Ware.

'No trouble,' Ware answered him calmly. 'Just Blaser. But if he goes off half-cocked again, in my direction, I'm going to have to forget about being a Ranger and come down on him like a brick off the top shelf. Sheriff, I'm going over to the Siding and send a telegram to Captain Durell about this. He and Lige Fyeback were boys together, Rangers together, you know. Want me to take any wires for you?'

'I reckon not. If I decide to do any wiring, one of the boys in the office can ride over to Dub Murdock with 'em. The more I think about this murder, Steve, the easier it looks. It's a lot like bear hunting, this chasing criminals: you young fellows don't feel like you're earning your pay unless you do a lot of hightailing up and down, kicking up the dust. Us old has-beens, we have got to have up our li'l' bit of strength. So we don't take out on the tracks unless we're crowded. We get up on a hogback and watch the country for our bear. It's got to be the right hogback, of course! But when Brother Bear *do* come by—overcoats! Bearskin overcoats!'

'Verde your hogback?' Ware asked politely, when some of the men behind Loren laughed. 'Murderer coming by the office door where you can kill him out of your chair?'

'About that—though I'll take a posse out tomorrow when it's light, and I reckon you'll want to ride with us? No-o, our man won't likely come back this way. But, you see he's going along figuring that all he's got to do is make a li'l' distance and forget he ever was in Verde. But that's because he do'no' Lige Fyeback's way of writing down who he sold knives to. *He* won't guess that we know about him and his Plumb Bob horse; about him buying the knife that murdered Lige.'

Ware grunted and lifted his reins. Blaser had disappeared—into the saloon, Ware thought.

'Likely you're right,' he admitted to Loren. 'But I'm still going to send Durell the wire.'

He pushed Rocket on the seven miles of road to the Siding, where the telegraph operator was a boyhood friend. Dub Murdock, hammered up at his mother's house in the tiny village, swore incredulously at Ware's news, then unlocked the office to send a wire to Captain Durell. They sat smoking, talking, for two hours, until a reply came. It was typically brief; Durell had more than the frontiersman's usual gift for curt, but explicit speech:

> TAKE AFTER FYEBACK MURDERER ASK LOREN IF ANY OF PRYDE GANG LATELY REPORTED VERDE NEIGHBORHOOD STORE ROBBERIES THEIR SPECIALTY CONSULT FUGITIVE LIST FOR DESCRIPTIONS PRYDE, TIBB, ANDRESS, BURR I HAVE NOTIFIED SHERIFFS TEN SURROUNDING COUNTIES WATCH FOR PLUMB BOB BAY AND RIDER KEEP IN TOUCH WITH ME BY WIRE OFTEN AS POSSIBLE

Ware drew a long, slow breath and Dub Murdock looked curiously at him.

'First big lone wolfing?' he asked.

'You could call it that. Not so big, if it's just a bad cowboy on a Plumb Bob horse. But if it should be one of Pryde's bunch, cutting his sign might mean just anything. It's more than that, though, Dub. You see, I never had folks all around me, like most of you. After Pa died, I was all by myself. Lige Fyeback was like—like an uncle, say; nicest kind of old uncle. He was all alone, too, same as I was. Maybe that made him feel kindly toward me; maybe it was just his way to act like he did. Anyhow, the man who hit him was hitting me—hard. And I damn well mean to show him that!'

'And—you know, Steve, I just think you'll about do it!' Dub Murdock grunted. 'There always was something different about you; you could find stock the rest of us couldn't; you could see into the insides of tricks and puzzles—Boy! Damn' if I don't put my stack on your number! And Chick Graves actually admitted he owed you something . . . Steve, you've already done plenty in Verde, doing that! Knowing Chick, making him own up you saved his neck looks bigger to me than saving him, neat, the way you worked it.'

'Loren would have thought of checking up in the book. He does tickle me on raw places a lot, Loren, but he's a good officer. He would have cleared Chick.'

'Yeh! Yeh, cleared him after Chick was swinging to a limb!' Dub Murdock scoffed. 'There's enough of Blaser's kind in Verde to hoolihan the town on a proposition like that. You stopped Blaser's talk at just the right time, the only time, way it looks to me. Maybe just in time to save Loren's bacon, too. Well, I reckon you'll ride with the posse?'

'Start with that,' Ware said briefly, staring at the wall. 'It's like Loren said—maybe! This man may not guess that his horse brand was left big and plain in the store. He may be riding the running walk right now, feeling safe. Maybe one of the sheriffs Durell has notified is already jerking him right out of the middle of that peaceful notion. But—maybe not! I'll act on the idea that I'm the only one after him. I—— So long, Dub! Certainly good to wawa with you again. Be seeing you— I reckon.'

Rocket made the return trip as quickly as he had gone to the Siding, but without straining. When he stopped before the little courthouse in Verde he was ready, Ware knew, for a day of traveling that no ordinary horse could do, however fresh.

There were lights in the little stone building. Horses

stamped in the darkness under the oaks beyond the courthouse. Men talked in the sheriff's office. Ware swung down, stretched, and went with *clink-clump* of spur chain and boot heel, to the door. Loren and McDonald of the Spade and other ranchers and townsman were at the pine table which served the sheriff as desk. Loren was writing painfully and talking to Bugs Lydell, one-time Wrench cowboy, now wearing a deputy's shield. He looked up at Ware and sighed gustily.

'Well!' he cried. 'Now, we're all right. I swear, Steve! Didn't realize how much we leaned on you till you rode off. But now everything's going to be all right. Hear from Durell? What'd he 'low?'

Ware came over to the table and put out his telegram. Loren and the men about him bent to read.

'Uh-huh,' Loren said at last. 'Well, Bugs, reckon this saves you a ride to the Siding. I was going to get out wires to the sheriff's around, Steve. Durell saved Verde County some money on telegrams and we won't forget it. Now, we'll take a good look behind the store as soon as it's light, try to cut sign, and head out. This kind of boogers up your fence-cutting case at Wind Mountain, huh?'

Ware moved over to the wall, to squat and make a cigarette. He pushed back the bullion-trimmed sombrero from his eyes and watched Loren without expression.

'You got to follow orders, of course,' Loren went on gravely, while he rammed food and tobacco into his saddle pockets. 'But, Steve, if you do happen to run into any fence-cutters, it might be a pious idea to tote 'em in. Many a deer hunter, you know, he's filled the pot by taking cotton-tail rabbits when he couldn't get deer . . .'

Some of the listeners laughed. But not so many as had shown amusement the night before in Fyeback's, before the murder. Ware lighted his cigarette, drew in smoke, and nodded.

'I appreciate that advice,' he drawled through a smoke

cloud. 'I take it you wouldn't warn me this way, except you've put more cottontail than venison in the pot, in your time. But at the start, anyway, I won't bother rabbits. I'm after wolf!'

McDonald banged Loren on the back and laughed until the tears ran down his weathered face.

'I—I been waiting for somebody to come along—to hand you as good as you been giving out—all these years,' he told the sheriff. 'Reckon you better quit *trying* to hurrah a Ranger. Like Lige told you, it's bad luck.'

'What about the Pryde outfit?' Ware asked Loren. 'You had any news of 'em since last year, when they rode through Verde to stick up the train at Frayme?'

'Not a thing,' Loren snapped. 'This was no Pryde job. Of course, if Durell wants to sit off and read tea leaves and figure different, it's all right with me. But I reckon I know that gang's ways and marks as well as he does.'

IV. *'He rode fast'*

In the first gray light Ware and a half-dozen men particularly skilled in trailing worked around the back of Fyeback's store, stooping, calling to one another to pass judgment on a particular smudge in the marked earth. Slowly, they moved away from the jumbled tracks on a trail that each of the trackers had come to know as he might have known the face of a man studied, the shape of a hill long watched.

'A nervy son!' Bugs Lydell told Ware, with something like admiration in his snarl. 'Walked off after you jumped him and he got his horse. Walked up to right here; then he figured he could risk a li'l' trot——'

'Then a lope, yonder,' Ware said grimly, staring

ahead. 'I reckon we might as well get going, Sheriff! We can follow this out of the saddle, now.'

They trooped back to the courthouse and to hitch-racks along the street, to get horses. Ware rode over to the Flaherty back door. Mrs. Flaherty, looking more than usually huge in her wrapper, filled the kitchen doorway as he came up.

'Y'r lunch!' she said, holding out a big package wrapped in newspaper. 'We've been at the making of 'em since three, knowing they'd be wanted. A half-dol-lar, Steve—and may you be straddle of that dirty knifer's neck when you put y'r teeth into the first of them steaks! Luck to you, boy. He thought of you like you was his own. Go after that killer like Lige was y'r father!'

With growing light Ware and Bugs Lydell pushed ahead of the posse at the trot. The trail of the Plumb Bob horse led straight into the northwest, toward the county line, the trail of a fugitive pushing his mount at the fastest run the animal could make. So it went for three miles and more, then slowed for a half-mile to the running walk. But soon the murderer was at the gallop again.

A Wrench cowboy met them. He had seen nothing, heard nothing. He turned to go with the posse. Two miles more and Ware pulled in Rocket and jerked his arm up, then waved to indicate the west. The Plumb Bob horse had been turned from the county road into the mesquite and greasewood of the caliche flat. He and Bugs Lydell separated slightly and rode through the straggling vegetation of the mesa, slidng down into shallow arroyos, topping out on the far bank of each dry watercourse, finding deep scars where the murderer's horse had slid and climbed before them, then going as much by instinct as by actual sight of marks, on hard stretches between arroyos.

The going became harder as they drew toward the harsh crests of the Verdes. On stony ground the trail was seen less and less frequently. At last Ware and Lydell looked at each other hopelessly and shrugged. Loren rode up to them, lifted himself in the stirrups, and looked all around.

'Scatter out,' he grunted. 'Go right and left and straight ahead. Looks like our only chance to cut it again.'

But Ware held Rocket motionless when the posse moved. He stared at the hills ahead; at the rough scope of semi-desert to westward. The mountains . . . Somehow, you always expected a hunted man to head for the mountains. But the Verdes were very rough. Traveling would be slow. What a man might gain in cover he would surely lose in speed. And—if this murderer were a man of the cold nerve Bugs Lydell had suspected, he might also be a man of some shrewdness; he might guess that the mountains would be thought his natural goal.

'Hey, Steve!' Loren yelled across fifty yards. 'Ware! Oh-h, Stephen F. Austin Ware! General Stephen F. Austin Ware! Come on! I would hate for this li'l' bitsy bunch of ours to jump a desperate man, without the Rangers along.'

'I'm not siding you any farther!' Ware yelled back. 'But if I loop him, I'll wire you. Let you clean up your books.'

'All right, then. I'll move my blankets down to the Siding as soon's I get back. I'll sleep with Dub Murdock, so's not to miss the telegram. Might even get married there and raise a family, to pass the time while I'm waiting. So long, General!'

Long after the posse had shrunk in the distance to dark beads rolling across a yellow floor, Ware smoked and studied the country, trying to put himself into the skin of that cool and merciless killer. But the difficulty was, he had no good, clear picture of the man. One type might do one thing—must do it! Another sort must move in quite another fashion.

He put Loren and his edged tongue out of mind. He thought of Lige Fyeback. What was it the old man had said—that had been echoed by Dub Murdock? That he

owned an ability not common, to see backward and forward from what he looked at? Something like that. He
knew that he had it; it was instinctive in him to think
backward to the reason behind actions he saw—murders,
for instance. He had done it in the Amargo case, facing
what seemed a causeless killing. José Amargo was in a
death cell today, because of that ability.

'But all I can see in this case, looking backward, is
a high cloud of dust,' he thought irritably. 'Going on,
without a track to follow, is just blind guesswork.'

Then he shrugged and gathered up the reins. Rocket
moved westward. For it·seemed to Ware that the mountains to northward would be well covered by Loren's
posse. The south might well be chosen by a man running from a crime. But the west offered even more to a
fugitive; there were places like the Little Bend, like
Satan Land beyond the Bend; wild stretches where men
were the savage creatures to be dreaded, more than
wolves and rattlesnakes.

Something after midday he met a cowboy hunting
strays, a cheerful young redhead from the Bug north
and east of the Verdes. They ate Mrs. Flaherty's sand-
wishes together and smoked and gossiped. Four years
before, Ware had ridden the Bug rough string for a
time and this stray-man, hearing his name, assured him
that his reputation was still green on the Bug. He had
heard nothing of the murder, nor had he met anyone
coming down from the hills.

'Of course, I been out two days,' he said, making his
cigarette where they hunkered beside the drowsing
horses. 'The country I been covering ain't popular with
travelers. I wouldn't be a speck surprised if Dave Loren
cuts that jigger's trail in the Verdes. If you'd wanted
to be in on the kill, you ought to've stayed with Loren.
That's a blood-hound for you; I rode on one posse with
him. You can learn all the tricks, siding him.'

Ware said nothing. The cowboy's insinuation that a
young Ranger should study an old sheriff was natural,
and the Bug man had stated it without thought.

'No use in everybody standing at one door,' he drawled. 'I might accidentally stumble over the hairpin, going west. *He* wasn't running on rails. He could head in any of three hundred and sixty ways, from that patch of hard ground where he killed his trail. You know the country west of this?'

'Far as Los Alamos. I was to Alamos last year with some horses. You might be right about that killer going west, at that. It's certainly a country you can lose yourself in; and a country where nobody much is going to ask your pedigree. Looky!'

He smoothed a patch of gray dust and with a greasewood twig sketched a map.

'Right here's where we squat. Nearest outfit's Eagan's 66, the Hooks. Kind of south and west, see? But due west is Ten-Sleep Norman's Lightning Rod. Salty outfits, both of 'em. Seems to me I heard that they don't love each other. Down on the River is Little Bend, about south of the Hooks. Olin, fattish man, runs a store there. He knows about anything you'd want to ask, about all the goings and comings between the Verdes and south of the River. But he ain't going to tell a thing he knows! Not Olin!'

Ware nodded, keeping his face blank. He knew of Olin from talk of Durell's. The captain had said about what this Bug man was saying. But, twice Olin had passed a quiet word to the Rangers which had resulted in capture of a much-wanted man. There was no point to remarking this, now.

'You can go on up the River from Olin's to a Mex' *plazita* they call Vado, account there's a ford there. Plenty wet stuff has gone both ways over that ford, too, if you can believe part of what you hear. From Vado, you can head kind of north and west past Two-Day Water in Satan Land and make for Carlos Smith's D-Bar-D beyond Three-Jag Hill, or—Capen's Open A. Me, I ain't a superstitioning man, but I still think I would pick the D-Bar-D . . .'

'Account of what? Superstition?'

'Well, Capen's got the name around Satan Land—and Los Alamos and south to La Piedra and beyond—of being a queer kind of jigger. Foreigner of some kind. He's got a big, fine house like one in town, all Turkey carpets and pianos and fixings like that. Sets down to dinner with white tablecloths and silver dishes and waiters in white coats—and what started out to be Capen Castle the Mex' around call "The House of Whispering Shadows" account they believe ghosts walk around the place. But—suit yourself! You can hit for Alamos from Capen's or Smiths, or from Piedra that's up the River from Vado.'

'Well, thanks for the map. I think I'll head for Olin's. It sounds like the kind of place my kind of man might hit for, if he knew about it. But that's the trouble: I don't know whether I'm trailing a hard-case cowboy with just one murder and robbery on his tally, or some real highliner.'

'Either way, you'll maybe wish you had tough old Dave Loren to side you, if you come up on this fellow,' the redhead said cheerfully. 'Dave is hell on wheels with his hardware——'

Ware's right hand snapped under his *charro* jacket, flashed out with the Colt from slanting left-hand holster, and, with what seemed no more than the snap of that motion, the .44 roared. As the cowboy gaped uncertainly, Ware came to his feet and took three long steps to look down upon the thrashing length of a huge diamond-back rattlesnake.

'Not so good,' he drawled solemnly. 'I aimed to crack him between the eyes, but I was 'way off—more than a sixteenth of an inch off.'

The cowboy came to stare. Then he grinned.

'Ex-cuse! I take back and eat what I said. But you didn't have the name, your time on the Bug, for being streaky lightning with the sixes, Ware. Rangering must have give you that. Loren never seen the day he could make a draw that fast. I never seen it; you just never had a gun out and—you was shooting.'

'Practice! Who's sheriff at Alamos?'

'Deputy name' Briggs is acting. Going to run for the job next election. Reckon he'll make it, too. Theo Ribaut, the county attorney, is backing him. If you want to know anything around Alamos, you go to Ribaut. If he ain't got some good reason for not telling you—or telling you the truth!—Ribaut will give the straight of it.'

Leaving the Bug man, Ware did not turn directly south, toward Olin's lonely store on the River. Instead, he worked a little westward in the direction of Eagan's 66. It was as he had said to the stray-man: not knowing whether he hunted a hard-case but inexperienced cowboy-turned-criminal, or a veteran *buscadero,* he was uncertain about the fugitive's movements.

'A tough cowboy thinking he'd left no trail might hit for the closest ranch and play chuckline rider,' he thought irritably. 'But a highliner would know the layout of the country from hearsay, anyway; and he wouldn't take chances the beginner might. It's a puzzle! Regular spiderweb of a trail.'

In late afternoon a Mexican youth showed plain in the glasses, topping a ridge. He came toward Ware like one with clear conscience, drew in, and stared admiringly at the big black, the silver-trimmed Myres saddle, Ware's bullion-embroidered sombrero, jacket of soft-tanned goatskin, wide-bottomed *pantalones* with scarlet insert at the seams and twin rows of tiny silver buttons. He nodded absently at Ware's question.

'This morning, early,' he said. 'It was a bay horse, but I was not close enough to see the brand or more of the man than that he was Anglo, not Mexican. He rode fast, and twice, as I watched, he looked behind him. I said to myself that someone was on the trail behind him! He went as toward the Little Bend.'

'*Milgrácias!*' Ware drawled. 'One is on the trail behind him.'

V. 'Talk is cheap!'

DARK found him still on the lonely way to the River and that loop of it called the Little Bend. In the wilderness of greasewood and mesquite he made his dry camp in a shallow arroyo, hobbling Rocket. When he had eaten his last thick sandwich and lay with head on saddle seat, smoking, he was not too hopeful.

'Loren's just as likely to be on the right trail as I am,' he confessed mentally. 'In spite of his double-edge tongue, he is a good officer. Good enough that the first telegraph office I come to I'm going to wire him and ask if he came up on our man! But——'

But he hoped that it would be himself, not Dave Loren, who overtook the killer! He had been very close to the old storekeeper—closer, he felt, than anyone else in Verde. The thought that Fyeback had been mercilessly killed while *he* stood close enough to hear that husky cry of agony, but not close enough to prevent the murder, roused cold, deadly fury in him. He knew that he would never be satisfied if another caught the murderer and sent him to the gallows.

He was up and saddling before dawn. Rocket headed over the trailless flat, and within five minutes of riding Ware pulled in to stare incredulously at the ground. There were the tracks of three ridden horses. He turned and followed them back for a little way, moved by an irritable sort of curiosity. Coming even with his camp, he stopped. It seemed impossible that three men could have passed within a hundred yards of where he slept, without rousing him.

As he went on he consoled himself with memory of what Captain Durell had once said of this region: 'There are men in plenty, around Little Bend and Satan

26

Land, who could ride full speed through a spiderweb and never break it!' But that was poor consolation for a young man who prided himself on wolf-keen hearing. It was in no pleasant humor that he followed the trail of the silent riders on toward the River. For they seemed to be of his mind about visiting Olin.

But when in mid-afternoon he came down a last slope to the *bosque* on the shore and saw a squat adobe building with smaller 'dobes behind it, only the tracks were to be seen. Olin, fat as the Bug cowboy had described him, with a moon-like yellow face, clean-shaved and expressionless, seemed to slide into the door. He watched Ware with little eyes that shone like bits of gray ice set in wrinkles above round cheeks.

'Howdy,' was all he said, then waited as Ware quite openly stared about store and sheds.

'I'm Ware, out of Durell's X Company,' Ware told him frankly. 'I was just wondering about your last three customers. They passed my camp last night and all but stepped on me, without waking me. Good thing I don't have gold in my teeth! They might have done some dentistry on me and I wouldn't have known about it till mealtime.'

'Three Mexicans. Strangers. Went on to Vado,' Olin said. 'You—happen to be after 'em for anything?'

'Not a bit. Got something I can feed this big fellow of mine? He had more moonlight than grass, last night.'

When he had seen Rocket eating corn behind a shed, surrounded by Olin's scrawny chickens and a family of pigs, he went back to the store.

'My woman's fixing you some steak,' Olin said. 'So you're a Ranger, and out of Durell's company . . . Long time since Durell used around Little Bend. Long time since any Ranger come by. And I always like to see one. Like to have somebody once in a while I can talk to with bars down. Can't do that with many of my customers! Even the honest cowmen—honest, you know, for Little Bend—lots of times they've got something private in their heads.'

While he gossiped of Durell and other veteran Rangers and spoke of affairs in and about the Little Bend in general terms, a pretty Mexican woman brought steak and biscuit and coffee to Ware. He ate and listened and studied his host. Finally, he told Olin of his errand.

'Fyeback! I be damned!' Olin grunted. 'I kind of knew him. But I don't use Verde much; couple times is all I ever was there. So you figure Loren's on the wrong track?'

'Not exactly,' Ware said slowly, pushing plate and cup from him and getting out tobacco and papers. 'He may have put the cuffs on our man already. But if he does happen to be on the wrong trail, I may be on the right one. And Loren can't go out of his own county, unless he goes along with the other sheriff. A Ranger is different, of course. Well, all along I have been wondering if this man I want may not be a real highliner, one of Black Alec Pryde's gang, even. If that is a good guess, no telling how many counties he may cross. His notion would be to split the breeze away from the county that's waving a hang-knot his way.'

'You're just guessing that he might have headed this way?'

'Not much more. I met a Mexican who'd sighted a nervous hairpin on a bay, coming toward the Little Bend.'

'He got here, too,' Olin said calmly. 'But whether it was your man—— Yours was on a Plumb Bob bay. What the iron on this fellow's horse was, I don't know a bit more than what was on Pharaoh's nag that got drownded. It was late yesterday and I was busy with a bunch of *vaqueros* from across the River. He put the bay out yonder where yours is, then come in and eat a meal and had a drink or six. Paid up for him and the horse and went off.'

Ware leaned a little. He could not help his tension. There was a war-flame in his green eyes.

'But—he was not yellow-haired. More brownish. Brown eyes, too. Kind of high-pocketed, slimmish man.

No talk in him. Shut mouth was his racket! But, shucks! In the Little Bend that's a lot like saying he had two arms and two legs. Where he come from, fast enough to sweat that bay like it was sweated, or where he was heading, fast as he went off, I do'no' a bit.'

'I do wish you'd got a glimpse of the brand,' Ware said irritably, but more to himself than to Olin.

'Uh-huh,' Olin grunted softly.

He was not listening to Ware. Some faraway sound held his attention. He was like a drowsing hound lifting one ear, Ware thought, trying to identify something barely heard. To Ware no outside noise had carried. He watched Olin curiously. It was easy to see the fat man leaning upon his counter day after day, all day long, alert for every thud of hoofs or rasp of feet, wondering which might be dangerous . . .

Olin heaved himself up, where he had slouched with both elbows on the rough counter, big chin in both thick hands. He crossed to the door, and as he stood there, with what Ware could see of his face expressionless, his fat body was suddenly no longer slack. It had stiffened. Not with any jerk. It was just that, in one instant, he was slack as a saddle string; in the next that leather had become steel.

The tension was contagious. Ware folded his arms and slid from his seat on the counter to stand before it, leaning with appearance of lazy ease against the edge. Then Olin was slack-muscled again. He turned—Ware could hear hoofbeats, now—and came back to the counter. But now he went around to sit on a stool behind it, hands out of sight.

The pound of hoofs grew louder, then ended in the sound of horses sliding to a stop beyond the door. Saddles creaked. Feet scuffed sand. Olin looked blankly at Ware and, meeting his narrowed green eyes, let one eyelid sag.

Five dusty, beard-stubbled men crowded through the doorway. The leader was lanky, hatchet-faced, middle-aged, brown as a Mexican. He stood with thumbs hooked in a sagging shell belt, narrow black eyes shuttling from Ware to Olin, thin mouth very tight.

'Olin,' he snapped, 'I come to talk to you.'

'Preach ahead,' Olin invited him. 'But I warn you beforehand, I'm a Free-Thinker and a Henry George Single-Taxer; a mighty hard man to convert. But whoop her up, Eagan. Talk is cheap!'

'My kind ain't!' Eagan snarled, clumping over to glare across the counter. 'My kind of talk costs plenty. That fat neck of yours, maybe. Olin, you harbor too damn' many shady customers! It costs me too much. I don't aim to afford it.'

'Shady customers . . .' Olin seemed to be thinking aloud. 'Quaint preaching, for the Little Bend!'

'Yeh? Doggy Tibb, just for one. I hear he's been here more'n once.'

Behind Eagan, the 66 cowboys moved forward a step. Ware, still leaning with folded arms, hands under his jacket, cigarette sagging from a mouth-corner, looked them over carefully. Young or past middle age, they were hard cases, he decided. But Olin's weary, disgusted drawl seemed to check them.

'Ah, don't be a bigger jack than you was born! You know and I know that the men using that trail outside, they ain't Sunday-School boys. They don't hand me visiting cards when they come in buying grub and whiskey and tobacco and horse bait. Huh! If they was to give me names, they'd be a long way from right names. You say I've been harboring shady customers. All right, I'll bust down and say you're dead right. I harbor plenty of 'em. Always have, ever since I opened up here, years back. Matter of fact, when have I dealt with anything else, huh?'

He moved fat shoulders irritably, staring up at Eagan. His hands, Ware noticed in a flashing side-glance, were still under the counter.

'Doggy Tibb, is it?' he growled. 'And what would *you* know about Doggy Tibb? Your whole corralful wouldn't know a thing. Has he been here? Maybe! Him and his whole family. Think he'd come around telling who he was? Talk's been going around this neighborhood like a tumbleweed rolling. Somebody says Doggy Tibb done this. Somebody else says he done that. He's been using around the Little Bend, off and on, for a couple of years—so they say! But who's actually laid eyes on him? You? Some of those bowlegs that ride for you? Nah! Or nobody else I know. How do I know if he's been here? Tell me that, if you can!'

Suddenly, Eagan wheeled upon Ware.

'I don't know you,' he said belligerently.

'Which makes us about even,' Ware drawled. 'And it suits me well enough.'

'Well? Who is he?' Eagan snapped at Olin.

'We-ll, he looks to me a lot like a fellow that bought some crackers and cheese—and paid for 'em. That's enough for me. You want to remember, Eagan, you ain't running this store.'

'You want to remember, Olin, I'll maybe run the storekeeper!'

'Not this storekeeper,' Olin said very softly. 'I'm too fat a man to run. It'd overheat me. So I don't start.'

The 66 cowboys moved another step toward the counter, as if pulled all at once by an invisible string. But now they lowered at Ware, instead of Olin. A younger copy of Eagan lurched from among them and leaned with his hatchet face almost in Ware's, his hands almost on the butt of his Colt.

'Fellow!' he snarled. 'You're maybe hell on wheels where you lit out from, but in the Little Bend you——'

'If you don't haul that ugly face of yours away from me, in the Little Bend I'm going to be the man that worked you over,' Ware interrupted him coldly.

'Oh!' young Eagan cried. 'It thinks it's——'

This time Ware interrupted with a short and savage swing, whipping from jacket front to Eagan's cheek. The heir of the 66 grunted; his head snapped back under the smash of Ware's hard right fist; then he staggered back against the others. Ware drew his left Colt flashingly, then his right.

'Take it easy!' he counseled the stiffening cowboys. 'Bad luck to bother a Ranger.'

'Ranger?' the elder Eagan cried, stopping his own gun hand. 'What're you trying to peddle? You—a kid like you—a Ranger!'

'My legs are long enough to touch the ground,' Ware said, grinning. 'I've got the regular number of arms and eyes, too!'

VI. *'Who wants grief?'*

OLIN's wheezy laugh was loud and startling, in the tense silence of the store. Eagan and the 66 men looked his way. Ware continued to watch young Eagan, who stood between two cowboys, gash-mouth working, gun-hand fingers crooking and straightening over, but not on, his pistol butt. For very accurately Ware had sized that young man, just as he had placed him in relation to Eagan; the signs of the bully, the would-be gunman, were as plain as the Eagan features.

'All right, Ware,' Olin said easily. 'Eagan passes for straight—in the Little Bend. He's a notionate man. Sometimes it takes his mind a draggy time to catch up with his idees; and he's got a trick of starting his jaws to waggling and expecting 'em to say something, eventual. But he passes for all right—Little Bend grade. He owns the 66 north of here, joining Ten Sleep Norman's Lightning Rod that's west of him. Yeh, Eagan passes for a honest cowman, more stole against than stealing.'

'You can put them cutters back in their holes,' Eagan grunted, nodding. 'If you really ain't lying about being a Ranger, you're safe with us. Burt! Mind your own business and don't ram your nose so much into mine.

I ain't got so feebling I can't handle a button this size
if I figure he needs handling!'

'I'll handle him! I'll handle him, all right!' Burt Eagan mumbled shakily. 'Ranger or no Ranger, I'll handle
him!'

'Not while I'm careful about my back, you won't!'
Ware assured him. 'No more than your big-talking papa
will.'

Eagan seemed to be thinking of something. He ignored the thrust at him, regarding Ware with narrow,
fixed stare.

'Ne' mind the wawa,' he snapped. 'Looky! I got a job
just a Ranger's size. Thirty head of my long yearlings
have got stole in the last three-four days. I know damn
well they was stole by some of Olin's favoryte customers.
And I know well enough Ten Sleep Norman was mixed
in the stealing. Likely, they went across the River between this and Vado up the River. I want you to take
after Norman, first——'

Ware spun his Colts on the trigger guards, let the
butts slap into his palms again, then reholstered them,
shaking his head and, smiling pleasantly.

'Got a murder case on my hands. Rustlers don't interest me. Anyway, I couldn't mix into this unless your
sheriff asked for my help and my captain ordered me
to drop the murder and loop your thieves. Tell your
sheriff about it.'

'Got no sheriff! Just a useless deputy that's going to
run, account Theo Ribaut's backing him. Now, about
my yearlings: Nobody can make me believe that all this
talk about Doggy Tibb being around come from nothing! My notion is——'

'I told you he was a notionate man,' Olin reminded
Ware.

'Yeh?' Eagan snarled at him. 'You want to watch out
about a notion I've been holding a long time—that
there's a cottonwood right outside with a high straight
limb, that'd look decorated fine with you strung to it!
My notion about my yearlings is, my stuff was run off

by a mixture of Ten Sleep's thieves and Doggy Tibb men; and that they've been doing the stealing and holding up of cowmen—yeh, and the sticking up of banks and stores and such for miles around—we had lately.'

'Lately,' Olin drawled softly, as if speaking only to himself. Then, to Ware: 'I said his mind takes time to catch up with his notions, or anybody's notions, for that matter. Anything since Sam Houston's day is lately, to Eagan. Rustling and sticking up banks and such have gone on for miles around here ever since there was a cow or horse or bank this side of the Gulf of Mexico.'

'It's interesting,' Ware told them. 'Some day when I've got a furlough, I'd like to sit down and hear all about it from the beginning. But, right now, unless rustlers and the like run across my corns, I'll stick to the trail I'm on.'

Eloquently, then, he turned his back upon Eagan; loafed across to look through the door. The 66 men in a body moved to that end of Olin's counter which served as bar. While Ware leaned against the jamb and considered his problems, the reference to Doggy Tibb of Alec Pryde's highliners coming into his thoughts persistently, he heard the rattle of tin cups and the jerky talk of the drinkers, without giving it attention.

He knew a good deal about the Pryde gang. The *List of Fugitives from Justice*, often called the Rangers' 'Bible,' and certainly read with attention the Scriptures rarely got, held the descriptions of Black Alec Pryde, Doggy Tibb, Rip Andress, and Baldy Burr, principals of what was, currently, the most dangerous, as it was the most cunning and elusive, criminal band in the Southwest. Whatever the authorities had learned of the four was printed by the Adjutant General—and memorized by the Rangers. So Ware knew that Doggy Tibb had once punched cows in this neighborhood.

'Maybe he'd come back here,' he reflected. 'Alone, or with the others, or some of 'em, to hole up. But, maybe it's just because he's known to know this country that

these rumors Olin mentioned get going. Toss-up, which
is right. I'd like to believe he's using around here! Like
to meet him! Eight thousand——'

Quick footsteps on the warped planks of the floor behind him jerked his thoughts back. He turned a little
to face Burt Eagan, who almost ran toward him, hand
at pistol. At the counter old Eagan and the 66 punchers
stared tensely, while Olin watched with his moon face.
blank. Suddenly, Ware wondered if Eagan's warning to
his son had been pretense; if Eagan could *want* a Ranger wiped out here?

Stranger things than that had happened by all accounts, in the sinister Little Bend! As Olin had inti-
mated, even so-called honest men had private purposes
which they tried to keep secret. There were always cur-
rents and cross-currents along this River; strange con-
nections . . .

But Ware's thoughts occupied him only the merest
fraction of a second. He jumped like a startled wolf
through the door—and flattened himself against the wall
with a pistol lifted. Burt Eagan yelled like another wolf
and came faster toward the door. Someone—to Ware it
Ware it sounded like the elder Eagan—shouted a warning. But Burt was coming through the door. Ware
swung his Colt up, then down. Burt dropped the pistol
he had drawn. He crashed to the sand, face down, to
sprawl motionless.

Ware moved as quickly into the doorway as he had
moved out of it. It was a desperate chance, but better
than fighting Eagan and the three 66 cowboys outside,
if fighting was in their plan. His eyes were dazzled still
by the light, but he had both Colts out when he
whipped back into the store.

'All right!' he yelled viciously at the four who were
coming toward him. 'Who wants grief?'

They stopped short as he blinked in the gloom. He
drew a long, slow breath, wondering if some nervous
one would loose the shot that might turn the store into

a shambles. But no shot came. His eyes cleared and he
saw them rigid three yards away, none with Colt out.
Eagan cleared his throat raspingly.

'What? Just Burt on the prod?' Ware snarled. 'Nobody else anxious to take a bite out of a Ranger?'

'Ah, it's easy to talk big from behind a cocked cutter!'
one of the cowboys burst out. 'If you was——'

'You mean, if I wasn't!' Ware interrupted him. 'If I
wasn't an officer, I'd cut the bunch of you off at the
pockets. Now, Eagan, you're dragging it. *Pronto!* I don't
like your looks, and as for your smell——'

They muttered. Eagan leaned and seemed about to
object, but when Ware gestured savagely with a gun he
moved toward the door with jerk of the head toward
his men.

'Come on! He's got the drop. No sense to running
against rope,' he told them. 'Reckon we got grief enough
on our hands without killing a fool kid of a Ranger.'

Ware stood back to let them pass, then watched from
the door. Burt Eagan had got to his feet and stood swaying, both hands at his head. His father reached to scoop
up Burt's Colt.

'I'll take care of this for a while,' he said raspingly.
'Next time you start out to pistol-whip somebody, you
better stop and ask him please can you!'

Burt snarled, but there seemed to be no more fight
in him. He staggered after the others to the horses,
mounted, and turned his horse mechanically with theirs.
One of the cowboys rode over to reach for Burt's hat.
Straightening, he faced Ware, a youngster of hard, devil-
may-care face. Calculatingly, he looked Ware up and
down, then grinned.

'Maybe you was kind of lucky that it didn't seem
quite like my fight,' he drawled cryptically, then spurred
off.

'Well!' Olin exploded, with Ware's return to the
counter. 'Keep that kind of doing up and it won't be
long before you'll find a rep' hung onto you. That's a

hard outfit! If there's another as hard, among them that passes for honest, it's the Lightning Rod, and that's part Mex' and part boys from over where the winds come from. Want to watch your step, Ware. The 66 ain't going to forget you one little bit!'

Ware shrugged indifferently.

'It won't be Burt Eagan who'll rub out my mark, anyway,' he predicted. 'If this country's a tenth as hard as it's called, he'll paw the air with somebody who won't just wrap a sixshooter around his nut, the way I did.'

He looked inscrutably at Olin. He was recalling the storekeeper's calm air of detachment as Burt Eagan rushed him. That might have been due to confidence in the outcome, he admitted. But Ware thought that, if he and Olin stood together in tight places, he would trust to his own eyes and hands. Like everyone else in the Little Bend, the storekeeper seemed to have his own troubles, his own axes to grind.

'You got stopped by the Hooks in telling me about my man on the bay. When he split the breeze so, leaving, which way did he head?'

'Up the River. The way he was going, he could've made for Vado, or turned north towards the 66 or Lightning Rod or Open A. Or he could've passed up Vado and gone on toward Piedra or Carlos Smith's D-Bar-D or Alamos.'

'Or San Francisco, or China,' Ware supplemented the tally very dryly. 'They're west, too, my old geography always said. Anyway, all I can do is head that way. I reckon I'll charge up the time spent with Eagan to experience; the kind a Ranger collects and keeps in the back of his head and sometimes finds use for, years afterward. But it looks like waste, now.'

'Been spending time with Eagan, have you?' a voice drawled, just outside the door.

It was a big man, blue eyes and graying mustache very light against the dull mahogany of his skin. He came inside with a slow, sure way about him, a man of forty or thereabout, Ware guessed, his grayness premature. He ignored Olin, to look Ware closely, deliberately, up and down.

'Ten Sleep Norman, the Lightning Rod man I told you about,' Olin said after a moment.

'Oh,' Ware grunted. 'Your place seems to be right popular, today, Olin—but it's a good thing you get your customers in separate layers. If Norman had walked into the Eagans——'

'What I walk into, I aim to walk into, and I'm ready to walk into,' Norman told him in his deep, even drawl. 'I made out the Eagans here. I can smell anybody off that outfit for a mile against the wind. So I waited.'

'I'm Private Ware, X Company,' Ware introduced himself, on sudden impulse. 'Eagan complains that he's lost some yearlings. He claims that you and Doggy Tibb rustled 'em.'

Norman's face did not change, but he cursed Eagan and all his ways and works. Ware shrugged, lifting a corner of his hard mouth contemptuously.

'Of course, Eagan's not here . . .' he meditated aloud. 'I wonder if you'd do that to his face.'

'I'm going to do *this* to his face. Same as now—to your face!'

He whipped out his low-swung Colt and aimed it at Ware.

VII. *'Let your wolf loose!'*

WARE regarded the big, quiet man very steadily. Norman's reaction had been one of the moves he had expected to rouse the Lightning Rod owner into making. But, he admitted to himself, Norman's manner prevented more than a guess at his thoughts. He might be the thief Eagan called him. Or——

'Maybe he just was born bull-headed!' Ware speculated. 'The kind of man that *will* run against rope, until he's certain he can't break it.'

'No baby-faced kid is going to haul me around,' Norman told him flatly. 'I don't give a hoot if he calls himself a Ranger or the Angel Gabe! I have got other things on my mind besides answering every damn lie the like of Eagan can tell. So, young fellow, I'm going to bother you to reach up and get a solid hold on your ears. Then we'll have to borrow your hardware for a while. You can split the breeze down to Vado and tomorrow come back and Olin'll give the gun back to you. Olin! Don't be pawing around! I never yet winged a storekeeper, but——'

'You act like a man trying to act like a man that didn't rustle the Eagan stuff,' Ware said, grinning. 'I take it that you mean to act like that . . . The trouble is, I can't make up my mind whether you're just acting, or if you really didn't!'

'*Muchacho*—boy,' Norman drawled tolerantly, 'if you happened to be older and more knowing about places like the Little Bend, you wouldn't go off half-cocked on a windy yarn told by the like of Eagan. That's the trouble with starting a kid off on a man's job. People in Austin act like they can just tell a young button he's a Ranger; to go off and always act like one. Or do they give him a book to read? Anyhow! Chances are, nobody lifted a head of stuff off the Hooks! Out of all the plenty liars in and around Little Bend, Eagan's the fanciest.'

Ware, leaning comfortably with arms folded, nodded gravely. Norman lifted a shoulder, made a disgusted sound.

'Eagan's just trying to bother me, sicking you onto me. But he can't bother me a bit on his own and he's not going to bother me through somebody else. Where I come from——'

'Wyoming . . .' Ware said, as if he knew. 'The Ten Sleep country. It has the name of being salty, all right.'

'Huh?' Norman grunted, staring. 'Well! The button does know something. You're damn right it's salty country, and——'

'But salt's not always brains. Put that cutter up, Norman, or—let your wolf loose! I've been holding a gun on you, under this *chaqueta* of mine, for five minutes. All right! Make up your mind. Reckon neither one of us can miss. Just a question of who gets hit hardest. And'—he grinned savagely—'you're the big mark, the easy one.'

Norman stared at Ware's concealed hand, but kept his pistol trained steadily.

'Oh!' Ware grunted suddenly. 'About Eagan and the yearlings: Maybe I'm just a button, Norman, but I don't believe everything I listen to. Nobody wants to haul you anywhere. In fact, the reason the Hook outfit pulled out, making it safe for you to come in, was my asking 'em to please drag it.'

'Right!' Olin put in. 'You didn't stop to ask for good advice, Norman. Now it's not my way to bull into people's doings. Else I could've warned you that your eyes ain't too good; that you was misreading Ware's brand—as well as missing the guns he packs in that cross-arm vest. Put up the cutter, man! Else they'll be renaming you Eleven Sleep—ten sleeps before you hit Texas; eleven being your last, in the graveyard!'

Norman grinned and reholstered his Colt. Ware stretched and yawned, bringing out both .44's in the motion, then sliding them back into the pockets of his vest. Olin looked with amusement from him to Norman.

'Just a button . . . But he happens to be the button that went into as tough a Mex' settlement as you'd find in a year's ride and took a killer right out from the middle of his kinfolks, not so long ago. Never shot a shot, either. Just outnerved 'em.'

Ware stared. He had not guessed that Olin had heard of José Amargo's capture. Norman shrugged.

'I'll buy the drinks. And I take it back, what I said

about kids. Reckon I went off slaunchway when you mentioned Eagan.'

'What do you allow about Doggy Tibb being around?' Ware inquired, when they lifted their tin cups formally.

'Nothing! Just a tale that got started.'

'Ever see him? I mean, would you really know if he used around this country? If you met him on the range?'

'No-o. But going on what I've heard of him and the whole Black Alec bunch, I don't expect any of 'em to hang around a country like this, or pull little jobs of rustling.'

'Well, I'll be leaving you. Trail that man you saw, Olin. Likely I won't catch up with him; and if I do, hundred-to-one he won't be the man I want. But when you serve under Durell, you keep moving!'

He had a final drink with them, then went out to Rocket. Riding westward along the plain trail to Vado, he shook his head. Eagan, Norman, Doggy Tibb . . . He saw no connection between them—any or all of them—and his own special business. But it was hard to get them out of mind. Particularly, he thought of Doggy Tibb; of the persistent rumor that Tibb was about here.

Norman, too, persisted in returning to mind. One of the few things known of the Pryde gang's beginnings was that Black Alec and the little red killer, Rip Andress, were Wyoming men. Baldy Burr and Doggy Tibb were Texas cowboys-gone-wrong. But Pryde and Andress had owned Northern records before Kansas, Oklahoma, or Texas had seen them.

'Of course,' Ware conceded, 'a cowman from Wyoming, even one settled in the Little Bend, might not know a bit more about Wyoming highliners than I do. But when one of the partners of that Wyoming gang is said to hang around the neighborhood of that cowman from Wyoming—well, it's interesting to think about.'

Then, grimly, he dismissed them all from mind and concentrated on his own particular interest, the stocky

man on the Plumb Bob horse. His automatic study of
the ground around Olin's had found no mark of those
remembered hoofs. But the soft sand had been so
smudged that he could not feel sure of any print seen.
Now, as he rode, he watched the trail close ahead—and
shrugged irritably.

'Too many have kicked up the sand; and the wind
moves it,' he told Rocket. 'We'll try Vado, horse! See if
anybody knows anything—that he'll tell.'

But when he reached the little clutter of adobes, near
dusk, his casually voiced inquiries brought no information about any sort of Anglo on a horse of any color.
Ware had the feeling that the *cantinero* who served him
a drink and the Mexicans who accepted *tequila* and
aguardiente at his expense told truth. He knew these
people well and they showed only polite indifference, not guardedness, in saying that no Anglo had been
in Vado for days.

'It may be that your friend turned north to Los Alamos,' the *cantinero* told him. 'There is little here in
Vado for a man who carries money and thinks of a spree.
But in Los Alamos—*ay de mi!* That is a big town. Fine
liquors to drink. Pretty girls to dance with. Monte,
poker, faro.'

Ware agreed that his good friend might well have
gone to Alamos. When he had poked about the place a
little longer, and talked during a meal with two men
who were eating at the same table, he decided that Alamos was as good a goal as any. He rode a few miles on
the way, lighted by the moon, then camped.

All the next day, the trail led him across arroyo-
gashed flats studded with greasewood, mesquite, ocotillo,
bayonet weed, and prickly pear. Occasionally he saw a
snake sliding across the sand, or a cottontail or jack
rabbit bounced into air from behind bush or rock and
skimmed the greasewood tops with racing jumps. Dusky
eagles coursed patiently back and forth, hunting; buzzards made dots against the intense blue of the October

sky. But of men he saw nothing in all that vast land between hill and hill.

He was too much a part of the country to be lonely. Mechanically, he watched the skyline to right and left and ahead, with occasional shifts in the saddle for a glance behind. That night when he made his second camp, after he had killed two cottontails for supper, he settled comfortably beside the fire and studied his *Fugitive List*. Once more he re-read the descriptions of Black Alec Pryde, the renegade cowman, and the three notorious *buscaderos* he led. There was nothing new to be learned from the book of Pryde, Andress, Burr, and Tibb.

'Killers, all,' he summed it up when the fire died beneath sand and he smoked his last cigarette of the day. 'But Burr's not so quick on the shoot as the others; and Rip Andress is the worst—what Durell called a homicidal maniac. And Tibb used to ride in this country . . . I—wonder! It would certainly set Dave Loren back on his heels if I could dab a loop on Tibb. Eight thousand . . . What a man could do with that much! Add the rewards on the rest of 'em, and you wouldn't have to beg a calf to set up as a cowman! I wish Durell would let me work this country, after I settle this case . . .'

In the following forenoon, he saw riders twice. But they were only vague shapes on the far ridges. From the main trail side-tracks led occasionally—toward ranches, he thought. But he had set his mind on going direct to Los Alamos and working out of the county seat. This country was too big for haphazard searches; his man might have turned into any of those ranch roads, but to check meant days of riding. He had cottontail for lunch, as for breakfast, and in mid-afternoon, came to a wider road, marked by wheel ruts and many hoofprints.

A cowboy rode out of the greasewood ahead of him, reined in for a look, then addressed Ware in Spanish.

'Yeh,' Ware replied, in English. 'Los Alamos. How far, now?'

'Hell,' the cowboy grunted. 'Thought you was a *charro* in that fancy rig. Close up, I can see you ain't black-eyed. Why, we'll make town around dark or a spell before, if we don't set down to pick posies—if there was any posies in this forsaken country!'

He was a North Texas man, less than a year in the country, he said. He missed the creeks and woods and grassy prairies. Ware inspected him carefully and put him down for what he claimed to be, a restless cowboy. He was young and cheerful, with nothing about face or manner to set him apart from fifty dark-haired, dark-eyed, shabby youngsters on any range.

'Come by Piedra?' he asked presently. 'Or——'

. 'No. By Olin's place. What's special about Piedra?'

'It ain't about Piedra; it's about the road between it and Alamos; and old Theo Ribaut—and his kid, Jules.'

'What about 'em?' Ware demanded. 'I've heard of Ribaut, of course; big auger in Alamos; ten fingers in twenty pies.'

'And then some pies!' the cowboy agreed. 'But it kind of looks like his pie-stirring days is over. Yeh! plumb over. He just up and disappeared and left no more sign behind than—than cows that disappear in the Little Bend! Had seven thousand in the buckboard with him, too! Been missing a week or more.'

'No reason for thinking that he might have had something to do with his own going?' Ware asked shrewdly. 'I don't know enough about him and his affairs to more than guess, but—it wouldn't be the first time a man just got and skipped.'

'I do'no' much, either. Seen him a time or six in Alamos and around—I been riding chuck line my whole time in this damn' country and I got around a lot—and heard lots of talk about him and his doings. But the way I heard the tale yesterday on the JV, old Theo was dry-gulched som'r's along the road to town from the D-Bar-D. But hunting ain't found the place.'

He knew very little more. A cowboy had ridden out to the JV, where he had been making an extra hand, bringing with him the news he had just told. Ware was slightly irritated; he had counted on getting a certain amount of help from Ribaut in his hunt for the man on the Plumb Bob bay.

'Well—nothing to me!' he told the cowboy carelessly.

VIII. *'You're promoted'*

Los Alamos was the largest and most prosperous town for many miles in any direction. Viewed as Ware viewed it, its red tiles shining in the last yellow light of the sun, it seemed almost a little city. A spur of the railroad came to it. Farms and small ranches, irrigated by Red Creek, were green all around the outskirts.

But when they came down the last slope, just before sunset, to ride into the tree-bordered main street, Ware found all the familiar Southwestern cowtown look about stores and saloons. The cowboy turned off, leaving Ware to jog toward a livery corral. When Rocket was comfortable in a stall, and his saddle and Winchester locked in the saddle-room, Ware went back to the busier section of the county seat.

There was a huge adobe store with sheds and corrals behind, centered on the south side of the street, a little back under huge cottonwoods. Ware turned that way for tobacco and papers. As he came into the deep veranda, where men sat comfortably on the thick adobe half-wall or on boxes upturned, a big and dandified cowboy stepped from the store doorway beside a slender, dark, and vivid girl. Ware looked first at the big man's expensive hat and shirt and boots, then at the small figure beside him. Meeting her eyes, he forgot the man!

She was in white buckskin jacket and skirt, fringed and embroidered, a crimson stock about her slim, round throat. Her hair—blue-black, shining, loosely coiled at

the back of her head—was bare. She swung a white Stetson against her boot as she talked to the cowboy.

'Now, Miss Georgette!' he was saying. 'You're too nice
and kind a lady to do a man like that!'

To Ware, the girl appeared anything but kindly. Ar-
rogance was in her dark eyes, the set of her red mouth,
the way she carried her head. At Ware she looked quickly, searchingly, then seemed to label him—and forget
him. But he continued to watch her admiringly, wondering who she might be—and who the big man might be,
who seemed on such easy terms with her and who, in his
own devil-may-care way, was as much a figure to mark.

'You're wrong, quite wrong, my friend,' Georgette informed her companion. 'I'm neither nice nor kind. I
dislike both words, by the way, pinned on me! Capens
are this, or that, or something else. But hardly nice, or
kind. Just to prove it, you may walk to the Watson gate
with me. But you can't come in! Loraine Watson and
I will do nicely without you. So you'll come back and
put my horse in the Watson corral.'

'Nothing but a carpet—me!' he complained, grinning.
'A nice big carpet for you to be a-tramping on.'

'Not a carpet—a convenience! What on earth is a man
good for, otherwise? I've never known but two kinds of
man: the man who's a convenience for his betters—
women!—and the one who won't be! Wait a minute!
Hold those horses! I've known both kinds, but the second kind I won't have around me. Now what?'

She laughed up at him and he shook yellow head and
groaned dismally, continuing to grin.

'I take it back—about you being kind! How a hundred
pound of pure loveliness could be mixed with so much
pure cruelness——'

They passed Ware, walking very slowly. Georgette
looked his way as if he were not there. Then they
stepped from the veranda and went up the street. A man
who, like Ware, had been watching and listening shook
his grizzled head.

'She's a pint-sized hellion,' he drawled. 'But she is

pretty as a red wagon. Always was. Remember the day Capen got off the stage with her, Ike? She wasn't no more'n three-four, but smart as a whip, and the way he had her dressed up she looked like one of them big Christmas dolls.'

'Man that gets her,' Ike predicted sourly, 'he won't never get a chance to set down. He'll be busier'n one dog with four dogs' fleas, jumping to wait on her.'

'Well, that leaves this neck of the woods aiming to set,' another man snapped. 'Because Capen don't figure anybody in this tol'able scope of country is good enough for his niece!'

Ware went on into the store, meeting curious stares with blank face. He got his tobacco, listening to the talk of a group there about Ribaut's disappearance. But it seemed that Los Alamos really knew little more about that vanishing than he had learned from the cowboy on the trail. The talk of these townsmen and cowboys seemed to be concerned with the question of Ribaut's actual fate. Some argued that the money carried by Ribaut had surely caused his murder for robbery. But a loafing cowboy, a thickset man newly barbered, said drawlingly:

'Well, I got to see that damn old twisty fox laid out for the bone yard before I believe he's dead! Yeh! And I got to know he ain't wiggled a finger for a week, then! He always had a lot of behind-your-back deals on. How do you-all know but what he had good reasons for sliding off somewhere? Nobody located the buckboard and his team. Bingham and Logan never even cut his trail past a point when Marie Ribaut sent 'em out. They got the name of trackers, too!'

'Let's see, now,' a thin-faced, shrewd little man said, grinning. 'It couldn't be Capen you ride for, Hannom?'

The cowboy turned slowly, so that his heavy, expressionless face was near the townsman's. Reddish brows drew down in a slight frown over unwinking little blue eyes. He was a bulldog type, Ware decided stolid, not too quick of mind.

'Meaning?' he inquired slowly.

'Capen and Ribaut haven't been *compadres* for quite some time. So——'

'I think you talk a sight too much with your mouth!' Hannom interrupted, but speaking deliberately.

The little man began to back away, but the counter was behind him, and Hannom's big hand caught his coat and pulled him back. He jerked and threw up his arms defensively. A clerk called—in no excited voice, though—to Hannom. But the Open A cowboy slapped the little man heavily, a half-dozen times, then shoved him violently. The little man fell and Tannom turned to the clerk.

'I ain't going to really hurt him. Just learn him some manners. You damn' town mice, you set around and you gabble so much amongst yourselves, you think everybody's like you; you can say anything you like and nobody'll do a thing but say back at you. Nobody's going to hint around that Capen bushwhacked Ribaut while I'm around to bang his teeth for him!'

None there seemed to care about objecting to his contemptuous words and manner. So he went slowly out and Ware followed, while a quick gabble of voices began in the store.

'I think I'll send Dave Loren a telegram,' Ware decided on the street. 'No sign of my Plumb Bob horse at any hitchrack I've seen. No sign of him in the livery corral. But if Loren hasn't found my man, I'll take a real look around.'

He found the station agent in his tiny office beside the cattle pens at the spur track and got a message blank. In his slow, neat hand he wrote his four words of inquiry and asked for quick reply. The station agent read it without show of interest until he came to 'Stephen F. Austin Ware.' Then he grunted.

'I'll be swizzled! If that's not funny . . . Here I was setting wondering how I was supposed to find a Ranger corporal I never had laid eyes on or heard tell about——'

'Private,' Ware corrected him. 'I'm in Durell's X Company. You don't climb away up to the rank of corporal, under Durell, unless you do something he likes a lot. He's afraid the height will dizzy a young fellow. He seasons him first.'

'Well! Then you must've whanged the dishpan plumb center. For this is addressed to Corporal Stephen Fuller Austin Ware. Says in the message, too, that you're promoted. Here you are.'

Ware took the yellow sheet and looked quickly for the notification of promotion. It gave him a pleasant thrill, for, as he had said, promotion was not easily gained under the grim and watchful Durell, who expected the unusual of his men as a matter of routine. But when he had read the line three times he began at the first, and as he read he frowned:

INVESTIGATE DISAPPEARANCE THEODORE RIBAUT ACTING SHERIFF BRIGGS AND RIBAUT FAMILY HAVE ALL INFORMATION THIS TAKES PRECEDENCE OTHER CASE RIBAUT'S MADE REQUEST ON GOVERNOR FOR RANGER STAY ON CASE UNTIL SETTLED OR YOU RECEIVE OTHER ORDERS PRIVATE AMES, FORMERLY U COMPANY, NOW X COMPANY, IN STONEWALL COUNTY ON HORSE THEFTS THIS MESSAGE HIS ORDERS TO ASSIST YOU

'So you're going to explore into the Ribaut business, huh?' the station agent said curiously. 'Begins to look like a right tough detail. Marie—Theo's oldest girl—has been pawing the ground ever since he didn't show up from his trip to Piedra. She got after Ben Briggs and Alf Mullit, the man she's going to marry, and I reckon she was on their necks plenty till they hunted all over and couldn't find a trace of Theo and the kid. Theo had his ten-year-old boy along, you know. Then she sent out the two best trackers in this part of the country. They haven't found a thing yet. But they went out again. Marie run 'em!'

'Seems to be considerable difference of opinion about Ribaut,' Ware remarked. 'About whether there's really a case to clear up. But I do wish he'd picked a better time for his disappearing. I wanted to get that other job finished. Well, send that wire to Loren for me. I'll stop in tomorrow for the answer.'

Going back along the street, just now pleasant with the smells of suppers cooking, Ware wondered about this Private Ames who was to be withdrawn from the neighboring county to help hunt Ribaut. The name was vaguely familiar—— Suddenly, he remembered some gossip of months before.

'That must be the man they call "Bar Nothing"! Sandy Ull was on a scout with him. Used to punch cows for the Bar N, that was so salty it got named the Bar Nothing outfit. Sandy said he was plumb good—and knew it . . .'

He looked for the Plumb Bob horse, as he had watched while going toward the station. But none of the bays drowsing at hitch-racks wore the iron he searched for. He stopped at a Chinese restaurant and, when the grinning little waiter suggested fried rabbit, stretched himself wrathfully across the table.

'I don't reckon I've killed forty Chinese cooks in my life,' he snarled. 'But if you say "rabbit" to me after I've lived off the critters for two days, I just won't be responsible. I want a big steak, with fried potatoes and onions mixed, lots of coffee, and about half an apple pie. *Pronto!*'

He was eating when that big dandified cowboy seen with Georgette Capen came into the restaurant with two townsmen. The three looked at Ware; then the tall cowboy said something in an undertone and all laughed. Ware continued to eat placidly, as if he had not observed their amusement.

They ordered supper, and while they waited talked of the Open A; of 'King' Capen and his 'castle'; of the stories told by Mexicans of the 'House of Whispering Shadows.'

'I never heard ary shadow whispering,' the big man told his companions, grinning. 'But I swear! I heard more orders than a range boss ever handed out, every time I got in reach of Georgette. Looks like it downright hurts that li'l' lady to see a man comfortable. Well, I reckon I won't be around long enough to get wore out fetching and carrying for her. Now that I got my horse-thieves settled in Stonewall, I'll wire the Cap'n and find out what's next for a big, strong, pretty Ranger like me. Still and all, I'd kind of like to stay around here . . .'

'Quite a few felt like that,' a townsman said grimly. 'I notice they none of 'em stayed too long. Be the same for you, Ames. Capen's got plans for his niece. Lucky you're going.'

'But he's not going,' Ware drawled, looking at them solemnly.

'Huh?' Ames grunted. 'When'd you buy into my affairs, son?'

'About the time Durell wired me to—son,' Ware answered. 'Here your next job. Our job, that is.'

He held out the telegram and Bar Nothing took it, read frowningly, then shrugged.

'All right—Corporal!' he said coldly. 'Powders are powders!'

IX. *He'll want trouble'*

WARE dawdled over his coffe while Bar Nothing Ames and the two townsmen ate. He could understand the big Ranger's coolness. But this worried him very little. Instead, he considered what he had heard of Theo Ri-

baut and that trip from Alamos to Piedra on which the
politician had vanished.

Presently Bar Nothing came over to straddle a chair
and look sharply at him.

'Have you happened to talk to Briggs, or the Ribaut
family?' Ware asked tonelessly.

'Briggs ain't in town. I know that Marie Ribaut has
had a couple trackers on the job. She's going to marry
a cowboy named Alf Mullit that used to ride for Capen
and had some trouble and quit the Open A. Well, she's
had Mullit on the trail, too. He ain't in town, either.
What's your notion?'

'Take a look at the road, I reckon. What about this
money Ribaut was packing?'

'Carlos Smith on the D-Bar-D paid Ribaut his mortgage money. The old man drove on down to Piedra and
come back and stayed with Smith a night, then went on
the road home. Somewhere along it he just disappeared
into air, him and the buckboard and span of mules,
looks like. And seventy-six hundred dollars . . .'

'You happen to hear about the storekeeper in Verde
being murdered?'

'Fyeback? Yeh. Briggs told me about getting a notice
by wire. We looked around for a bay Plumb Bob horse.
No luck.'

'That's what I was on, until this wire stopped me,'
Ware told him very grimly. 'You see, Fyeback was about
the best friend I had in the world, and the night he was
killed I was close enough to hear his last yell. I'm not
likely to forget that. I'm sorry this Ribaut case has come
up.'

He asked Bar Nothing about the Pryde gang; if he
had heard anything of them in this section.

'Nothing but the regular rumors. Doggy Tibb is always popping up around the Li'l' Bend and Satan Land.
But it's all hearsay. It——'

Hannom, the hard-faced Open A rider, came through
the door and stopped to look blankly at them. Ware

sensed, rather than saw, the tension in Bar Nothing. Then Hannom came deliberately over to stand above Ware. He ignored Bar Nothing.

'So they put you on the Ribaut case, huh?' he drawled. 'I wonder what you figure you can find out about that crooked old son? Looks like the Rangers is getting runtier and runtier. Used to be, they might not amount to a hell of a lot, but they had some size to 'em and some rings on their horns.'

'Don't need 'em like that now,' Ware said courteously. 'We don't have anybody to buck bigger than—oh, squirts like you. Foolish to have big, strong fellows for that. But, about the Ribaut case, you certainly do sound interested in it.'

As in the store, Hannom scowled faintly.

'You talk too much with your mouth!' he growled, as to the little man he had interrupted. 'Learn you some manners!'

'Wait a minute!' Bar Nothing thrust in angrily. 'You——'

But Hannom had already whipped out his hand, reaching for Ware's jacket. Ware slid from his chair, twisting away from the lunging hand. He snapped a pistol from beneath his jacket, jerked it viciously down upon Hannom's wrist, up and across his temple. Hannom fell stiffly across the table.

'Well!' Bar Nothing grunted. 'You're a kind of sudden proposition, Ware! Never give me a chance to horn in.'

'We've got more to do than hair-pull with every thick-headed bowlegs trying to play tough,' Ware said contemptuously.

'To say nothing of playing safe!' Georgette Capen snapped from the door. She came in, with a blonde girl and an elderly man following. 'Hannom eats little boys like you between meals. All you've done is delay his meal. As soon as he comes to——'

Ware looked her up and down with a tolerant grin,

then stooped to search Hannom deftly. The cowboy had a .45 between skin and shirt in his waistband. Ware reholstered his own Colt and put Hannom's gun on the table. He reached for a glass of water and poured it over Hannom's face.

'He won't like the lump he'll wake up with,' he told Bar Nothing. 'But this solid bone kind of head takes a lot of hammering. Different from men with less bone and more brains. But the lady's right; he'll want trouble when he comes to. So—trouble's what he'll get.'

Bar Nothing scowled uncertainly from Ware to Georgette. She was glaring at Ware's blank face.

'He come in on the prod, way he always is,' Bar Nothing began to explain. 'And he knew Ware's a Ranger, too——'

'Who? A Ranger?' she cried loudly, theatrically. 'He's a Ranger? What *has* happened in Austin?'

Hannom stirred, growling. He pushed himself up from the table and blinked stupidly around.

'Well!' Bar Nothing said cheerfully. 'How you feel now? Looks like that bunch of manners kind of back-fired and landed between your mind and your mouth, Hannom.'

Hannom straightened with a snarl, his hand streaking inside his shirt as he faced Ware. Bar Nothing laughed as Hannom withdrew his empty hand.

'I've got it, Hannom,' Ware informed him. 'But you can have it back. I'm not going to be bothered wondering about you. If you want trouble, you can have all your clothes'll stand—right now, out in the street. Just make up your mind and we'll get it over with; no dodging around corners trying to bushwhack me.'

He waited and Hannom stared unwinkingly, silently. The men crowding the doorway, like the handful of customers, watched stiffly. Ware thrust out the .45 abruptly, muzzle first, one hand out of sight under his jacket. Hannom took his gun and slipped it into the band of his overalls.

'Be seeing you,' he promised flatly, then wheeled and pushed by the staring ones, to disappear.

'Come on, Georgette, Loraine,' the white-haired man said uneasily. 'No place for you gals. Oughtn't to have rammed in here in the beginning, Georgette. Come on, now!'

Georgette hesitated. Ware, looking around the room warily, saw her frown, but stared blankly as if he had forgotten her—or as if she were not there. To Bar Nothing he suggested going.

Some of the men about the door wanted to ask about the trouble; talk about Hannom. Ware was informed that the other girl was Loraine Watson; the big elderly man her father, Job whose freight outfits trailed far and wide. He learned—also without needing to speak—that Hannom was a dangerous man; that nobody had ever checked him as he had been stopped tonight.

'He picked Ware account of his size,' Bar Nothing explained generally to the group going along the street with them. 'He passed me up, figuring the li'l' man would be the softest. Which was his big mistake. I'm big, but I'm awful good-natured. Hannom and his likes, they could take and tromp all over me for years and I wouldn't do a thing. But the Corporal, he ain't like that. And, too, he's busy in his head. He has got to do all the scheming and figuring for us. He ain't going to be bothered by the like of Hannom busting in on his thinking.'

'Let's get off to the side,' Ware mumbled to him. 'Away from this wawa.'

Bar Nothing grunted and began to lag behind the talkers. When the group thinned, he turned suddenly to Ware and remarked that his report had to be written. Ware offered to help him and they walked briskly away together.

'Talk to the Ribaut family, huh?' Bar Nothing said when they were alone. 'Reckon we might's well start at the beginning. Besides, if it was the political pull of old Theo that got the Adjutant General to sick us onto the case, the Ribauts will expect to be consulted with. This Marie has the name of brainy; she's more Ribaut than Gonzales. Been to school in San 'Tonio—convent. Where she gets her looks, I do'no', but she's pretty as a red wagon. Her ma is plain *pel'ao*; black as an old saddle. Marie's fair and got big blue eyes.'

'Pretty as Georgette Capen?' Ware asked innocently.

'Yeh, in her way. But Georgette—damn' if I know what it is about her Ware. She treats every man around her like——'

'Like a convenience! I heard her tell you. She's got the same trouble lots of rich kids suffer from. But worse with her. For she's got behind her not only King Capen, but her looks. Hasn't met the kind of man that won't be a convenience for her; not enough of 'em, anyway.'

'*Por dios*! I think she met one today, when she run into you!' Bar Nothing disagreed suddenly. 'I do'no' if you're as cold-blooded as you look from outside, but you acted like she didn't mean a thing more to you than a— a chair.'

'She didn't. She won't. My best girl is locked in the saddle room at the corral. Her last name's Winchester. What about this Alf Mullit that Marie's going to marry?'

'He's a biggish, right good-looking cowboy. Brunette as a Spaniard. Scar on his left cheek or he'd be too handsome to have around. Worked for Capen two-three years. Then quit and tied in with Ribaut. I do'no' all the ins and outs of this country, of course. But from what I hear, Marie got home from the convent and Mullit started hanging around her. Capen and Ribaut haven't made a team in a long time. So Mullit had to quit the Open A. Maybe it didn't happen just that way, but that's close enough. Yonder's the Ribaut place, that big 'dobe behind the trees.'

They came up to the low, white-plastered wall that separated the Ribaut yard from the dusty street, and Ware looked across thirty yards of fruit and shade trees and flowers to the dark bulk of the long, low house. It seemed deserted. Then he saw a single light at one end of the front wall, a long, golden line at the edge of shade or shutter.

They went through the solid wooden gate in the wall, and mechanically Ware noted the silence with which the hinges worked. For all his size, Bar Nothing went almost as noiselessly as Ware along the path to the house. Somewhere in the dusk ahead, where moonlight did not shine, there was what seemed a murmur of voices. Ware called:

'Hello, the house!'

'Who is it?' a woman answered, after a full minute, from the end of the long, roofless veranda that ran across the house front. 'Ben?'

'Miss Marie?' Bar Nothing countered. 'This is Ames, the Ranger. Corporal Ware got a wire—orders from Austin.'

They stepped up to the veranda, and now Ware could see the white figure down it, standing beside two big chairs, plain in the shaft of moonlight that came between the cottonwoods in the yard.

'All by yourself tonight?' Bar Nothing asked Marie Ribaut.

'Right now, yes. The family went over to see our cousins. Mother's worried sick. Have you been ordered to hunt for my father? I wrote Austin. My father knew—knows so many people there. I thought we might get some Rangers in——'

'And you did,' Ware told her. She was all that Bar Nothing had said, but not precisely what that description had led him to expect. For she was a large, handsome woman, not the girl he had pictured. 'Ames and I have been ordered here. So if you'll tell us all you can, to start us off——'

He waited and she stood looking at him, nodding.

'Yes. Of course. I'll tell you all I can. But—not tonight! I—I've got a splitting headache and I was about to go in and lie down. Will you come back tomorrow? Besides, I don't know but what you might just as well go out toward Smith's place and look around. He was coming this way——'

She put her hands suddenly to her head and gasped.

'My head! I'm sorry, but I just can't talk any more——'

They said good night and she passed them, going into the house. At the gate, Ware hummed tunelessly.

'Certainly wanted to get rid of us. Wonder who it was that jumped over the edge of the porch—and left his chair rocking—when we came up? What's two and two when it's not four?'

X. *'He hit you'*

BAR NOTHING was quiet for fifty yards, as they walked back toward the lighted fronts of store and saloon on central Main Street.

'Well?' Ware asked abruptly. 'Still feel about working with me the way you did at supper?'

'No-o,' the big man answered slowly. 'I reckon I don't. When you popped up before me with that fancy *charro* outfit, I misread your brand; figured you was some kid-cowboy. When you handed over the news about being a corporal—I'm taking it now that you didn't collect that rank from being Durell's company clerk and the white-haired boy. The way you put a quietus on Hannom. Then, seeing what I ought to've seen and never noticed, about that chair——'

'Funny!' Ware said amusedly. 'Durell has a big hand-some man like you for clerk! Volks; out of the German settlements around Fredericksburg. Wears great big yel-low mustaches that he keeps waxed. Biggest hat in

Texas. Two fancy .45 Smith and Wessons with pearl steer-head grips. Volks looks more like a Ranger than the rest of the company put together when he sits up on hs big black horse——'

'And never goes out on a scout or detail!' Bar Nothing finished. 'Heard of Volks. Used to be a deputy at Dallas—office deputy. Writes a pretty hand. Wiz' at bookkeeping. All right! I take it all back and—how do we work this Ribaut case?'

'Tomorrow, I think I'll drift out along the road Ribaut is supposed to've covered. I'll leave the town to you. Marie Ribaut'll maybe tell you something if I'm not around. We'll put what we both know in the pot and stir it and see if we've got something to put our teeth in. We——'

Ahead and off to the right, as if behind the row of houses they were passing, a shot crashed with a flat sound. Then another; then several very close together.

Without speaking, Ware and Bar Nothing jumped into a run and turned from the street along a blank wall. They stopped at the corner and looked around. There was no noise. It was as if the whole town held its breath. Nobody moved in the moonlight.

Ware edged around the corner and, keeping close to the back walls of the buildings, went quickly down to where someone's yard wall projected beyond the line of houses and stores. He stopped there to listen and at the same instant he and Bar Nothing heard stumbling footsteps; gasping. Ware thrust bared head around the corner.

Twenty feet away, edging backward toward him along the wall, a tall man seemed to be watching his back-trail and menacing it with a pistol. Ware withdrew his head, as did Bar Nothing. He shrugged and waited until the man came around the corner and leaned as if very tired—or sick. Then Bar Nothing's hand flashed out, to twist the pistol from the other's fingers.

'What was it, Mullit?' he demanded. 'Who's shooting at you?'

Mullit gasped and whirled on them. Then he shook his head.

'Don't—know,' he said painfully. 'Opened up on me—down yonder. Both of us—shook out—all our loads. He got to his horse. Got away.'

'He hit you,' Ware grunted, seeing the coat bundled around Mullit's right arm. 'Just guessing—who was it?'

Mullit shook his head again and straightened. He seemed to have got control of himself somewhat.

'Might've been just anybody. Don't know. I'm not bad hurt. If I can get to the house—Ribaut's—they'll fix me up. I—I reckon you wouldn't keep quiet about it? About it being me that was shot?'

'Why?' Ware asked curiously. 'Because it's got to do with Ribaut?' he added on purest impulse.

'How's it got to do with Theo?' Mullit countered. 'What do you mean? Because I don't want to be answering a million fool questions tonight—that I can't answer anyhow.'

'All right! We won't say anything,' Ware promised him. 'Ames will help you home. I'll take a look around and see if I can cut the sign of your man. Talk to you later.'

He went on around the corner and men coming out of stores and saloons and houses called to him. He answered vaguely and joined them to course back and forth across weed-grown vacant spaces in search of a dead or wounded man. Apparently none there knew more than he, if as much. For no one mentioned the man's running to a horse and riding off, or Mullit's slipping away. Then someone yelled from over in the dusk of the buildings:

'Somebody got hurt, all right! Here's blood—and empty shells!'

In the doorway, Mullit had evidently taken time to reload his pistol and wrap his coat about the wound in his arm. Ware grunted when some of the townsmen, having identified him as a Ranger, asked his opinion.

'Looks like a private war; the gentlemen didn't think they needed anybody's help,' he said easily. 'So they opened up on each other, and when they had finished they went off. Had any trouble around lately that might have popped up here?'

Nobody remembered feuds, or was willing to speak of them if remembered. Bar Nothing edged into the crowd and was greeted by several. He looked solemnly at the blood and the shells and shook his head.

'We're just helpless about it. Got to wait till Ben Briggs comes back. Ben'll straighten it all out—right after election. You voters just put him in for sheriff and he'll tell you who it was that fit and bled here.'

'Yeh! About the time my grandson's old enough to vote!' an anti-Briggs man jeered. 'Capen's the man we'll put in.'

'Suit yourselves about that,' Bar Nothing invited him cheerfully. 'But don't expect the Rangers to worry about li'l' private puzzles like this one.'

He got close enough to Ware to mutter: 'He was right about his arm. Nothing but an ugly snag. Old Lady Ribaut's doctor enough for it. He's lying about not knowing who it was. He told Marie, but I couldn't catch it. Reckon it really is hooked up to the old man going?'

'Something tells me that we've got to find that out, along with forty other things. Good thing there's two of us. Now, if we only had about four ears apiece, we'd be set for the job.'

They went with the others to the nearest saloon, and while he moved his glass aimlessly about the bar Ware studied the people, and from their faces and talk tried to make a picture of all this great stretch of country. Men were fitting into place on his mental map—Capen and Theo Ribaut and Alf Mullit and Hannom, like Olin at the store and the enemy-ranchers Norman and Eagan. But there was much too large a part that was blank . . .

He heard Hannom's name down the bar and listened

without seeming to. It was a dusty, stubbled cowboy, asking questions about the shooting. He had seen Hannom while on the road in.

'Or anyways it looked like him,' he qualified. 'He was not on the road. He was off to the side, going toward the Open A. And he got his come-uppance, huh?'

'That reminds me,' Bar Nothing told Ware, grinning. 'I've been kind of waiting for Hannom to make a play at you! And he decided to take his pistol-whipping and hightail. Funny! Not a bit like I'd figured him.'

'Might be a good reason besides my fierce shiny eyes,' Ware said, in tone too low to be heard by anyone else. 'Suppose it was Hannom behind the other gun tonight?'

'Can happen! But—I doubt if it's going to mean a thing to us tonight. Well! If things hadn't been tangled, beyond just understanding with a look, we wouldn't be on the case. So it's no use complaining that they are tangled.'

He looked at the clock, poured himself another drink, and like Ware stared blankly at the back-bar.

'Hannom is a good deal more'n just a hand on the Open A,' he said slowly. 'In the time that I hunted thieves around Stonewall, I covered some of this country. Went out to the Open A a half-dozen different times. Got a sort of line on things. Yeh, Hannom was always kind of important-looking. I noticed that because we just rubbed one another the wrong way from the start. Well . . . Mullit quit Capen and tied in with Capen's enemy . . .'

'Careful, now!' Ware advised him, grinning. 'You're guessing. The way I'm so sure of that is, I've been guessing along the same line. It can happen, but that's no reason for swearing it did happen. You know what's really bobbing into my mind, and bobbing away again, before I can dab a loop on it? Mullit! Something about him I ought to remember. See what you can find out about his back-trail, will you? Maybe he stole a calf off my grandpa, one time. I know it wasn't one of Pa's! If

Pa had lost a calf he'd have had to get out of the cow business sooner than he did get out; and he was flat-broke, then!'

Around ten o'clock they went up to the room Bar Nothing had rented in the Alamos House. When Ware had bathed in the painted tin tub that represented the 'Baths' of the hotel sign, he came back to the room to find Bar Nothing checking a copy of the *List of Fugitives from Justice,* whistling contentedly.

'Two boys that'll be out of the next printing of the book,' he said. 'Hundred and sixty-five—and fifty—that's two hundred and fifteen towards the li'l' old homestead nestling under the shade of the cottonwoods on the banks of the crystal stream, where the birdies sing sweet in the springtime, uh-huh. And I'm going to really save those rewards. No putting my hard cash on the red or the black while the wheel spins. No, sir! For how do I know which'll win?'

Ware sprawled comfortably on his cot with a cigarette and looked curiously at the big man. Bar Nothing put away book and pencil and stared as openly.

'Sandy Ull told me about that scout you all made in the Alice country,' Ware remarked presently.

'He's a great Sandy,' Bar Nothing drawled reminiscently, grinning. 'We run onto a hard-case bunch in a crossroads store, that time. Sandy'd been telling me for fifty mile how a man that had been trained in the prize-fighting ring to hit knew things cowboys like me never would know—reckon you've heard that sermon of his. Well, this bunch decided to hoollihan us, account they was five to our two. Sandy wasn't more'n up to the shoulders of some of 'em. But he lit into the middle of 'em like a mink killing hens. I saw he was doing all right, so I stepped back and rolled a cigarette. When the five was all spread out on the floor Sandy turned around to me with blood running down from a cut over his eye—the eye that wasn't swelled up—and he wanted to know how come I hadn't backed him up.'

'I know! He told Durell that you said you was afraid

of hurting his feelings when he was showing you how to hit, so you just *stacked* 'em for him.'

They talked of Sandy Ull and Durell; of other Rangers and sheriffs; of their own beginnings. Out of the jerky talk came what each was hunting, understanding of the other's character. When Ware put out the light and settled himself again on the cot, he felt very well satisfied with his partner.

Ware was waked at dawn by Alamos roosters crowing. Bar Nothing roused to curse sleepily, yawn, and get up. They were among the first in the Chinese restaurant, but the station agent was there before them. He gave Ware a telegram from Dave Loren, grinning as he handed it over.

'Came last night,' he explained, 'but it didn't seem worth while hunting you to deliver.'

'You mean you have not captured him yet?' was all that Loren said—collect—in reply to Ware's query about Lige Fyeback's murderer.

'I reckon I'll have to forget that for a while,' Ware confessed grimly to Bar Nothing and the agent. 'But it'll just be for a while, if I have to resign!'

After breakfast he saddled Rocket and left Bar Nothing to talk to Marie Ribaut and Alf Mullit. He was well pleased to head into the open again. Towns had never appealed to him, but today he was restless, anxious to be working at the Ribaut mystery because it stood between him and Lige Fyeback's killer.

XI. *'Capens hate Ribauts!'*

BEYOND Red Creek semi-desert began. From hearsay, Ware knew that the land would become more desolate as a man rode east or south: broken flats of chalky caliche; great sweeps of yellow sand; the tallest vegetation, mesquite trees head-high to a rider. Everywhere he looked, distant red-black mountains hemmed him in, the green stripes of *bosque* showing where shallow streams ran were very few.

He shook his head bodingly. Somewhere, anywhere, Theo Ribaut and his son were. The caved lip of an arroyo bank might hide their bodies; or any of thousands of sand dunes; or the stone-closed crevice of any rocky hill . . . They might be prisoners in some isolated house or camp of desert or mountain . . . Or Ribaut might be, at this very moment, a free man sitting comfortably in El Paso, San Antonio, Fort Worth, intent upon some scheme, meaning to come back in his own time—or never to come back. Ware laughed suddenly at his own hopeless picture.

'It's not the best way, of course,' he told Rocket as the big gelding fox-trotted comfortably along the south road, 'but when you can't see all of a stick you have just got to grab it somewhere. If it turns out to be a snake and you get him by the navel, he'll probably bite. But we don't see the ends of this stick, so we'll take a flyer, *viejo*. We'll grab and yank.'

He had ridden more than a mile when he heard the horse behind him and turned. Distant as the rider was, he recognized Georgette Capen instantly, and grinned.

'Now, if it was Bar Nothing he'd be happy for the day,' he said solemnly to Rocket. 'But we're not calico-chasers, so we'll enjoy it in a different way.'

He turned when she was only a few yards behind, looked at her indifferently, then kneed Rocket to the side so as to let her pass. But she drew in the black she rode, a horse as tall, if not so well shaped, as Rocket. So, almost stirrup to stirrup, they looked blankly at each other. Then she smiled.

'Where is my large cavalier?' she inquired. 'Shouldn't he be along to guard and protect? This is a wicked country. Hannom may very well be somewhere close along the road; it's our trail to the Castle.'

'Hannom . . . Oh. veh? Hannom. Fellow whose reach was bigger than his grab. Not that I want to belittle him. He's got a way or two that I like. About handling talky fools, for one. Yeh, I would put Hannom down as a pretty good man—in his class.'

'Boy-Rangers, of course, are not in his class! *Muchacho*! Something tells me that your stay among us, even if it happens not to be permanent, is going to be painful but also educational——'

'Rangers often have that effect on counties they have to look after,' Ware said blandly. 'But there's nothing in the Constitution of the State of Texas ordering us not to be painful. In fact, so long as the Ranger's constitution can stand it, the State's can. You want to remember that we do it for your own good!'

'Why, it's a wit!' she cried. 'And I thought it was a solemn boy—solemn because not too bright. Ah, me!'

'I'm taking Bar Nothing's place for the time, you see. If he was here, he'd wrangle the kindergarten and tell 'em funny stories. But he's not, so I have to take my mind off business——'

'So that's your opinion of him, is it? All he's good for is telling funny stories? You consider yourself the better man——'

'Worse! Poorer, anyway. He can do the girling as well as the Rangering. I'm nothing but a bloodhound, or a bulldog. When I see a pretty girl, it's the same as seeing anything else pretty—I look at 'em and go on. This is the first time I've worked with Bar Nothing—I generally lone wolf it. But I know his reputation and I can't think of a man I'd rather work with.'

She stared at him levelly, gravely, with one of the flashing changes of expression that he had come to think were typical of her.

'It seems queer, you being superior in rank to him.'

'Luck and service!' he said, shrugging. 'I've been a little longer in the Force; happened to be lucky enough to mix into some tough jobs and settle 'em.'

'Do you expect to settle this mystery of Theo Ribaut?'

'Too soon to say. Suppose somebody killed him and the boy to rob him, then hid the bodies and the buckboard and the mules. Well! Settling it means finding what's hidden, and how hard that may be depends on how well it's covered. I know that I could hide an elephant train in certain places so it never would be uncovered, not this side the Crack of Doom!'

They went on silently for a while. But Ware, keeping his eyes levelly on the country before them, was conscious of her study of him. A thought came. Very solemnly, he said:

'That Marie Ribaut is certainly a beauty! Are there some more Ribaut girls? If they're as pretty——'

'A beauty? Marie? That cow! Of course, to a cowboy who hasn't seen any women except——'

He turned in the saddle to face her, forcing a puzzled expression. The viciousness of her tone amused him.

'Why, she's sort of tall. But as Bar Nothing was saying, when a woman's beautiful, she's—just beautiful. No difference if she's dark or fair, or big or little. She's still a beauty. But don't get excited about it! She's not going to put a spoke in your wheel, being about the same as married to Alf Mullit.'

'Imagine Marie Ribaut affecting me!' she cried, and began to laugh. 'She—I'm not saying anything against her. That would be silly. She caught Alf Mullit after my uncle booted him off the Open A. I suppose that contented her. The twisty Alf is just about Marie's caliber. If they do marry, she'll be happy.'

'You mean, if Alf lives long enough to marry her,' Ware said, nodding. It was a shot in air, but she nodded, also.

'He's not too popular. He repeats every lie and rumor he hears; doubtless invents more. Men don't like that, and around Satan Land, what they don't like they usually do something about!'

'I reckon it didn't make him what you'd call popular to go over to Ribaut and begin to talk about the Open

A,' Ware drawled. 'A man as clever as old Theo could make it look like Alf bringing real secrets. I figured that was what put Hannom on. the prod in town.'

'Theo Ribaut was the perfect combination of snake and wolf and—and fox and buzzard!' she said between her teeth. 'The whole Ribaut family is off the same bolt. Your beautiful Marie—*beautiful!*—is as clever in her way as Theo. Alf Mullit's nothing but a handy stick to poke the Capens with. Theo and Marie tell him what to do, the same as they tell that jellyfish, Ben Briggs, whom they're trying to make sheriff. If you're going to investigate the disappearance of Theo and Jules, there's one thing you can paste in your hat: Don't look for help on the Open A!'

'You could put it another way: Capens hate Ribauts! Ribauts hate Capens! But, you see, Georgette, the only thing about this feud that interests the Rangers is the fact that one of the feudists is the man disappearing. That ought to interest the feudist who didn't disappear. I mean, he ought to want to make it plain that it wasn't his doing; want to help prove what really happened. That's just common sense.'

'Common sense . . . Listen, Corporal Stephen Fuller Austin Ware, Detective! When you get out to Capen Castle on your explorations, you'll meet—King Capen. I think that even a boy-Ranger will understand, after that, how little Capen cares about common sense! He simply does what he wants to do and lets the world think what it wants to think. You'll come to know that.'

'Maybe,' Ware admitted. 'One thing about this Ranger work: You meet the mixed-upedest bunch of people! But I take it that you're saying Capen had nothing to do with Theo flapping his li'l' streaky wings; and that he lets people think whatever they want to think. But not say what they want to say!'

'Just about! As Hannom showed that little gossiper in the store, it's not wise to go up and down hinting that the Open A——'

She stopped and, under Ware's narrowed stare, turned

very red. He thought that she had suddenly seen the double meaning of her boast; or the meaning that could be taken. He grinned, and she drew herself erect and stiff to glare at him.

'You're pretty clever, now, aren't you!' she snapped. 'You think you can pump me—make me say things that you can use in building up some silly theory——'

'Goodness, no!' he protested gently. 'Imagine a boy-Ranger, a—a pore thickhead cowboy, pumping a Capen! It jist ain't possible a lady with all your book-learning

and—well, I reckon if Capen's a king, you must be one of them prin-cesses like I seen pictures of in fairy tales—could be pumped by me. I jist love to hear you talk! Talk some more, will you?'

'I could talk in a way you wouldn't love to hear! I could tell you what I think of you, with your little head swelled by that promotion you just got, and the privilege of ramming your little nose into everyone's affairs and——'

Ware instantly put both hands to his head, then his nose.

'Dadgumit! That's what was wrong this morning! I knew my head used to fit my nose better. But don't bother about telling me more. You've already got me puffed up—way you know my whole name and when I made corporal and—I wouldn't bet that you don't know about my strawberry mark. No, sir—I mean, ma'am—I wouldn't. But there's one thing you don't know . . . It's the kind of thing you'll find it hard to believe, too . . . Not being the marrying kind, the fact that you're the prettiest girl I ever laid eyes on means not one—single—solitary—thing, to me! I'm the kind of man you won't have around; the kind that won't be used for a convenience by any woman. All your prettiness; all your smiling and eye-rolling that you've practiced on every man you ever saw—nothing at all to me!'

She stared, furious of eyes, her mouth tight. Then abruptly she laughed and leaned toward him.

'The little boy whistles as he passes the graveyard; to

keep his courage up. Corporal Ware says over and over to himself that Georgette is not going to get him! *He* won't be one of her victims. Steve . . . If I crooked my finger . . . What?'

But she did not crook the finger. Instead, she put her hand upon his and watched him, smiling. He turned the hand and looked down, shaking his head.

'I see your life in that palm,' he singsonged. 'A lovely girl—niece of a rich man—petted by everybody all her life—grown up spoiled—thinks every man was made to jump at her whistle—nothing in the world important but her notions——'

'Nothing about my going away to school, or the wolf-hound I lost on a Tuesday three years ago?'

'Yes, sir—thinks the whole world spins around her—or stops if she wants it that way. What if you crook your finger at me? I'll tell you: I'll go on about my business. You'll have to straighten your finger or point it at some-body else.'

Still she smiled at him, vivid dark face disturbingly close, letting her hand rest in his.

'Captain Durell put you on this case because you're specially able, didn't he? You've cleared up other puz-zles; I'm sure of that. Tell me about them! Tell me about you!'

'He put me on the case for the same reason that he ordered Bar Nothing on it. Two men can find out more than one. We happened to be handy. I'm the youngest man in X Company in age and in service. Except for Bar Nothing, and he's just out of U Company. No need to tell a girl with your brain anything about me. You can see me! And you've certainly heard me.'

'Oh, well,' she said cheerfully, 'you're nothing much for a girl to have around. Bar Nothing's much better company.'

'That's the sensible girl! Don't moon around over something that's clear out of your reach. Take what you can get and claim it's what you want.'

Patronizingly, he patted her hand and smiled. She

jerked the hand away and her horse jumped to the side, rearing under the dig of her rowels.

'You— I—of all the conceited—— One thing! You won't last long enough in Satan Land——'

The big black jumped again, this time into the gallop.

XII. *'A very sad business'*

WARE watched her go, grinning faintly. She kept the horse bearing eastward and disappeared over a ridge.

'*Amor de dios*! but she's a beauty,' he told Rocket. 'No wonder she's been spoiled; thinks people are just made for her to walk on. From all they say, Capen *is* king of this country; the ones who don't make up to her for her looks would knuckle because of the loop he spins. Well! We know what we think about each other. Not that it matters. For we'll see little of her.'

If she had been a different sort of person, he reflected, there were a hundred questions he might have asked: about Ribaut and his pulling of strings about Los Alamos, the amount and kind of crimes in the region, the people in general. Even about his stocky man on the bay Plumb Bob horse. Somewhere, he would have to ask someone those questions, to build up his picture of Ribaut's goings and comings. For he had little hope of finding the actual trail of buckboard and team on this road, if natives had failed. Too much time had passed.

As he continued to jog southward he studied the road, looking mechanically for the ruts of a buckboard among hoofmarks and the prints of wagons. The country grew hillier, with occasional domes and pillars of stone and masses of boulders. Somewhere along here, according to general belief, Theo Ribaut and the boy had been stopped, or had turned aside. Ware whistled tunelessly and shook his head.

'I think I'll hit straight for the man who paid him

the money,' Ware decided. 'He's supposed to have left the D-Bar-D. So that ought to be a starting point for me.'

He looked at the landmarks and turned from the road in a direction more east than south. Rocket foxtrotted through the greasewood and mesquite, avoiding bayonet weed and cactus like the native he was. Ware kept watch as mechanically. But time passed without event, until at last, near noon, he saw two riders on a low hogback, very evidently watching him.

They waited without movement either hostile or friendly until he sent Rocket up the slope to them, then nodded. Both were Mexicans, one a man in mid-twenties, the other hardly more than a boy. Ware looked at their horses, the boy's a D-Bar-D bay, the other a bay also, but wearing a tangled Mexican brand.

'*Buenas dias,*' he greeted them pleasantly, 'Are you *vaqueros* of the D-Bar-D?'

They shrugged. The man looked Ware's smallish figure up and down, face blank, eyes watchful. The boy was openly admiring of clothing, saddle, horse.

'Why—perhaps,' the *vaquero* answered. 'Or of the Open A. Why do you need to know? Are you a stranger? You came from Los Alamos?'

'I have no need. But I am a stranger and I look for the house of the D-Bar-D. The young one, there, he rides a horse with that brand. It is of no import. Perhaps he bought the horse and did not vent the brand. Your customs are not known to me. The house lies ahead?'

The man studied him, as if even this simple question needed thought. Then he nodded slightly.

'It lies ahead. Keep that great monument of stone always on your left and go on toward the desert. You will see the windmill. One might ride it before the night.'

Ware offered tobacco and papers, and in turn they made cigarettes. But there was no relaxation of their guarded manner. He smoked and spoke of this and that natural range matter. They listened, and the man who alone talked gave brief replies or nodded.

At last, shifting straight in the saddle, Ware said, 'A sad business, that of Ribaut, *no es verdad?*'

'A very sad business,' the *vaquero* agreed stolidly. 'If you think so.'

As he rode his way and they went on out of sight in the arroyos and small rocky hills, Ware grinned without humor. The manner of the *vaqueros* seemed entirely typical of the region. Nobody trusted his neighbor, much less the stranger. As he kept the great monument-like rock on his left and rode the slopes and flats automatically, he summed up what he knew of Ribaut from Bar Nothing's talk.

The man was like so many on the frontier, a mystery. In his cups, he had been known to hint that he was from an old and famous family 'back East,' but whether that was a Ribaut family, or he had assumed the name Ribaut years before, none knew. An able, well-read lawyer, famous for his eloquent orations in and out of court, he preferred the string-pulling of politics to practice. Owning the manner of a great gentleman, with the finest homes of all the border country open to him, he had married a slatternly Mexican woman out of a *peon* family.

Partly because of increasing competition, but also because of the distrust or actual hatred felt for him by the country, he had been for three or four years losing his hold on the region. Of late he had barely controlled Los Alamos. Money no longer came easily to him.

'Plenty who'd kill him to rob him,' Ware had summed it up, talking to Bar Nothing. 'Plenty who'd just kill him! And—good enough reason for him just to get together as much as he could and light a shuck.'

Two riders popped up as by a mechanical trick, close ahead of him, to disappear as abruptly. He had only the flashing sight of them, two men on bay or sorrel horses. He pulled in, frowning. The *vaqueros* he had met should be behind, not ahead. But in this broken country it would be very easy to head a man and hardly be exposed; and he had been riding deliberately.

The pair did not reappear, and Ware hesitated. There had been nothing hostile about the two Mexicans, but——

'It could just as naturally be somebody else,' he thought. 'Question is: Did they see me, same as I sky-lined them? And if they did, are they maybe not looking for company? This is a sudden range . . . I think I'll take a thoughtful look!'

He turned Rocket to the right, where an arroyo offered cover. As Rocket moved, from that spot where the men had gone a Winchester shot sounded. A bullet fairly breathed upon his neck. The next instant he was flat over the horn and Rocket surged toward the arroyo. The Winchester *hranged*! time after time. But Rocket jumped into the dry watercourse before the rifleman had corrected his range. Ware slid from the saddle with his own carbine out. His sombrero dropped. He scrambled up the arroyo bank until high enough to look over, head masked by a greasewood bush.

'He certainly did set the air afire over me,' he thought. 'Now, I wonder! My *vaqueros*? Or maybe Hannom and another Open A gunman? Or would it be a couple of Smith's D-Bar-D hands, trying to make 'emselves impolite to strangers?'

There was still no movement in the stony rolls where the men had vanished. Ware studied the land's lay. The arroyo in which he sheltered ran toward the ridges from which the shots had been fired. Apparently the men were in another. They could come at him only by working along it and into his. He watched, green eyes narrow and bright, grinning faintly. Then he lifted the little carbine and drove two shots at the rock nearest to where he thought they lay.

His fire was answered quickly and accurately. Lead tore into the greasewood close by him and whistled away across the arroyo. He slid down, scooped up his sombrero, and mounted. Rocket moved at the walk, ears pointing forward, as if he watched for an enemy. It was not the first—nor the dozenth—time he had carried Ware into a fight. He chose his own path now, putting his hoofs down carefully among the rocks, making very little noise. A horse ahead was not so quiet. Ware pulled in short with the clink of a horseshoe on a stone

The rider came on. Ware slipped from the saddle and moved toward a boulder near the arroyo wall. Rocket came after him. The big horse stumbled and the rock on which his hoof had turned crashed against another. Instantly, the man up-arroyo whirled his horse. Ware ran to the side and forward. He had a glimpse of a smallish figure on a bay horse and began firing without touching butt to shoulder. The bay stumbled to its knees. The rider came off like a cat and plunged toward a jumble of boulders. Ware stopped and lifted his Winchester steadily. With the echoing crash of his shot the horse collapsed.

Wolfishly, then, Ware began to work toward the man's shelter. But out of the boulders came a burst of shots and he had to hug the wall. Worse—from the cross-arroyo carried the thud of galloping hoofs. The other man was coming to the battle without troubling to ride quietly. Ware looked at the bank by which he stood, then began to climb carefully. The galloping horse had stopped; no more lead came from the boulders. The only sound was that made by the wind in the grease-wood, the little rasp of Ware's boots, and the swish of sliding dirt.

He wriggled over the edge and listened, then began to work forward, to get over the dismounted one's position. Before he had taken his third cautious step, a heavy rifle bellowed from the original position of the pair he hunted. The slug came only close enough to prove that he was its mark. He jumped to a low shoulder of stone. Bullets chased him, but he squatted behind the rock without being touched. There were noises in the arroyo under him, but he peered at the spot from which that unexpected attack had come.

'Three of 'em?' he wondered. 'Must be! Even if I did
only glimpse two . . .'

He waited with Apache patience, watching for movement on the left, listening to the small noise below. At
last, in the stones and greasewood clumps of the cross-
arroyo edge he saw the movement of a dark body. It
was not clear, but he aimed carefully at its center, fired,
and whipped down the lever to fire again. Without waiting to see the result of that shot, he rolled toward the
brink of the arroyo under him. Nobody was in sight,
but he sent two bullets whining and ricocheting from
boulders, past the dead horse and toward the cross-
arroyo.

The shots seemed to send a horse, or more than one
horse, into a frantic gallop. The sounds went to the
left, toward that other rifleman. Ware looked that way
again, but there was no more movement. So he slid
down into the arroyo and went along it to where it
crossed the other watercourse. He could no longer hear
the horse, or horses; and the arroyo was too twisted to
let him see more than thirty or forty yards. So he went
back to the horse and looked quickly at it.

' "Skillet of snakes" iron,' he grunted, giving the border cowboy's reading of the tangled Mexican brand.
'But not the same horse that the careful *vaquero* was
riding . . .'

The saddle was a worn center-fire tree, and the length
of the stirrup leathers told of a man no more than
Ware's height. There was a blanket-and-slicker roll behind the low cantle, and Ware was tempted to cut it
loose to see what might be in it. But with three explo-
sive fighters in the broken country beyond him, policy
seemed to dictate getting back to Rocket and trying
to locate them.

Mounted again, he rode alertly up the arroyo, straining his ears for sound of the enemy. When he came to
the crossing of the arroyos once more, he dismounted
and worked slowly from boulder to boulder, going hardly more than a step at a time between halts for listening.

Tense as he was, ready for a wolfish leap to cover, or a snapshot at anything moving, he found the stalk pleasant. Fear of being killed—even of being hurt—he had never known. Fighting was a game in which each side used all its skill and cunning, and he was confident of his own ability to play that ancient game.

'Three of 'em, but only two horses,' he thought while he hunted them. 'If I could kill another horse——'

But evidently they were watching, too. Two rifles blazed into a volley, pounding wall and floor around him so closely that he huddled behind a boulder and hid his face behind his shoulder, squinting against the splinters and pebbles flung up. The firing stopped and he wriggled to the far side of the wagon-sized rock. Tell-tale smoke rose lazily above a litter of boulders ahead. Ware grinned and shoved his carbine forward, sighted, and began to fire.

He sprayed the rocks as with a hose, hunting cracks between them, trying for ricochets, watching for sign of them. When the Winchester was hot and empty he drew back to the other side of his shelter and waited for re-turn-fire. But none came. He reloaded, and still the line of boulders was quiet. So he ventured to dash to the next cover, then the next, until he could climb to the lip of the arroyo and look all around.

He could see neither man nor horse; and there was no sound anywhere except that of the land. He worked toward the boulders, came up to them, slid around the largest with carbine shoved out—and found only the litter of brass shells to show where his men had been.

With more and more boldness he looked for sign. When he saw where two horses had stood for a time, he knew that he had won the skirmish, if no more. The horses had been turned and ridden away at a walk. He trailed them, disappointed because there was no sign that his shooting had been better than theirs. Then he rounded a red rock slab and looked down upon a dead man.

It was a Mexican, grizzled, scarred of face, one-eyed,

shabby except for a broad belt of carved saddle leather spotted with gold and silver, with heavy buckle of engraved gold. Near him was a long .45-70 Winchester, and Ware, with a glance at the arroyo wall above the body, understood that this was the man who had fired upon him while the other two were at the crossing of the arroyos. He had died on the rim from a bullet through the head, then slid down here.

XIII. *'Meaner'n twin rattlesnakes'*

Ware went quickly back to Rocket, piecing together the background of this fight. Three men had seen him and set out to bushwhack him. He wondered grimly if their reason had been general or particular: if they wanted to kill him only because Satan Land disliked strangers, or because he was known to them.

'Could have been my two *vaqueros*,' he speculated. 'But that would mean one of 'em changing horses with Number Three—the one who tried to part my hair and couldn't quite get there . . . For I have got a dead horse and a dead man and I don't know either one of 'em! Of course, it could have been Hannom and a pair of his Open A friends. But, somehow, two of 'em hightailing from one doesn't match up with my notion of Hannom. I expect better than that of Hannom, yes, sir! Might just as well have been town mice wanting to discourage me on this Ribaut job. Georgette seemed to know as much of my detail to it as I do; so, likely, the whole town knows. So—I do'no' a thing for certain except that I showed one of the bushwhackers you don't shoot without being shot . . .'

In the saddle, he turned Rocket for another look at the dead horse. There was nothing about the saddle to tell him more than he had seen at a glance—that it was not a typical Texas tree, being of the single-girth type more often seen on Northern ranges. But the slicker and blanket, unrolled, assured him that the horse had been ridden by an Anglo, not a Mexican.

For besides the new flannel shirt, the pair of socks, the plug of chewing tobacco, was a letter. Salutation and signature had been torn away from the penciled sheet of cheap ruled paper. But it was in English and intended for one who spoke, not merely English, but rangeland English:

Yor leter comm saif was offul glad to hear. Times ben offul hard hear not like time we dun thatt othur. Stores and bankes gott no mony nothing to paye you all comming. I am roling my bedd ende of munth wood like offul well to wurk with you all agen. You no I will nott nede to sende off for a bakbone. Writt befoar ende of munth saye if I can wurk with you all. I will hit thatt waye pronto.

Ware nodded grimly. If he had needed more proof than their actions, the scrawled note would have made him sure that the men who had tried to kill him were outlaws. He could almost see the writer, a weak cowboy good enough to 'stake out' bank or store for highliners, even to make an extra hand during the robbery, but not of caliber for a regular.

'My li'l' friend wrote a letter,' Ware deduced. 'Asked this *gunie* if Jonesboro or Smithville had put on some fat since the last time the bunch hit 'em in the pocketbook. I—wonder! All that talk at Olin's about Doggy Tibb . . . Could that have been Doggy I shot a horse out from under? Yeh! *Could* have been. But——'

He moved over to the tumbled boulders, behind which the man had gone frog-like. And with sight of the blood red-black upon the sand, he understood why the two had run away from a fight with one. But he saw nothing more to be done here. Both men were now mounted. The wounded man was plainly able to ride the horse of that dead Mexican. In this broken country trailing them would be next to impossible—and the advantage would be always with the ones trailed.

'I still think that we'd better head for Smith's!' Ware told Rocket. 'Maybe he knows my dead rattler with the .45-70 fangs. Or Acting Sheriff Ben Briggs may—if Marie Ribaut lets him look!'

He sent Rocket at the trot back to the dead man. Here he made methodical search of the Mexican's pockets. But either the escaped pair had been before him, or the man had carried nothing more than tobacco and cornhusks, a stock knife, three silver *pesos*. The belt drew Ware's eyes. He unbuckled it, pulled it off, then covered the man's face with his battered hat.

The belt went into an *alforja* and Ware swung up. He made a cigarette as Rocket topped out of the arroyo, then squinted at the sun. It seemed a long time since he had jumped the big horse into shelter, but in reality, he decided, not two hours had passed from first sight of the hostile riders to this moment. He looked at the monument of stone and pushed Rocket into a lope, grinning sardonically at a thought which came.

'It'll be funny, Horse, if our riley friends happen to land at Smith's before we do! For they'll know us before we know them. It'll be funny, but we may not get time to laugh!'

There was no sign of the pair during the afternoon, as Ware watched for the windmill the *vaquero* had mentioned. He saw it on the flat ahead, well before dark. Beyond was a motte of cottonwoods. Now, he pushed the carbine back into its scabbard and rode more watchfully. But when the fort-like adobe of the D-Bar-D house showed, with its bare dooryard and row of smaller buildings behind, he found nothing hostile about its look.

Rocket halted at the corral and Ware stared curiously about. A man came around the corral and looked calmly at him. In every detail of feature and dress he was the *pelado,* the Mexican laborer.

'Howdy,' he drawled. 'Light and rest the saddle.'

'Thanks!' Ware said slowly, and the man's teeth flashed.

'I'm Carlos Smith. Reckon you thought I was a Mexican. And you was half-right. The old man drifted down to Satan Land and squatted here, thirty year back. Couldn't find a woman handy in them days except among the Mexicans. So he married Ma at Piedra and I take after her folks in looks.'

Ware got down and stretched.

'Glad to meet you. Reckon I met a couple of your hands this morning. One was riding a D-Bar-D bay, anyhow. Just a boy. The other was older, sort of hatchet-faced. Skillet-of-snakes brand on his horse.'

'I sell a good many horses around,' Smith drawled vaguely.

'Queer business about old Ribaut, wasn't it?' Ware said easily. 'Peculiar even for this country.'

'Sure was! They tell me—couple fellows from Alamos that come hunting him—that I'm likely the last to see old Theo. Except them that rubbed out his mark. If—' he grinned— 'he was rubbed out a-tall.'

'You don't mean you—that there's doubt he was?' Ware demanded in as amazed tone as he could manage. 'Why, the way I heard it, somebody killed him and the boy while he was driving back from Piedra. The money they say he had in the buckboard was certainly enough to buy him lead—through his back.'

'Seventy-six hundred and forty-two dollers,' Smith agreed, 'is plenty even for .45 slugs. Maybe he had more. I do'no' what he was about at Piedra or on the road there. But I paid him that much, principal and interest, on my mortgage. And I'm plumb happy I got back that mortgage, I tell you. It was due the day after I paid, and if I'd had to monkey around trying to find out who could take it and give me back my headache papers, Marie might've found her a law-shark to prove my place was forfeit. And it's worth two-three times that much. You'll stay the night?'

Ware nodded. He had been watching, listening, for the men he had fought. It was a little hard to frame the question he wanted to ask about them. Smith answered it for him.

'You're certainly welcome. I don't see many folks drifting by I can wawa with. Old Theo, now, he come out just to collect. Then he went on to Piedra, him and the boy and some Mexican I never see before. Then he come back—that is, they come back, him and the boy and this mean-looking li'l' *cholo*—and stopped overnight. A week or so after, Buzz Bingham and 'Pache Logan, they bulged along from Alamos, hunting him. You're the first to wander along since then.'

He indicated the corral and stood by while Ware unsaddled. Then he led the way to a shed and showed him where to put his gear. When Ware brought his carbine outside with him, he grinned.

'Know how you feel. Pet gun, huh? Bring her along and stand her in the corner.'

Ware grinned faintly. He was studying his host, wondering if that rather lengthy tallying of Ribaut's visits and the coming of Bingham and Logan had been artless or artful; the indirect alibi of a man who knew a good deal, or merely the garrulous way of a man much alone. It seemed to him proper to be suspicious of everyone who might have had contact with Ribaut on that last trip of the lawyer. Certainly, Smith's contact had been closer than that of anyone else he knew. He stopped abruptly.

'Oh! Nearly forgot. Wait a minute.'

He went back into the shed and from the *alforja* took the belt the dead man had worn. Outside again, he held it up.

'Know a Mexican that this belongs to?' he asked.

Smith looked at it frowningly, then shook his head.

'Can't say as I do. Reckon I'd have noticed it if I'd been around it before. Shines enough! Why?'

'Just wondered. You are kind of off the trail, here. Lonesome country! Seems funny old Ribaut would take chances carrying that much cash around. You'd think he'd have collected from you on the road back. Saved the packing and the danger.'

They were at the house now. Ware stepped alertly into the dusk of a big room and automatically slid to the side so that solid adobe masked his back. Smith followed and crossed to a door while Ware looked about, eyes refocusing. He called to 'Carmencita' to get supper ready.

'Set down! Set down!' he invited Ware. 'Take that big chair and make yourself easy. Why, Theo wanted to hold off our business till he got back, but I wasn't that big a *tonto!* I've known that old fox all my life. He's cute, and he's meaner'n twin rattlesnakes. Time he got back, my mortgage would've been overdue. Likely he wouldn't have come back by; just gone on back and foreclosed. Uh-uh! I made him take the money and hand over the mortgage. I told him he could go out and hide the sack somewheres till he got back, but all I wanted was my paper. I know that old devil too well, Ware. I ain't saying he was too crooked to sleep in a round corral, but it would bulge out the pickets if he was to!'

Ware hid the surprise he felt at use of his name. So, Carlos Smith had known him from the beginning. Evidently, then, he knew the reason for this talk of Ribaut. Ware wondered why the man had not voiced his recognition directly at first, instead of letting it show now by inadvertent use of his name.

'May not mean a thing,' he reflected. 'But in this business you have got to think of the little things as well as the big—and often and often, I do remember, some of the little ones showed up at last as pretty big . . .'

XIV. *'I smell murder!'*

CARLOS SMITH produced a quart of tolerable Bourbon whiskey and they drank. He was very much a talker. As he listened to recountal of what he already knew of Theo Ribaut's history, with much that he had never heard of Ribaut's political and financial and personal moves over thirty-odd years, Ware continued to study Smith and wonder if the man were talking just because it was his nature and he had nothing to conceal, or if everything he said was cleverly intended to give that impression.

They ate the meal served by a pretty, silent Mexican girl, and still Smith talked, Ware only steering the conversation by occasional questions or remarks. Back in the big room, which evidently served the rancher as bed-sitting-room, he spoke of Ribaut's reputed influence over men of the region.

'No trick roper in the Bill Shows ever had so many loops going at once as Theo,' Smith agreed, grinning. 'Clean back to Austin he had his lines. He could get him jobs with good pay and no work—and him a Republican! Seems like he just had to pull gentle on a rope and whisper to somebody that he wanted something—— Hell! he was packing more secrets than any two men had a right to guess at.'

'You really take stock in the notion that he just lit a shuck? You sort of talked like that, you know. Some around Alamos seem to hold with you, if you do.'

'He wasn't so easy to handle as you might figure, to look at him or hear about him! He packed a .45 under one arm and he didn't need no month's notice to get her out and smoking. And he could stitch your shirt with it, fancy. He went down to Stonewall one day with

84

a bad Mexican that Jimmy Quagson—Jimmy's county attorney in Stonewall—aimed to try for murder. On the stage the killer snatched a gun off his guard and he was going to shoot 'em all. But Ribaut got his .45 out and drilled him before he could let the hammer down on a cap.'

'Funny!' Ware grunted sardonically. 'I never was in this country before; never laid eyes on Theo Ribaut; and still I know the truth of that deal and it seems you don't: Ribaut didn't want that Mexican tried, for reasons of his own. The guard was a man of his. The gun the killer grabbed was empty. Cap'n Durell got the straight of it, but he couldn't prove a thing!'

'Do'no's I ever felt sure of Ribaut's account,' Smith conceded easily, shrugging. 'But, either way it happened, it goes to show that gun-slinging didn't bust his coperostus a bit. He was cat-eyed and, since Alf Mullit come over from Capen to work for him he was extra cat-eyed. Looks funny to me that anybody could've got the drop on him. If he was took by surprise, still he would have got him a lunch while the others was having dinner.'

Ware nodded. Smith poured them another drink, dark face thoughtful, shaking his head.

'He had plenty reason to hightail, Ware. Plenty! He was right up to the tassel end of his twine around here. *We* do'no' how much money he had, besides my seventy-six hundred. Maybe he thought about the men around who'd like a chance to even up with him; and about how much safer he'd be somewheres else. Maybe he just schemed it to skip without leaving a sign!'

'Can happen,' Ware conceded. 'Seems to me, Smith, you struck it lucky, having the money to pay him off when you did.'

'Lucky! Lucky your aunt's black cat's long, curly tail! I just about went down on my marrow bones to old Clem Tooley at Piedra to borrow that money off him. He finally loaned it to me—just as a favor—for a year—eleven per cent. Lucky! I just hopped out from between two bricks into a hard place. Clem Tooley has got a

mortgage on the D-Bar-D that covers it all—same a long
blanket covers a short Injun. Huuuh!'

'Tooley? That the storekeeper?'

'No. He's a lawyer. But mostly he's forty-'leven different other things. Partnering in one business or other;
trading ranches and stock—I do'no' what-all he ain't in.
He's fat and he looks sleepy as a cowpony in town and
kind of easy-going—and ain't none of that so except he's
fat. Say! I was just thinking about that belt you showed
me. Where'd you find it? My range?'

'Don't know about the range,' Ware said, shrugging.
'I got it off the Mexican who owned it. I had to kill
him.'

Smith was drinking. He gulped, coughed furiously,
shook his head, and regarded Ware with watering eyes.

'You—you killed him? And—you been setting here—
you been eating supper and talking about Ribaut
and—— You wouldn't run ice water, instead of blood,
would you? *Amor de dios*! I ain't boogery, special. But
if you ain't about the coolest I ever run into, you'll do
till he comes along.'

Ware shrugged calmly. 'He got first bite! I didn't even
know he'd been born when he let got at me. I certainly
won't lose any more sleep over him than I would over
a snake that hit at me and missed. When three Win-
chesterful hairpins choose me——'

Briefly, he told of the fight. Smith shook his head.

'One of my boys was in town and heard about you
backing Hannom down. I didn't take a lot of stock in
that, somehow. Rafael thought it was kind of an accident; that Hannom had something on his mind and
you was favored—Rafael said you was just a kid—But—I
wonder who it could've been . . .'

To Ware, watching, listening intently, he sounded sin-
cere. They talked without much point about the men.
When at nine he took the cot that Smith showed him
and the room was dark, Ware lay for a while, thinking
of the three men and of his host. Carlos Smith interested

him a great deal more than those riders so simply murderous. For in Satan Land there were altogether too many riders who shot at strangers from general policy. But Smith——

'His story's not worth a hoot unless it can be proved,' Ware decided. 'Same for a charge against him, if one was made. So—I have got to ride down to Piedra and see Clem Tooley.'

Suddenly, he recalled Smith's remark about a strange, 'mean-looking' little Mexican, going and coming with the Ribauts. No other person, speaking of the case, had mentioned that third one in the Ribaut buckboard. The mystery might very well be solved by no more complicated procedure than identifying and locating that Mexican—if he had not died or fled with the Ribauts.

'And, somehow,' Ware thought, 'I can't buy a lot of stock in the idea of Ribaut leaving the country. He might have got scared; might have decided to toss in his cards. But a man who pulled so many wires for so long would find it pretty hard to believe that he was done. He'd go on hoping. I smell murder!'

One thing he had rather completely assured himself of—Smith's lack of knowledge of the bushwhackers. He believed that if the escaping pair had come to the D-Bar-D and spoken to Smith, his manner would have been vaguely different when discussing the dead man's belt. For he would have known of the man's death. Which, of course, meant only that Smith had not identified them at the moment, not that he did not know them.

He was up with the first sound of Carmencita's stirring in the next room. Smith snored evenly and Ware looked down upon him intently, studying the thin, long-nosed face with its pointed chin and oddly small mouth. He decided that Carlos would never be a favorite of his; there was something weak and shifty, if more than usually intelligent, about the halfbreed.

Carmencita looked at him with a blankness of ex-

pression which somehow typified Satan Land and its
people. Ware smiled pleasantly at her and in Spanish
inquired how she did.

'Very well, thank you,' she answered in a flat voice.
'You wish to clean yourself? There is water in the trough
at the corner of the house. Wait! I will give you a cloth
for drying.'

Ware thanked her and smiled again, but there was
no lightening of her guarded manner. Splashing in the
trough, drying face and hands, smoothing his short,
black hair, Ware wondered about the girl. Usually he
got on very well with her kind, received at least an answering smile and light word.

'Maybe it's just her natural disposition,' he reflected.
'But—somehow I don't think so. My guess is that she's
sulking about something—or scared——'

Carlos Smith came to wash. He seemed quite cheerful. Ware smoked a cigarette while the D-Bar-D owner
ducked in the trough and rubbed himself dry, talking
briskly the while.

'I'll take Rafael down with a gentle horse and gather
up that fellow you drilled. Got to go into Alamos, anyhow. So I'll take him along to Briggs. You better gi'
me a note to that Ames and to Briggs. I don't want to
have somebody accusing me of killing him! Well, ready
for breakfast?'

He talked while they ate the steaks Carmencita
brought and drank her very good coffee. This morning,
he had no doubt at all about Ribaut: The old man had
taken all the money he could get together and cleverly
escaped from the country. Ware shrugged.

'I wish an affidavit from you, to that effect, would
satisfy the family,' he said grimly. 'I—well, I reckon I
oughtn't to spill this to anybody, but you've helped me
so much with information about the country that I feel
like opening up. This Ribaut case is just a side-issue
with me, Smith. I'm on another trail; one that started
'way back over. But'—he looked at the wreathing smoke
of his cigarette, preparing to make a skillful mixture of

fact and fiction—'the Ribauts can pull strings in Austin. So I have got to make some kind of show at looking into the case. Same for Ames. If I see the killer—if there was a killer—I'll loop him. But if you'll show me a dark, heavy-set hairpin with bat ears, riding a bay horse branded Arrow Head, I will thank you!'

'Oh! Like that!' Smith grunted, grinning and nodding. 'Arrow Head . . . Nearest to that I know about, on ary horse I seen rode around the country lately, was what I took for a Plumb Bob. And the fellow straddling that bay wasn't dark. Do'no' about his ears; I glimpsed him three-four days ago on the east edge of Satan Land. Watched him awhile through the glasses. Seems to me like he was yellow-haired; lock was down on his forehead. I never showed; that's a lonesome country, and lots of men riding it don't hunt people to meet. Besides, I was busy with some rustler tracks and they was made by Mexicans. But I thought about that Plumb Bob iron, account I always heard that outfit was 'way over in the Devil's River country.'

Ware lifted his cup with a hand rock-steady and drank. He drew in smoke and blew rings upward, as if what Smith had said was of so little importance that it needed no answer. But inwardly he felt a surge of savage exultation hard to control. His man was still ahead of him! Here, at last, was proof that Loren, not he, had been following the wrong trail.

'This fellow was heading kind of north,' Smith continued, as if bent upon drawing some answer from his audience. 'If you're heading for Capen's, you might run onto some sign of him. But it was a Plumb Bob, not a Arrow Head, iron on that bay.'

'Capen's? Huh! With that girl there? I can make a motion just as good by heading for Piedra and asking if anybody down there killed Ribaut. Besides, I kind of figured that my man on the Arrow Head *caballo* would stick to the River. You see, Smith, there's a reward for him . . . If the Cap'n wants me to hunt Ribaut killers to satisfy the family, I might just as well hunt 'em where I might stumble onto fifteen hundred accidentally.'

Smith laughed. It seemed to Ware that his manner was easier.

'Tricks to all trades, huh?' he said, with sag of an eye-lid. 'Well, luck to you, Ware! I certainly am glad you come by. It gets plenty lonesome out here, and half the time when somebody does come by he ain't a man you want to talk to. When you pass this way again, don't you miss stopping. I do'no' when I've cottoned to any-body so much in a dog's age.'

He came out to the corral, protesting friendship, and stood by while Ware saddled Rocket and shoved the carbine into its scabbard, the ornamented belt into an *alforja*. A slender Mexican youth appeared and stared admiringly at Rocket. Smith ordered him to catch up a packhorse and get ready for a ride to town.

'I won't have trouble finding him,' he assured Ware. 'I know that scope of country from what you said. *Hasta la vista!*'

Ware rode vaguely southward for most of that long day, meeting nobody until in mid-afternoon he came back to the road. La Piedra was a tiny place, some twenty adobe houses and stores making a thin double row through which the road ran. It stood on a low mesa just above the tangled *bosque* of the River, willow and cottonwood and tornillo and low bushes, threaded by stock-trails. A well-beaten road turned toward the River beyond the *plazita,* evidently leading to a ford.

Ware looked at the single two-story building which dominated the place. Both stories were fronted by deep verandas. The lower floor was a prosperous-seeming store. Mexicans and one or two Anglo cowboys loafed on the earthen floor, smoking, eating, talking. A dozen horses were at a hitch-rack down at the end of this build-ing. But above them, sitting like a great Buddha on the upper porch near the rail, was a man with what seemed to Ware a black stick set crosswise at his mouth.

As Ware came abreast of the store the loafers looked

at him curiously. The fat man looked over the railing but did not lower the stick. Faintly, over the gabble of talk, Ware caught a thin piping sound and understood that Clem Tooley was playing a flute. He knew that the fat man could be none but Tooley. He rode to the hitch-rack and swung down. As he turned, he heard hoof-beats. From behind the store, riding away, a slim cowboy appeared. He turned in the saddle and Ware saw his face.

'I thought I recognized that buckskin!' he told him-self.

For it was the devil-may-care youngster of Eagan's 66, who had told him that he was lucky, at Olin's. He rode on, seeming not to see Ware.

XV. 'Somebody's watch charm'

WARE stared after him, frowning. There was no mis-taking that man of Eagan's. When he had ridden over to get Burt Eagan's hat, there at Olin's store, and stopped to speak, there had been both time and reason for a good look at man and horse.

'Now,' Ware asked himself, 'how-come he's over here?'

But short of riding after the cowboy and putting that question, there seemed no easy way of getting an answer. Unless Clem Tooley or some other Piedran knew—and would talk.

Ware shrugged it off and went around the corner. Stairs led up to the second-story porch and, while the loafers stared, he climbed them. The notes of the flute came down to him, a vaguely familiar melody. Then he recalled where he had heard it—in a San Antonio variety theater months before. He hummed it to him-self softly as he went on up.

The huge man in a great handmade chair looked owlishly at him over the flute and continued to blow until a discordant squeak sounded. He stopped, blew again, squeaked once more in the same place.

'Doddern it!' he complained irritably, lowering the flute. 'Don't know how many times I've done that. You know anything about a flute, young fellow?'

'Just what they look like and sound like. Know that tune, though: *Pinafore*. There was a clown singer in Red Ed's at San Anton' singing it. It runs about the Cap'n and winds up:

> I am never known to quail
> At the fury of the gale,
> And I'm never, never sick at sea!
> What, never?
> No, never!
> What, never?
> Well—hardly ever!'

'Oh, I know the song, too. Know what it sounds like. But, doddern it! I can't make it come out of this stick the way it's supposed to! But I'll get that run right or bust a hamestring!'

Ware grinned faintly, moving over to half-sit on the porch rail, studying Clem Tooley. Without Carlos Smith's description, he thought that he would have judged this fat man correctly. So he met the tiny eyes levelly.

'Reckon you know who I am,' he drawled.

'Doddern it! That's not fair,' Tooley grunted. 'A good, safe lawyer, he never admits anything. Might be a confession. But, since you put it that way—yeh. Leave your long-coupled partner in Los Alamos?'

'Somebody had to talk with Marie Ribaut. In cases like that I always try to make it somebody else. I'm just riding over the road that Ribaut was on, to get the lie of the land in mind. On the way, I pick up this and that.'

Tooley nodded and got a black Mexican cigarette from the small basket on his chair-arm. He scratched a match, set the flame to the tobacco, and drew in smoke.

'And, naturally, being a pretty bright young man, you want to test out and check what you pick up. I can set your mind to rest on one thing: I really did loan Carlos the seventy-six hundred. You wanted to ask me that . . .'

Ware frowned slightly, then nodded. Here was a man after his own heart! But it was no part of an investigation to trust anyone, anywhere, without knowing him. Least of all, he reminded himself, in Satan Land.

'Of course!' he conceded, in surprised tone. 'I have got to test every step of the way. Smith told everybody that he'd paid off Ribaut and got his mortgage back. Sort of funny, no? I mean, paying at the ranch; Ribaut riding around with that mortgage in his pocket. Seems to me that the paying would have been done in town.'

'Now, as to that, I just wouldn't know. Theo had his ways of doing things and they mostly weren't my ways—thanks be! I loaned Carlos the money and he signed a mortgage on the D-Bar-D. Plenty security to protect me if I have to foreclose. He had got back his mortgage. I'm in the clear.'

'Suppose he hadn't paid Ribaut? Suppose he'd just rammed the money into his pocket and Ribaut had foreclosed?'

Clem Tooley blew smoke into the still air and regarded it with slitted eyes. His fat sides shook gently.

'Technically, that would have been bad. No security for me. Seventy-six hundred out on a personal loan. I see what you mean. It would have been downright bad—for Carlos. These boys around here, Ware, they know me right well. I just can't think of one of 'em who'd hand me the dirty end of a stick—unless he was absolutely certain I was more than just usually dead.'

He flipped away the stub of his cigarette and turned a sleepy smile upon Ware.

'I loaned Carlos the money for one year and I charged him interest right up to usury. Because I don't like him and I never did and I couldn't abide his shifty-eyed father before him. He told me his troubles and I handed him the money on no more than a witnessed receipt. But—and this is important—I said:

' "Pay off Theo and get your mortgage. Then bring it here and we'll tear it up and make out mine. Be you sure"—I said to him in my plainest voice—"that you do that, and just that." He did, for reasons I've hinted at . . .'

Ware was watching two riders coming toward the edge of La Piedra along the road he had covered.

'What do you allow? About Ribaut disappearing?'

'Oh—*quién sabe*? Too many ways it might have happened—by pure accident of circumstance or the coldest kind of intent. It might have been a murder, but just as well it might have been a plan of Ribaut's hatching—as you've heard. If he skipped with that favorite boy of his and all the cash he could rake together, anybody who wants him found may have to circle around a lot, to pick up the .trail outside of this neighborhood. If it was murder——'

He shrugged and repeated what Carlos Smith had said, about the politician's many enemies. Ware nodded toward the oncoming riders, recognizable, now, as the two *vaqueros* he had met before the battle of the day before. He asked Tooley who they were.

'Valdez and Murillo; couple of Smith's hands. Why?'

'I met 'em yesterday and they wouldn't admit a thing— not even about the weather,' Ware told him dryly. 'Right after that, three gunies began to play the Winchester for me. I wondered if there might be a connection between Valdez and Murillo and that interesting session.'

'That I wouldn't know about. But I have always figured the two of 'em average good men, even if they do ride for Carlos Smith. In Satan Land, you might easily run into three travelers so stuck up they would kill a man who might want to associate with 'em.'

'Why did Ribaut come down here?' Ware demanded abruptly.

'Politicking for the sheriff's race, partly. He's backing that useless Briggs for sheriff. Partly a cow-trade.'

'Who was the mean-looking little Mexican with Ribaut?'

'Mexican? With Ribaut?' Tooley countered, staring at him. 'Oh! Why, that was the ghost of King Ferdinand of Spain, not a Mexican. He was in two parts. Half of him rode on Ribaut's right shoulder, the other half on the boy's lap. Isabella and Christopher Columbus traveled with him. But they weren't in the buckboard. Chris had his snowshoes and Isabella rode on the handlebars of a tandem bicycle. All invisible to the naked eye, of course.'

'Meaning?' Ware drawled.

'Meaning that I was sitting in the store below, when Ribaut finished his cow-trade and came in to ask if he could buy a plug of chewing tobacco. We've been on the outs for a good twenty years and he knows I am Hack Kinney's partner in the store. I said to Hack:

' "Well, you advertise to serve man or beast and I reckon if you can't rightfully sell him on one count, he slips in on the other." So he took his plug and paid his money with the Ribaut teeth showing like a coyote's. Then he went out to the buckboard and I watched him clear out of town. It's a straight road. He didn't stop this side of Two-Mile Grade to pick up a passenger, and there certainly was nobody with him and the boy coming into Piedra or going out.'

'Of course,' Ware suggested, 'he could have left the man beyond Two-Mile Hill coming in and picked him up again.'

'But showed a man who hated his insides—Smith—a Mexican he was afraid to show La Piedra? Maybe. Hardly that. I take you for a young fellow with brains to make up for what you may lack in Durell's experience. And from what I've heard about you—experience is what you're likely to get, fast! Well, look at it this way:

'Plenty of times, Ribaut traveled with a bodyguard. But always it was somebody he could trust; and that means somebody other people know. Carlos Smith knows just about everybody in this country. He told you—I reckon—that a mean-looking little Mexican was with the Ribauts. But he didn't know the man. Ribaut is going to have lots of money to watch. Well? Will he have a strange Mexican—strange anybody!—with him?'

He shook his head, and Ware nodded agreement.

'It's not a bit of skin off my nose what happened to Ribaut,' Tooley went on placidly. 'I'm old enough and mean enough to not give a hoot if he's alive or dead— the boy I do feel concerned about. But as a citizen of the neighborhood, naturally I want to help an officer. So I'll tell you this: If I had your job I'd think a lot about Carlos Smith. Not that Carlos is likely to ever kill anybody! Not even from behind—for he'd be mortally scared that his man might turn around. But because he's Capen's dog and Capen is—is Capen!'

He took another cigarette and lighted it. Ware waited.

'Capen first came into this country years ago, with Georgette, his niece, and a tale of being from South America looking for a location. He found Theo Ribaut ruling the roost. For a time, he worked with Ribaut. Until he knew the ground, you might say. He won the old, run-down Open A from young Holker who'd inherited it, in a string of poker games—maybe honest games! He somehow got possession of a good mining claim. Nobody has seen old Druscovich, the locator, since . . . Selling that property gave Capen money for making a crazy place of the Open A, with a castle and all sorts of picture-book touches.'

'Pianos and Turkey carpets and silver dishes and waiters in white coats,' Ware supplied. 'I've heard about it.'

'Yeh! He called it 'Capen Castle,'' but the Mexicans— they have a sort of feeling for that kind of thing—they named it "The House of Whispering Shadows." They say that it was built with dead men's gold. Young Holker blew his brains out. Druscovich the prospector disappeared. Others have had dealings with Capen and evaporated into thin air or been found dead in such ways that you could only suspect Capen. The Mexicans claim that the shadows of all these dead men move around the place at night, whispering that it belongs to them, but only whispering—because they're still afraid of Capen! You know how they tell ghost-stories.'

'Sometimes the ghosts are pretty solid,' Ware drawled.

'I'd take the ghosts quicker than the gang that usually works for him! Capen's mixed into about everything a man could figure, over the years: wet stock traveling both ways across the line; smuggling; jumping claims; plain and fancy bushwhacking . . . The Open A bunkhouse has generally had a crew in it chased by enough warrants to fill a Monday clothesline. Once or twice an officer went out—but the man he wanted was always gone. By accident!'

'Then Alf Mullit left Capen and went to work for Ribaut,' Ware said thoughtfully. 'He told Ribaut things and these began to get around. Capen is running for sheriff against Briggs, the Ribaut man. If Ribaut's out of the way——'

'Capen's in! You can imagine what kind of place the county will be when he's really King Capen.'

'That's off my line. The thing I'm interested in is covered by an old Ranger question. You always ask it when you can't tell who committed a crime: Who profited? Trouble here is, more than Capen might profit—the man who got the money Ribaut carried; the man who settled a grudge. But it does sound like a case that Capen would be interested in . . .'

Up the stairs a cheerful, freckled man came. He was grinning, looking at something in his hand. He held it out to Tooley.

'Somebody's watch charm,' he said. 'Look at the edges.'

XVI. *'Shadows may whisper'*

CLEM TOOLEY took the gold piece and stared at it.
Then, in a drowsy voice, he asked where it had come
from.

'This is Hack Kinney, Ware,' he added. 'Hack runs
the store. Well, Hack?'

'Murillo and Valdez come in to buy some peaches
and neckerchiefs. Valdez asked me about Ware. Reckon
he seen his horse at the rack, or maybe seen Ware ride
in.'

He laughed softly, looking over the railing while Tooley and Ware watched him.

'Must've scared 'em!' Kinney cried. 'They're dragging
it!'

He threw back his head and fairly roared, rocking on
his heels. Tooley turned to Ware.

'Things seem funnier to Hack than to most people,'
he explained dryly. 'He does get more fun out of life——'

'—I just took a chance,' Kinney gasped. 'I leaned
over the counter and kind of whispered that he'd been
looking over Carlos's range for evidence in the Ribaut
case; and that he'd found some. I said he s'picioned it
was murder and likely done by some of the D-Bar-D
hands. Valdez and Murillo both had give me twenties—
wages from Carlos, of course. I took the gold and acted
like I was setting it in a matchbox off to itself. I said
Ware had asked me to hold any money the D-Bar-D
people brought in, to look at because of evidence.'

He threatened to go into another fit of laughter, but
Tooley's rasping growl checked the attack.

'Murillo bust' out telling me it was just their wages;
Carlos paid 'em couple days back at their line camp. It
wasn't gold off Ribaut. Valdez just looked at me. But

I reckon I run off two customers. They are going to bulge back to the D-Bar-D, I bet you.'

'Hack,' Tooley told his partner in a weary tone, 'if I didn't know you pretty well, I'd think—the way Ware's thinking, now—that you're as big a fool as you act. That practical joking of yours is going to get somebody killed, one of these days. A lot of people in the county will hope it's you! But—ne' mind that, right now. I'm going to tell you-all something:

'If this twenty is not Ribaut's watch charm, that hung on his big gold chain as late as the day he bought plug tobacco in the store, I'm badly mistaken. And in a long and wicked life I haven't been mistaken many times —not so badly that I couldn't explain myself out of the tight anyway. I was born to see things and remember 'em. I can tell you right now, without looking, how many silver buttons are on Ware's pants-legs—and that Theo Ribaut was wearing one gray and one white sock when he stopped in the store—and that this gold piece or its match was in a little gold frame, hanging to his chain. I saw the date on it! I noticed just how much it was worn from rubbing against his belly all these years past.'

'You mean, then, that when I thought I was hurrahing 'em, I was hitting the old dishpan plumb center?'

It was another and entirely different Hack Kinney, a brisk, shrewd-eyed, efficient man, who looked at Tooley.

'I don't know. That is, I don't know whether or not Valdez and Murillo got this particular twenty from Carlos Smith. It could be that they murdered Theo and the boy and robbed and hid 'em. Or that Carlos by himself, or with them, or others, did the same. If Ware wants a lot of glory without a lot of trouble, all he needs to do is bring in Valdez and Murillo dead or alive—better dead, Ware; they pack easier that way— and settle the Ribaut case. Carlos will deny giving 'em this money. There's no witness to disprove his statement. I'll have to testify that to the best of my belief this is Ribaut's charm. Black for 'em!'

'Some big reputations have been built on a lot less,' Ware agreed. 'But I was born so that puzzles bother hell out of me until I've untangled 'em. In the company, they laugh at me for it; call me "Puzzle Buster." In this case, I don't give a hoot who's guilty, or what he's guilty of. But I never would rest if I didn't *know* beyond a doubt who did what—and why!'

'Good man!' Clem Tooley drawled. 'Now, I still don't believe that Carlos owns the nerve for murder. And I've known Valdez and Murillo just about all their lives. Maybe I'm wrong in believing that they're average decent; and wrong in my opinion of Carlos. But I don't think so. I don't think that Carlos having this charm of Ribaut's and paying it to Valdez changes a word in the death-warrant that—I have believed all along—Ribaut and Alf Mullit have had out against 'em! Capen wrote that warrant!'

'Can happen,' Ware admitted, after a moment. 'In fact, if these *vaqueros* got the gold piece from Smith, as they claim, he's certainly mixed in a murder or holdup—— But it's not enough to go on! Lot of difference between suspicion and evidence. You con't *swear* that the charm was Ribaut's. Neither could anybody in his family; too many gold pieces of that date are circulating.'

'Right!' Clem Tooley drawled. 'So, while I'm not trying to tell you how to handle your case, Ware, I will say that if I happened to wear those expensive boots of yours, I'd start digging around the Open A. Might be so as one of those shadows'd whisper something. I'd remember, though, that Capen is clever as a whole den of foxes, able to turn most people inside out.'

Ware worked at the rolling of a cigarette, thinking hard. He had the feeling that Clem Tooley knew much about a good many things—and talked of only a part of what he knew.

'The same thing I've noticed from Little Bend up to Satan Land,' he reminded himself. 'Probably owns an axe he wants ground . . . Well! More than one can play shutmouth!'

In a careless fashion, he asked Clem Tooley about the men in Capen's employ. Both the lawyer and Kinney listed several, putting Hannom at the head as range boss.

'But nobody can say at this distance just who's on the place, or around, from one day to the next. They drift in and out,' Kinney said by way of summing up.

'What's the name of the one-eyed Mexican with the fancy gold-and-silver belt?' Ware asked casually. 'And the heavy-set, yellow-haired man with the Plumb Bob bay?'

'Must be two we haven't met,' Clem Tooley answered. 'But, as Hack said, that's not surprising. This is a great country for strangers!'

'Well'—Ware grinned at them—'I did see one man we all know, riding out as I rode in. A 66 boy——'

'Oh, yeh! Gall Yager,' Kinney grunted, nodding. 'He come in to——'

'Eagan's lost a pet horse,' Clem Tooley thrust in, smiling. 'If Gall can't locate it, fast, Eagan'll be wiring Austin for a company of Rangers. That big sorrel is gold-plated, to hear Eagan tell it. Now, are you heading for the Open A?'

'As soon as I can gather up some of Kinney's airtights for the trip. I like to keep a lunch in the *alforjas*. Thanks for all you've told me, Mr. Tooley. It's hard to come into a strange country and—know the men you can trust.'

'Nothing. Nothing at all. Glad I could help out even a little,' Tooley said heartily. 'If you get a chance to ride back this way, do that. I'll be interested to know what you find.'

He picked up the flute and blew softly into it, a few bars of *Pinafore*. When the discordant squawk sounded, he snarled.

'Doddern it! Maybe by the time you come back I'll

have that fixed. I won't endure blowing one thing into this squeak-stick and having something else come out!'

As Ware and Kinney descended to the store-level, the storekeeper grinned and jerked a thumb upward toward his partner.

'There's lots of Clems in the world,' he remarked, 'and likely there's thousands of Tooleys. But he's the one and only Clem Tooley. When he was made the mold was busted.'

Ware nodded appreciatively. But to himself he said:

'What I'd give to look through that fat face and see his mind! I don't know how many horses Eagan owns, or what colors, but I'd bet my last dollar there's not a big "gold-plated" sorrel on the 66 range!'

In the store, as he took his beans and tomatoes and bacon from Kinney, watched by lounging men, he spoke of Yager.

'He ain't worked for Eagan long,' Kinney answered with a shade of hesitation. 'I really don't know much about him. He's from towards North Texas, seems to me somebody was saying. But I really don't know. Seems like a nice boy; awful pleasant. But salty, too.'

'My notion, exactly,' Ware agreed. 'Does Burt get over this way much? If he does, Gall Yager must be a fine, big relief.'

'He comes in with his pa, Burt does, once in a while. But the 66 and Lightning Rod and outfits around 'em, they buy mostly from Olin, I reckon. Closer than we are. Most generally, when Eagan comes in, he's got a kick about losing stock and wants Clem to raise hell at Los Alamos with the sheriff.'

'Like about the sorrel horse,' Ware said gravely.

'Uh—yeh!' Kinney replied quickly, with shuttling of eyes toward Ware's blank face. 'Well! Reckon that's your load.'

'Reckon. I'll buy you a drink, Kinney, then be going. I'm getting anxious for a looky at that famous Capen place. Shadows may whisper to me, you know.'

They had the drink and Ware took his canned goods,

bacon, coffee, and tobacco to where Rocket drowsed. He packed all deftly in the saddlebags and caught up the reins. As he swung into the saddle, the sound of Clem Tooley's flute came to him—halting on the discord. He grinned faintly. Quite a person, this Clem Tooley! He had something in his mind concerning Capen; very possibly—Ware thought—something which also concerned the investigating Rangers. But what that might be——

'Eagan's in it, I'd guess. Gall Yager came here for something that Kinney wasn't to let out; 66 business. Eagan is down on Olin and Ten Sleep Norman and the like of Doggy Tibb. My Plumb Bob man was in the country the other day. Carlos Smith paid off Valdez and Murillo with gold that may have been on Ribaut when he was roped or murdered. But, they may have lied! Or! Or! Or! What I need is something solid to bite on!'

Clem Tooley waved to him as he came out upon the road. Ware jerked up an arm in return-gesture. It amused him to picture Clem Tooley when the lawyer heard of the fight on Carlos Smith's range, and discovered that he was not the only man who could tell only a small part of what he knew. From consideration of that, as he rode out of La Piedra toward the jagged rise in the desert that he knew to be Three-Jag Hill, he came to consideration of Clem Tooley himself, and his opinion of the lawyer.

He decided at last that the fat man was honest—at least, by the standards of Satan Land! But whether he could be trusted completely by a Ranger who had a particular job, was something else. Clem Tooley would quite naturally be more interested in his own jobs; might try twisting and turning that Ranger to his own ends.

The double trail of Valdez and Murillo was plain before Ware for a half-mile. Then the *vaqueros'* sign turned off the plain way, going into the savage waste of sand.

Satan Land seemed well named. Forty, fifty, miles of

sand stretched away to north and east, sometimes flat, often piled in dunes. Even the cactus and stunted grease-wood and mesquite seemed threatened with burial. The sign of snakes and rabbits were few as Ware rode watch-fully. Eagles and buzzards overhead were the only signs of life. Other trails, some tolerably plain, came into the Open A road. None had fresh sign of use, but the light wind blew the sand so that it was hard to judge.

He came to a stretch more rolling than he had seen; with higher dunes. As Rocket rounded such a wind-carved mound of sand, a rifle-shot shattered the still-ness, and with the roar of it Ware heard the familiar vicious whine of a bullet going past him, fairly close.

He backed Rocket into the shelter of the dune and without haste pulled the carbine from its scabbard. Val-dez and Murillo came instantly to mind, but, just as in the other fight, he could only guess. He dismounted, frowning irritably, and took off his sombrero. Then he moved to look around the dune.

XVII. *'More trouble in town'*

FIFTY yards away was another, smaller pile of sand, brush-crowned. Ware studied it, looked right and left at the rolling desert from which it reared, then nodded placidly. The man or men upon that dune could get away only by riding in a straight line that kept the hil-lock of sand directly between him—or them—and Ware's position. For there was no other shelter for two hundred yards; the greasewood and mesuqite were too low to cover a horseman.

Sure of this, Ware lifted his carbine and drove a bul-let into the brush on top of the dune. The echoes of his shot crashed like sheets of glass breaking. A grease-wood jerked violently and Ware shifted aim, to send the second slug at the sand below that bush. A heavy rifle bellowed at the base of the dune, and Ware heard the bullet thud into sand within a yard of his face. He drew back a little, squinting.

'It does seem to be Valdez and Murillo,' he thought. 'Two men over there; that's certain.'

The next shot assured him that he faced two riflemen. For the report was lighter than the first. He trotted to the left and peered out from shelter of a greasewood. Smoke rose in a hazy feather on the dune-crest, gray against the intense blue of the sky. He fired two quick shots, at the unseen man directly opposite on his own level then at the ridge. Both rifles answered in fierce staccato while he moved to the right, to shoot rapidly and withdraw after that shot.

Comfortable in his shelter, he reloaded the carbine, made a cigarette and lighted it, then repeated the maneuver which seemed to excite his opponents—shooting from the left side, then quickly from the right, of his dune. When shots from both rifles indicated that his men were still before him, he blew out smoke, tossed away the stub, and looked briskly around.

'This,' he remarked to Rocket, 'is interesting. It's one way of passing an afternoon. It beats checkers or most books. But it could get tiresome. So, *caballo mio,* we'll reach under the chuck wagon and get a li'l' trick out of the caboose and——'

He broke off, scowling. Between the dunes and rolls on the trail he had covered, something moved. He had only the one glimpse, but nothing in brush or earth was blue there; so it was a man. Ware took three steps to Rocket and got his glasses. But though he watched that area, examining it inch by inch, almost, the movement was not repeated within his range of vision.

The men ahead fired a shot apiece and Ware, very conscious that he might be now caught between two parties, trotted up to answer that shooting and discourage any charge at his position. Then he came back to Rocket and led him over to a hollow in the sand. He tapped the big gelding's near foreleg and Rocket knelt, then rolled to his side and remained there. Ware went past him and crouched behind a mesquite, head rolling to watch both danger points. He heard the soft scuff of feet from a ridge of sand beyond his bush, a muttered sentence, and grimly raised the carbine.

A greasewood on that ridge moved very slightly. Ware looked at it over the front sight. It was hardly fifty feet away.

'Ought to be close,' a man said behind the greasewood. 'In a minute——'

Above the dull, dark green of the greasewood lifted the bare yellow head of Bar Nothing Ames. Beside it, an instant later, appeared the dark head of Georgette Capen. Both seemed interested, only; they were like spectators of a play. Ware grinned faintly and eased himself very slowly to a more comfortable position. He heard them come forward softly, up to his cover. They reached the mesquite; came on until Bar Nothing's boot descended within inches of Ware's knee.

'Well, you certainly took your time,' Ware complained.

Bar Nothing grunted and the Colt in his hand twisted automatically to cover Ware. Georgette gasped and stepped backward.

'What—what's it?' Bar Nothing demanded. 'Who're you smoking up, Steve? We saw you—made you out through the glasses hopping back and forth like a flea on a hot stove——'

'Yeh. I heard you,' Ware drawled mendaciously. 'So I waited. Do'no' who's over there. They don't seem to have anything to do and neither have I, so we've been playing with each other. They can't get off that dune without leaving their backs open to me. I reckon it's time to scoop up our marbles, now, and go home. Gi' me a hand. Take over the hopping back and forth; keep 'em busy while I round 'em up from behind.'

Bar Nothing nodded, grinning pleasantly, putting out his hand for the carbine.

'Where's your horse?' Georgette demanded abruptly. 'They—they didn't kill that beautiful black? Steve——'

'No. There wasn't anything he could do, so he went over there and curled up. He's taking his *siesta*,' Ware reassured her blandly. 'Bar Nothing—hammer all around 'em, but whatever you do, don't hit 'em! Not for anything!'

'Huh? Don't hit 'em? Why—— All right! You're the Big Auger!'

He moved toward the dune. Georgette stared bewilderedly at Ware, but he was going down behind a low ridge of sand that ran off to the left. He moved quickly on hands and knees, rising to a crouch where the ridge was high enough, getting out a hundred yards on the flank of the enemy's dune. He heard the firing before he reached what seemed a safe distance, and looked back. Bar Nothing was not in sight, but Georgette stood where he had left her. She waved at him.

'Now, where did he find her?' Ware asked himself. 'And what brought him out from town, this way?'

But the men were of more interest at the moment. He worked off at an angle from the ridge that had sheltred him so far, covered another hundred yards, and looked cautiously from behind a clump of mesquite at the horses standing with heads sagging. Both had big-horned Mexican saddles, both were bays. He studied the kneeling figure, the man sprawled near the crest of the dune. They could be Valdez and Murillo, but he was not sure. He stood boldly, trusting in ther preoccupation with Bar Nothing, and walked straight toward them.

He was within five yards of the kneeling man when the man above called down to ask about cartridges. The kneeling one turned and showed the face of the young *vaquero* of the pair Ware had expected to find.

'*Pocos!* But a handful,' he called back. 'And he—— Why does he not go back, like a man of sense? We have shot at him for an hour. But still he holds us here! I

tell you, Valdez, I do not like it! He fires as if he had
cartridges by the thousand! When our guns are empty,
he will kill us——'

Ware had knelt behind a mesquite with the boy's
first movement. Now, as Murillo turned to the front
again, Ware looked up at Valdez, who had not answered,
then went noiselessly across to catch Murillo's shoulder
with his left hand and poke his Colt into Murillo's
back.

The boy gasped and dropped his rifle. But he was
moveless. Ware drew hm upright and turned him. Valdez was firing deliberately, long spaces between shots.
Ware walked Murillo up to a point just below Valdez.

'Come down, Valdez!' he called. 'Valdez! Come down!
But with care—and above all, without thoughts of wick-
edness.'

Valdez rolled over and glared. But he let his rifle go
and it slid down the dune ahead of him. He followed,
watching Ware sullenly. Bar Nothing fired two quick
shots and Valdez's head jerked that way, then back.

'I—we thought——' he said in a puzzled tone, then
stopped.

'Oh-h, Bar Nothing!' Ware yelled. 'Come on over.
Chickens are in the pot!'

Then he herded the pair to the side and stood before
them shaking his head, clucking reprovingly.

'*Por dios!* You have much of luck. What if I were not
one of kind heart, and a good friend of your *patron*?
Why, all this shooting at me might have made me angry; I might have killed you!'

'Collected 'em, huh?' Bar Nothing said cheerfully,
loafing around the end of the dune. 'Who's it—and
what's it?'

'Valdez and Murillo. Ride for Carlos Smith—when
they're home.' Then, in Spanish again: 'Why do you
shoot at me?'

They stared at his blank face, looked sidelong at each
other, then Murillo shrugged.

'But—but we wanted only that you should go back and not come after us. We did not shoot to kill or even to hit you! We knew that you came after us. We thought you came alone. These——'

Georgette had appeared, leading Rocket and the other horses.

'These?' Ware repeated. 'Oh! They were in Los Alamos. But when I needed them, I turned this button upon my *chaqueta*—so! It is a button given me by a *brujo,* a wizard. My thought went to him as the telegram goes over the wire. He wished them here. It is very simple wizardry. But—why should I come after you? Is it that you have committed some crime? What have you done?'

'You did not come after us? At the store in La Piedra it was said—Kinney the *tiendero* said—the money that we were paid—that we gave to him—because of that gold——'

Ware shook his head, turning to Bar Nothing and the frowning Georgette.

'It is this terrible land,' he said owlishly in Spanish. 'The people are not honest and kind like you and me. They live wicked lives, and so when a stranger comes they are afraid that their crimes have been discovered; they try to kill that stranger, thinking that he brings a rope to hang them. Even poor *vaqueros* like these, they are made afraid. So when I ride near them they believe that I wish to take them to prison——'

'To kill us!' Valdez said smoothly. 'We knew that we had done nothing. But it was said that you would kill us, then say that we had done some terrible crime. This would give you a great name and—and a reward. Or so it was said!'

'Well!' Ware grunted. 'I only hope it's not going to happen often. Where were you two heading for?'

'Looking for you! More trouble in town: Thornton, cashier of the bank, skipped with better'n twelve thousand. Reckon it wouldn't have made so much smoke if a gang had cracked the box the regular way. But when Thornton turned it inside out and upside down, after playing Model Boy for years, looks like it kind of discouraged folks. They're saying you do'no' what to do now, when you get skinned from inside and outside, both!'

'No trail?' Ware inquired, without much interest.

'No more'n Theo Ribaut left. Thornton went around town same as usual—you could set a watch by him, they say, on his way to the bank, dinner, bank, supper, home. He never opened up next morning, Wednesday, the morning you pulled out. So Fay Zyrall, the president, he went by the li'l' house where Thornton lived by himself. Thornton had packed up his grip and hightailed!'

Ware shrugged. A cashier absconding with twelve thousand was not likely to stay in Texas. He would have made his arrangements for flight to the East. Finding him would be a task, not for horseback Rangers, but for county officers using the telegraph. He said as much, and Bar Nothing nodded.

'Tell him about the letters,' Georgette prompted.

'Nothing to 'em, so far's we're concerned! Just that twelve thousand may not be more'n a beginning of Fay Zyrall's loss, Steve. He's got to check up the bank's books to see. Ben Briggs and Zyrall looked over Thornton's house careful and found part of a letter from somebody telling Thornton he'd lost again and had to send more money quick—five thousand—or his stock would be sold clean out. And there was a couple of "darling" letters; seems like Thornton had a girl somewheres awful in love with him and just waiting until he got his affairs fixed so's he could come back to her for all time—awful rich. Los Alamos had him married to Emmy Zyrall next month . . .'

'Oh! Gay deceiver, huh? Tell me,' Ware said gravely, 'was he a big yellow-haired hairpin with blue eyes—too?'

'You know where you can go!' Bar Nothing informed him, grinning. 'He was nothing like so pretty as me.

Li'l' man, neat, pleasant, darkish. Around thirty. Worked for Zyrall ten year. Orphan. Raised right in Alamos. Well . . . Briggs wants us to help him.'

XVIII. *'That's a Ranger's life'*

WARE showed his teeth, shutting his eyes and shaking his head stubbornly.

'No, sir! No, ma'am! In fact—no! Let Benjamin kill his own snakes. About time he killed *one* of 'em! Here we are, with enough work and grief to supply a whole company of Texas' Finest. Briggs is the pride and joy of the Ribauts. Still, and yet, he has to get the Rangers in to find the man who just about whittled him from a clothespin to a sheriff. Now, he's got a case just made to order all-same shop-built boots, for even a boogery sheriff. But is he happy? Not so's you can notice it! He wants Rangers to find his cashier. It does seem to me, Mis-ter Ames, that the county'd get along at least as well, and save a slew of taxes, if they just nailed up Ben Briggs's door!'

'It would be a lovely idea to nail Ben inside,' Georgette contributed viciously.

'Huh?' Ware grunted, turning to stare. 'You'll excuse me, Georgette, if I kind of think that over . . . It do seem to me that, most always generally, you got some awful good reason for whatever you say about your neighbors. Briggs is just hearsay to me——'

'Then we just don't turn the light of our countenance like the Scripture says on Benny, huh?' Bar Nothing interposed hastily. 'In fact, we draw back the hem of our garment slaunchways and antigodlin from him?'

Ware nodded, still regarding Georgette with amused eyes. She glared at him, reddened, seemed about to say something, but turned quickly away.

'Might's well be going,' Ware drawled. 'Open A is

next on our list, Bar Nothing. We ask Capen if he knows anything about Ribaut. He says, nothing you would want to tell before ladies. We come back to Los Alamos—and right back to where we started. And that's a Ranger's life.'

He crossed to scoop up Rocket's reins, rescabbard the carbine which Bar Nothing had handed him, and replace his glasses in an *alforja*. Bar Nothing helped Georgette mount and swung into his own saddle. His horse was a rangy zebra-dun, with a look of speed about him.

'But—but señor!' cried young Murillo, who had stood beside Valdez all this while, staring, listening. 'What of us?'

'You? Why—what of you, then?' Ware countered blankly.

'We are not arrested? You—do not want us?'

'Why should I want you? Because you listened foolishly to someone who made *tontos* of you? *Hombres!* This tall Ranger and I, we have affairs of importance to consider. We search for the señor Ribaut, alive or dead. If dead, we look for the murderer. "Big chickens do not eat small corn." 'We have no time for small things. Only—do not be so quick to shoot the next time you hear a tale.'

He caught a stirrup, grinning at the pair, and went into the saddle. Bar Nothing's face was blank, but his eyes were slightly narrowed. Georgette watched with a small frown. Ware kneed Rocket up beside Bar Nothing and the zebra-dun moved off. Georgette's black followed.

'Now, what, just what, was all that about?' Bar Nothing inquired. 'For whatever it looked like, *that* was what it wasn't!'

'You tell me and I'll tell you,' Ware answered blandly. 'Couple of nitwit boys. Hack Kinney at Piedra filled 'em up with a tale that I was out to collect somebody and by choice somebody from the D-Bar-D, to get a case settled. That made 'em nervous. When I happened to ride their trail, that made 'em good and nervous. No use killing 'em, to ease their minds.'

For a mile, he whistled softly. Georgette and Bar Nothng drew a little ahead of him and he watched them, as he had done at first sight of the pair on the store porch in Los Alamos.

'For his sake,' Ware thought grimly, 'I do hope that this is not the Prize Petticoat, and that he can get over being handed frosty mittens. For she's not the girl to go homesteading on that creek of his, with an ex-Ranger turned one-cow rancher. Thanks be! I'm not the man to let her worry me. For she certainly is the *loveliest* girl I ever set eyes on!'

They rode on at the fox-trot through the afternoon sunlight, Ware busy with his thoughts, the two ahead of him plainly busy with each other. Georgette's laugh carried frequently to Ware, breaking in upon his piecing of puzzle-bits together. The sound disturbed him, jerked his thoughts to her when he wanted to weigh what he knew of men and events one against another.

What kind of girl was she, really? What race, or mixture of races? Capen claimed to have come from South America with her. Ware considered Argentiños, Brazilians, Chileños—citizens of the other southern republics, Italians, French, Germans, English, Americans—— He shrugged that question off as unanswerable. Besides, he reminded himself cynically, there was only Capen's word for it that he had ever seen any state except Texas.

He was more interested in Georgette herself, much as he disliked admitting that interest. What did she think of her uncle and his ways? She was far too intelligent, she moved about much too freely, not to know the tales that were told of Capen. Did she shut her ears to charges of robbery and murder? Did she merely disbelieve them? Exactly what was under her manner of mocking superiority?

He had to give up, but he told himself that one thing about the girl was certain: neither Bar Nothing nor he was likely to know the real Georgette Capen. In spite of white buckskins and broad Stetson and sure, easy seat upon the horse, she was not like other ranch-bred girls.

Wider fields—Eastern cities, doubtless—would appeal to her eventually. He recalled what the loungers in Los Alamos had said: that Capen saw none in all this country 'good enough' for his niece.

Bar Nothing suddenly put out his hand to Georgette and she reined the black deftly away, whirled and came at the gallop toward Ware. She pulled in, smiling at him.

'I think I'll ride with you. Our large friend has ideas that are too large even for a man of his size.'

'All right,' Ware told her indifferently. 'But remember what I told you! I'm the kind of man you go around saying you won't have around, the kind that no woman is going to make a stick-fetching pup of.'

'You had better be remembering what *I* told you, about the little boy whistling past the graveyard. But you're safe—for the moment. Bar Nothing has been telling me what a lovely couple we'd make standing before the altar. I won't force you to make Number Two for the day.'

'Thanks!' Ware grunted, grinning at her. 'Everything all right at the Castle when you got there?'

'Of course! And why shouldn't everything be all right?'

'Do'no' a bit more than you do—if you don't. But in this business a man has got to ask so many questions a day. Else the Adjutant General thinks he's not working. Here comes Bar Nothing! That's the screw-tailedest dun I've seen in years.'

'King Solomon,' she supplied, laughing as she watched. 'A wise, wise horse—or looks it.'

The zebra-dun's short tail was like a revolving whiskbroom as his big rider sent him toward them at a gallop, swung him neatly in a close circle, and brought up beside Georgette.

'Don't you be a-cutting in on me, Steve!' Bar Nothing warned Ware. 'And don't you believe a word she tells you. She's the kind of girl that'd flirt with a wooden Injun in front of a cigar store, if no other man was there. But down deep under that lovely loveliness of hers and her fickle way, she's true as love's true posy blowing, yes, sir! True to me, account I'm the man——'

'—who takes the place of the wooden Indian!' Georgette finished. 'But I've changed my mind. Until Corporal Ware came into my life, I thought you were the man. Now, beautiful as you are, you just don't signify, somehow . . . Sad! But that's life, my large friend. Steve fascinates me! The first green-eyed man I've ever known who's really handsome. And he fights! All the other men have run after me. He says I'll have to run after him!'

'And you won't put a loop over me, then,' Ware assured her grimly. 'Uh-uh! One of these days, I'm going to own me a *rancho grande,* with cattle on a thousand hills like the Psalm says. I will be too busy to bother with petticoats. Besides'—he looked straight into the pretty, mocking face—'even in Satan Land, princesses don't arrange their marryings. You'll take the man King Capen chooses for you, and, from what I've heard of *him,* there'll be a good reason all his own for picking this man or that, instead of the one you might like!'

She sat the black gelding very quietly for seconds. From red, her color changed to paper-white as she stared at him. He lifted a shoulder awkwardly.

'Sorry I said that!' he began. 'It—I'm not much on joking. I don't do it well, with girls. I——'

She did not spur her horse away from him this time. Instead, she lifted her reins with a hand that shook, and pulled in the gelding.

'You two go on,' she said very quietly. 'I think I've had about all the conversation of a particular kind that I can endure, for the day. Of course, I brought it on myself——'

Ware found himself suddenly, unaccountably furious.

'You did!' he agreed. 'When you reach down from that top-lofty perch of yours to amuse yourself with the common herd, the non-Capens, you mustn't be surprised when they amuse themselves with you.'

He had stopped Rocket. Bar Nothing, scowling uncertainly, sat Solomon looking from one to the other. Ware pressed Rocket's sides and sent him on. Bar Nothing lingered with the girl, but Ware had ridden no more than fifty yards when Solomon thundered up and Bar Nothing looked savagely at him.

'Now, what the hell was the sense of that?' he snarled. 'We ride along, pleasant enough. Then you have to tell her——'

'There was plenty of sense to it! She ought to have been told that, over and over, a lot of times. She has been petting and poking and slapping cowboys around all her life. Why? Because her uncle is an uncommon brand of scoundrel who's made a fortune out of every sort of skullduggery a man can imagine! So he sets himself up for a little king, builds himself a castle, sends her off to school on money he stole so she can come back here and lord it over the natives! She——'

He drew a long breath, and Bar Nothing, who had seemed on the verge of carrying the quarrel further, checked himself.

'Listen! I've been checking on things,' Ware drawled. 'On Capen and his man Carlos Smith and Clem Tooley and some other notables of the neighborhood. Just to begin with——'

In form as brief as he would have employed in a written report, he told of the fight near D-Bar-D range, and the impressions gained in the night at Smith's; and of his talk with Clem Tooley and the watch charm that might have been Ribaut's. As he listened, Bar Nothing lost his frown.

'*Por dios!*' he swore softly at the end. 'You have had a busy time. And I missed that cap-busting! So that was why you acted so surprised with Valdez and Murrilo, huh? It was the only thing to do. You couldn't prove that they rubbed out Ribaut—or who was with 'em, if anybody was, if they had help—any more than they could prove Smith handed one of 'em the watch charm for his pay. So you just had to let 'em go and act like nobody even suspicioned 'em. Yeh! Now, what?'

'Talk to Capen. Just for luck. Probably won't mean a thing. But something may show around the Open A. I've got ideas. But the trouble with 'em is, they just make a story that could be true: Capen wanted Ribaut and Alf Mullit out of the way. So he had Ribaut wiped out somewhere on the road. Sent Hannom in to settle Mullit. Maybe Ben Briggs is on the list! Capen looks to be scheming to just take over the whole county.'

'What about this Gall Yager, bringing something from Eagan to Clem Tooley—something they ain't telling a Ranger?'

'That,' Ware said solemnly, 'is one of the extra chapters of this story of mine. Or maybe another story! I've got a bunch of baskets in my mind, and all these pieces that don't fit into my "What Happened to Ribaut?" tale I just drop in a basket. My man on the Plumb Bob horse, who's somewhere in the country by Carlos Smith's account, he goes in another. The Mexican I killed, with his two friends, takes up still another. Then——'

He turned to look for Georgette. She had ridden off to the side and was going in the direction they went, but at an angle. As he studied the slim figure broodingly, she pulled in short. After a moment or two of what seemed staring, she jumped the black ahead and vanished over a rolling crest of sand.

'What man Capen will pick for her to marry is still another thing,' Ware continued evenly. 'But I don't expect that it'll have a lot to do with our business!'

Abruptly, Georgette reappeared on the ridge. She beckoned them excitedly, and automatically they galloped up to her.

'It's a horse!' she called. 'A—horse without a rider. I just happened to catch a glimpse of it. It—— There's blood on the saddle!'

They raced up the ridge and over it. The big buckskin stood no more than thirty yards away, head down, weariness explained by the dried lather of sweat upon its sides in its look. They saw a stirrup caught on a greasewood when they stopped beside it. Bar Nothing put out a hand and touched the stains on the saddle, looked at his fingers, then at Ware.

'Not so long ago,' he said. 'Open A horse. I—wonder!'

Ware nodded. He, too, had wondered—if Georgette had not recognized this horse, unsual for color and quality. He shifted position and waited for her to ride slowly downslope toward them.

XIX. *'A California killer'*

HER excitement did not show now. She looked calmly at the buckskin, and it came to Ware that the very stillness of her face told as much as nervousness would have done. For she was too calm! She was holding herself hard; forcing this quiet of face.

'But whose horse is it?' he asked aloud in an irritable tone. 'One of your boys' *caballos*, Georgette; had an accident——'

'There are so many horses on the place,' she said, shrugging. 'But isn't the important thing finding the—man hurt?'

'Vented brand,' Bar Nothing contributed. He had moved around to look at the buckskin from all sides. 'Reckon your uncle sold this one, Georgette. Don't see the buyer's brand, either.'

'Do you know whose horse it is?' Ware demanded flatly.

But she shrugged again, meeting his eyes stonily.

'As I said—so many horses——'

Ware nodded when she let her voice trail off. She did know, and for some reason had no intention of telling. He looked at the trail, the track of a straying horse, not a horse running in fright. The dead or wounded man might be many miles away. Except that the blood not quite dry on the saddle limited the time somewhat.

'You'd better go on home,' he told Georgette. 'We'll back-track this fellow. It—might not be nice to see.'

'Then, when we get close, if it's not—nice, I won't look. But—I'd rather—I'll ride with you.'

Ware nodded again. Under the stony calm, she was afraid; desperately afraid. Small wonder, he thought Something moved behind those sandy ridges and clumps of greasewood and mesquite that was more dangerous, cruel, than any wolf or snake, more intelligent. The killer who had emptied this saddle might be watching from within a hundred yards, and there was no assurance whatever that he would hold his hand from a girl.

It was not that he felt impressed by the thought, by the danger; but he understood how she might be impressed. He reached for the trailing reins as Bar Nothing cleared the anchored stirrup. The buckskin came after Rocket, and Ware turned.

'I'll keep to the tracks. You two might go right and left and see if there's anything to see. But Georgette! Don't you get out of sight for a minute, even. Don't drop over any roll unless I'm watching you that minute. I—I don't want us separated.'

'I won't!' she promised. 'I'll watch you, too.'

He saw how she drew a long breath and caught lower lip between her teeth, before she turned the black off to the right and left them. Her back was straight and stiff as she rode out.

'Scared!' he grunted absently. 'Scared to get ten feet away!'

'Listen, Ice Box!' Bar Nothing snarled. 'You run so much ice water instead of blood, I reckon it don't occur to you that a young girl ain't a gun-toting, risk-taking Ranger. She——'

'Yeh, I know! I know! In fact, my friend, I know a damn' sight more than you do about that particular girl. One thing I know: She recognized that horse. So

she's pretty sure she knows who must have been on it—
and is dead or badly hurt ahead. And I wouldn't be a
li'l' bit surprised if she's made a guess about who did
the job!'

'Ah! You're just guessing, because you don't like her—
Why, Steve! It don't make a never-mind what Capen is,
what he's up to in this country! How could a girl like
that know the ins and outs of the kind of crooked,
bloody business they do in this kind of neighborhood?
Why, it's ri-dic-u-lous! Why——'

'Go on! Wake up that screwtail can-eater and go on!
She's waiting for us to start. If I run ice water instead
of blood, it may turn out a good thing. Else every time
a skirt drags across a trail we're following, you'll turn
off to follow it! They must have raised you on big sugar
valentines! I never saw such a big loving heart as yours!'

He moved on before the indignant Bar Nothng could
answer and the buckskin came after, walking, then
trotting, just to the side of Rocket. Looking left and
right, Ware saw that the others were flanking him at a
distance of fifty yards. The trail of the buckskin was easy
to see in the sand. He looked at it only occasionally;
most of the time he watched the girl.

'She's certainly worth watching, too, Horse,' he muttered to Rocket. 'But we mustn't trust her an inch! She
knows things and she's not going to let us know 'em—
she thinks! Because we'd use 'em against King Capen.
So, she's mixed in some of the Capen ugliness. Anyway,'
he amended that hurriedly, for it was not a pleasant
thought, 'she suspects a lot and—naturally!—she's going
to cover up her uncle.'

They covered a mile and half of another before the
wandering and leisurely hoofprints of the riderless buckskin changed pattern. It was as plain as if a painted
notice announced that the frightened horse had galloped
furiously, slowed to a trot, then to a walk, at the point
where the changes of gait had occurred. Ware tensed
a little as they passed the brief stretch of trotting. He

looked ahead and toward the others. They trotted easily,
heads shuttling, apparently finding nothing.

But it was Bar Nothing whose hand jerked suddenly
aloft as he topped a brush-crowned ridge. Ware beckoned in Georgette and she came at the tearing gallop.

'I think he's sighted the man,' Ware said easily. 'Now,
if you'll just wait here, I'll take the buckskin over
and——'

'All right,' she answered meekly. 'I'll stay here.'

When he led the buckskin up to where Bar Nothing
sat Solomon, Ware needed only a glance to find the
sprawling figure on the sand near an 'island' of mesquite.

'Let's sort of circle,' he suggested. 'See if he got it
there, or if he rode a way, then fell off.'

They approached the body from two sides and before
reaching it saw the triple-trail, of buckskin, pursuing
horse, second horse turning away. Also, they saw the
man's face.

'Well!' Bar Nothing remarked calmly, 'looks like
somebody was a better shot, or had better luck, than he
had in town. Alf Mullit would better have stayed in
town.'

Ware pushed up near the body and sat looking all
around, whistling softly, tunelessly. The killer had come
fast on Alf Mullit's trail, dropped from his horse to look
at the fallen man, then——

'Por dios!' Bar Nothing cried, seeing what Ware saw.
'He hunkered down and made him a cigarette and
smoked awhile. Maybe waiting for Mullit to cash in.'

Ware swung off and went very carefully closer. It
was easy to make a picture in his mind of the squatting
figure, smoking and perhaps talking to Mullit, mocking
him . . . He could even see the face of that triumphant
man.

Again, as he looked at Mullit, he was troubled by that
feeling that he should know Mullit. But staring at the
dark handsome face with its thin white scar across the
left cheek did not give him the recollection he hunted.

Then he leaned suddenly toward Mullit's outstretched hand, which had made a long trailing mark in smooth sand.

'He waited for Mullit to cash in, all right, but he *left* before that!' he told Bar Nothing. 'Look! He told his tale, in the sand: "Hannom got me." Hannom wouldn't have left that if he'd seen it!'

'Hannom, huh?' Bar Nothing drawled, eyes half-shut, grinning. 'I was thinking about that gentleman. This just sort of yells what I was whispering. Let's put Mullit on his horse and drift on up to Capen's and speak in Mister Hannom's near-ear . . .'

Ware nodded, and they stooped to pick up Mullit and set him across the saddle of his buckskin. The horse fidgeted, but Bar Nothing caught his head, and he stood quivering while Ware lashed the body with turns of Mullit's own lariat.

'You go ahead with Georgette,' Ware said when this was done. 'That trail of Hannom's, going away—it heads for the house? I'll follow it in. No use making her look at this.'

'Looks to point toward the Castle . . . But you don't know whether he turned off somewheres. No! I'll take charge of it and you ride herd on her. Somehow—and strange as it may seem and queer, to you—I am not anxious to talk to Georgette right now, over a few miles of greasewood. *You* do it!'

'*Sta bueno*! Consider her talked to, then.'

He mounted and watched Bar Nothing putting the buckskin on the end of his rope for leading. When the big man was in the saddle, he grinned tightly.

'Remember that Hannom's not much fonder of you and me than he was of Mullit,' he reminded Bar Nothing. 'You ride hawk-eyed and cat-footed! I just don't like the idea of losing you, somehow! Maybe because this is a country so cluttered up with petticoats on the Monday washline . . . You're handy to have along: All I have to do is watch how you act when the ladies are around, then do the opposite, to know I'm right. Oh!

If you happen to hit the place or see anybody on the road before we get there, keep the Hannom name to yourself. I want to see him before we talk.'

He rode back over the ridge. Georgette stood with shoulder against her horse, head down, flicking a boot with the lash of her quirt. Ware wondered if she had seen him and assumed that pathetic pose of weariness, of if it might be real. But since there was no way of deciding the question, he rode quietly down to her and shrugged as she looked up.

'We'll go on to the house the way we were going. Bar Nothing will take a trail he thinks he knows.'

'With the—— He *was* dead, then?'

'As Pharaoh. Why didn't you want to say that you knew the horse? You see, I knew you did!'

She stiffened, seemed about to reply angrily, then sagged against the black again.

'It's hard to explain. I didn't like Alf Mullit, after he turned on my uncle and began to spread lies and give the Ribauts material for bigger lies than Alf could have manufactured. But I'd known him for some three years, talked to him as I talk to other men on the place, ridden with him here and there. I thoroughly disliked him after he left the Open A. But I didn't dislike him enough to want him killed! And——'

'And when you saw his horse and knew that he had been killed, naturally you thought that it was an Open A job,' Ware finished relentlessly. 'For Hannom and others had as much as promised to kill him.'

'I didn't say that! You can't assume you know what I thought! You are a bright young man, but——'

'Now, let's don't get started on that line, again—ever again! I'm not one of your cowboys, to furnish entertainment for the people of the Big House. I'm a special man on a special job. You've got the big edge on me in education—of a kind. But maybe I've got the edge on you in education of another kind—the kind that's needed on this special job. So don't bother to pat me or cuff me or try to make fun of me. Either talk to me straight, one person to another, or don't bother to talk!'

He swung down and put out a hand for her foot. She mounted, then in the saddle looked long and curiously at his blank face. At last she shook her head.

'All right! I'll do exactly that. I'll admit that I believe you to be a special man, specially qualified for Ranger work and able to see more than the outsides of things. So—I know a great deal about the kind of talk that goes around, of King Capen's ways. I suppose every strong, successful man makes enemies who slander him. I don't usually listen to this talk, or think about it. But——'

'But some of it sticks with you, naturally. So much smoke means some fire . . .'

'But there are different kinds of fire!' she cried. 'He's not liked. I admit that. He's a strange man, and one of his peculiarities is absolute indifference to the world's opinion. Too, he has education and breeding—— But never mind that. The important thing is this: He came into this rough country where the strong man prospers and the weak man fails, a stranger. But he learned the ways of these people and he beat them at their own game. Under his smoothness of manner, he is stronger than anyone in all this savage country.'

She put up a hand to stop him, when he lifted dark brows sardonically.

'Wait a minute! What I mean is, he hits hard when he thinks it necessary. And I admit that I don't like the way he's hated. So, knowing all the trouble that Alf Mullit caused us, I was afraid that, no matter who had killed him, it would be called one of King Capen's killings. That worried me, very much.'

Ware said nothing as they rode back toward the trail. She looked at him frequently, seeming to expect an answer.

'I wonder who he really was!' she said after a while. 'A remittance man? Some boy who had to come West to fight Indians? A criminal—murderer hiding, perhaps? So many——'

'*Por dios!*' Ware swore softly, triumphantly. 'I've got

him, thanks to you. Junns! That was the name. They called him "Snake" in the Panhandle and Oklahoma. A California killer. He ran for Texas ahead of a rope, eight-nine years ago. He bushwhacked a cowman in Dallam County, just before I got into the Rangers. I read his description, even to the knife-scar, in the *Fugitive List*. But that was away back. I couldn't quite place him.'

'That's hard to believe! Why, he had a note to my uncle when he came. I remember the day he rode up to us at the corral. He handed over a scrap of paper and my uncle read it, and said there was a place here on the Open A for him. Are you sure?'

'Absolutely,' Ware declared flatly. To himself, he said that she had let slip more than she guessed about the manner in which King Capen filled his bunkhouse with 'reliable' men.

XX. *'Comes the King'*

GEORGETTE was like a different person, as they rode steadily across the semi-desert toward the headquarters range of her uncle's holdings. The half-flippant, half-contemptuous manner which had so irritated Ware was replaced by a seriousness he had never seen in her. It was mixed with worry, he thought, if not altogether caused by worry.

She had to talk, that was plain to him. So he nodded or grunted or said 'Yes' and 'No?' and divided his automatic watch upon everything around to include her face. Occasionally he asked a definite question and now she answered quickly, freely, without suspicious look at him.

So within a few miles he came to know a great deal about the people of Satan Land—or her opinions of them. Her own odd, lonely, twisted life was made even clearer. He heard of 'surprises' arranged by Capen for the 'princess' of Capen Castle, when great boxes holding hundreds of dollars' worth of clothing were opened— hats and frocks and shoes utterly useless to a ranch-girl who had no friends and, in most years, attended strict schools where uniforms were worn. She spoke of those schools viciously.

Ware listened as he might have done to some foreign child. It was a life like nothing he had ever met. Suddenly he thought of the book lent him two years before by an Englishman playing cowboy on the 10-Bar, a fat, green volume dealing with the romance of a huge farmer and a beautiful girl held prisoner in an outlaw den. *Lorna Doone* was no further from his kind of life than Georgette Capen. He thought grimly that, while she had hardly been the prisoner that Lorna had been, there was a good deal of similarity between the Doones and the kind of men King Capen was reputed to have around him.

'But you seem to be doing pretty much as you please, now,' he suggested. 'Riding around by yourself, giving cowboys and Rangers—some Rangers!—notions . . .'

'It's been different for the last six months,' she admitted, staring blankly straight ahead. 'Ye-es, I—I am freer than I've ever been and I don't know—— He's promised to let me go East, maybe even to Europe! Pretty soon. But——'

She shook her head and was silent for a half-mile. He wondered what was in her mind that worried her. For he was sure that whatever she thought of was not pleasant.

'It's all odd,' he said finally. 'I mean, this way of Capen's; your life. Odd to me. Not a bit like Texas. Not——'

He stopped himself. What he had been about to say was that it seemed to him not 'healthy' as a way of living.

'Where were you born? Where did you live before you became a Ranger? I suppose you were a cowboy, like most Rangers.'

'My father was a one-cow rancher with a number 12 itch in a number 5 boot. Always looking for a fine range—and I reckon the kind he pictured in his mind he never saw until he got where he is now: other side of Jordan River. But he hunted! I was born in a Studebaker wagon on the road to that range, right with the herd. My mother died when I was a long yearling and we kept on trailing. I never slept under a roof till I was eight, when we finally stopped and settled on the Slash W back of Verde. I taught myself to read out of an old patent medicine almanac. Even today'—he grinned absently at her—'I'll bet I can recite every symptom of every disease a woman can have and prescribe for her—if I can get Mrs. Louella Blueham's stock of pills and powders!'

She laughed. He made a cigarette and she reached for the sack and papers.

'Something that was *not* taught at Miss Lancaster's Select School—but learned!' she told him. 'We bribed the Irish cook to bring us in novels and tobacco. Chiefly because both were forbidden. But why did you leave the Slash W?'

He lighted her cigarette and shrugged.

'It would have made a grand rich man's ranch: needed a bank in town to support the cows. After my father died, the bank did get it. I was lucky, too young for 'em to make me keep it. I worked around, made a hand when I was fourteen, clerked in the store at Verde, even. Then I enlisted under Cap' Durell. And that's the whole, long, sad story of my life. One of these days when I get enough money together, I'm going to ranch it.'

'What! No love affairs? No childhood sweetheart waiting?'

'You ought to've stuck to Duke's Mixture at that school. That Irish cook could have carried more if she hadn't been bowed down and tuckered out toting novels, and you'd have been better off a long sight. I never had time or money—or even disposition—for girls.

Of course, when I get that ranch going, I will need a cook. They tell me, some of the men, that it's cheaper to marry 'em than to hire 'em. Then, again, some say it's not. I'll think it over and maybe marry a nice, fat, happy, healthy woman—that's tongue-tied.'

'I'll—bet! But you're certainly not complimentary. Don't you know that you're supposed to make the girl you're with feel that she's the one you'd give anything, do anything, to marry?'

'I'm jist plumb helpless and iggerant without Bar Nothing in cases like them! When I'm with girls—which is not often, thanks be!—I just talk to 'em the same as I would to anybody else, about the weather or cow-prices or did they see a cross-eyed murderer running down both sides of the road. Bar Nothing's a better man; he can talk about all that and make 'em all feel like the Queen of Hearts. But'—he looked squarely at her—'he never before met one as pretty as you, or with as much brains. That is *not* a compliment. It's just a fact.'

'*Thank* you! So, suppose I marry him? Regardless of King Capen and those plans you're so sure he has for me! What?'

'No affair of mine! Is that the famous Castle yonder? The house where shadows go around whispering?'

She did not turn, but for seconds continued to study his serene expression. Then her mouth tightened, and she lifted a slim shoulder and let it sag again.

'If it looks like the Castle, then it must be the Castle. I almost believe you!—about—marrying a fat woman because she can cook! About—having the wrong sort of disposition and——'

'Why would you marry Bar Nothing? Or anybody like him or me?' Ware demanded, turning in his saddle to face her. 'Why do you bother with men like us at all? We're not your kind. We couldn't be your kind if we wanted to be, not in a thousand years! We know it and you know it. Do you get a lot of fun out of hurrahing cowboys—pretending that they're just as good as you are, when you know well enough you don't think anything of the kind? Do you think you fool those cowboys—except, maybe, the nitwits among 'em? Do you—— Ah, what's the use!'

He shrugged off the outburst and turned grimly back to stare at the shallow green valley below them, threaded by a tiny creek and dotted with mottes of cottonwoods and willows. The buildings grouped beyond the creek were uniformly cream-colored, arranged about the massive bulk of the 'castle' Capen had built. It was no helter-skelter pattern like that of most ranches, but a design in which every building and corral had its planned place. In all his life Ware had never seen such a ranch, and as he looked admiringly a thought came, and automatically he turned to look at the desolate range beyond the valley and tell himself that one thing was very certain . . .

'Unless he brought money in, or has got money since, you could convict him before any cow-country jury of anything and everything Clem Tooley accused him of. For Satan Land cows and horses never paid for that place or kept it going!'

That thought so interested him that he almost forgot his flare-up at Georgette; he was surprised to see her eyeing him sulkily. So he grinned.

'What's the use of us rowing? I like you. I've talked to you more than to any girl I ever met, I do believe. But I'm a policeman on a beat just as much as if I wore a brass-buttoned uniform and walked up and down in Fort Worth or Kansas City. I have got a job to do here, got another job waiting while I hunt for Theo Ribaut. There's another one sure to pop up after that. I'll hit the Castle, then I'll bounce. Chances are, we'll never see each other again——'

'You might at least act as if you'd like to see me!'

She smiled, abruptly the sulkiness vanished and she looked at him as when riding behind Bar Nothing, before discovery of Alf Mullit's horse.

'A girl likes to collect victims. Somebody said that

we're like Indians hanging scalps to the bridles. No self-respecting woman wants to feel that she was lucky to get married, that if she hadn't caught her husband she wouldn't have had another opportunity. She wants to believe that she took her choice. So, naturally, I keep my list of proposals. And, leaving out the elderly ranchers and the dozens of cowboys, there's Bar Nothing—and Jimmy Quagson, the county attorney at Stonewall —a very nice young lawyer is Jimmy, he rides over quite often, to bring me books and things. Then——'

'He's the man!' Ware assured her briskly. 'Stop right there. Marry Quagson and keep behind him until you make a governor or congressman out of him. Get him over here to help Capen run the Open A. Glad I can help you with good advice. Now, we have got that settled and—yonder comes Bar Nothing . . .'

Her head jerked to the right. The veneer of gaiety disappeared as she looked at the tall figure approaching the buildngs, leading the burdened buckskin. She said nothing as they rode toward the creek and its bridge of solid planking. Bar Nothing had disappeared when they came by a graveled driveway to the side of the Big House. Ware looked at the smooth lawn before it, that held some greenness even in October, and shook his head marvelingly.

'A lawn! On a border cow-ranch! I hear there's a piano, too!'

'Oh, yes,' she answered, but staring ahead blankly. '*He* plays wonderfully, composes, too. But I'm not very fond of it. He has a weird sort of taste. I'm going in! You take my horse, will you? Straight ahead to the stables and corrals. Some of the men will be there to show you.'

She slipped from the saddle and ran across the lawn to a broad, arched opening that gave upon a great patio. Ware led her black on through a tall hedge of tamarisk, into a bare yard before a row of buildings and corrals.

Bar Nothing had dismounted and stood in the center of a little group of men, some of whom were helping to unlash Alf Mullit. They looked around at Ware, and he examined each face flashingly as he drew in by them and nodded.

A short, wide young man, beginning to be fat, resplendent in red silk shirt and dark blue pants and decorated boots, moved out to face Ware. He had a gold shield upon his shirt pocket and there was no need of introduction, for *Ben Briggs* was embroidered in orange script upon the right breast of his shirt. Ware swung off and looked at Briggs with instinctive dislike for heavy face and quick, loose grin and yellowish eyes.

'Glad to meet you, Ware!' Briggs greeted him explosively. 'Awful about poor Alf! Ames just told us how you run onto him. Does look like we're catching more'n our fair share of grief: Theo and the kid; Thornton skipping with the bank-cash; now Alf!'

'And ee-lection a-coming up, too,' one of the cowboys drawled. 'Certainly is hell, Ben. A full-growed man'd be some worried about a line of country like you're facing.'

Two other cowboys, those who had been helping Bar Nothing, laughed harshly. Briggs ignored the thrust. The fifth man was a tall figure in dark citizen's clothing and small gray Stetson, pants-legs in black boots, a tanned, hawk-nosed man of thirty or so, with a sort of pleasant grimness about his face. Briggs indicated him with nod and thumb-jerk.

'This is Quagson, county attorney from Stonewall. Jimmy is kind of interested in the Thornton business because of some accounts and deposits and things. He rode out with me.'

Ware nodded. He liked Quagson as instinctively as he disliked Briggs. One of the cowboys interrupted the introduction:

'Comes the King!' he grunted. 'Wondered where he was.'

XXI. 'Born to be hung'

CAPEN came deliberately from a gate in the hedge, a tall, slender figure in gray tweeds, cat-light of step, the yellowish brown of his thin face with its unmoving features giving it the look of a bronze casting. But when he came closer Ware saw that the large, dark eyes were bright, alert.

Capen looked at Alf Mullit's body, now laid upon the ground, then at Bar Nothing, Briggs, and Ware, in quick glances.

'So Mullit was killed, as he might have expected to be,' Capen said evenly, in deep, slow voice. 'What about it?'

'This Ranger says he found him on our range,' one of the cowboys volunteered officiously. 'Says Miss Georgette and *him*'—he nodded toward Ware—'was along and——'

Capen only looked at him, but he stopped short and swallowed. Ware looked up from the cigarette he had begun to roll.

'We were heading this way, Ames and Miss Georgette with me, when the horse showed close to our trail. We backtracked him and found Mullit. Didn't see anybody around. I thought it might be a good, pious notion to bring him here and ask what you asked: What about it?'

Capen looked steadily at him, then shook his head.

'When he left the Open A, he ceased to be a concern of mine. He worked for Theo Ribaut and I know nothing whatever of the sort of work he did or—what he might have been doing to draw a bullet toward him. Briggs, you were closer to Ribaut than anyone except Mullit. Perhaps you know something that will aid in investigating this? That is, if you're going to investigate; if the Rangers aren't to take over the sheriff's office while you're still in it . . .'

'I—I don't know a thing,' Briggs mumbled. He seemed uneasy upon Capen's stare. 'I mean—about Alf doing anything to special get him rubbed out. But he was shot at in town the other night; hit in the arm. Said he never seen the man that unloaded at him.'

Ware had his cigarette lighted. He studied Capen with very real interest, from the thick, smooth crown of gray hair to his gleaming shoes. Capen seemed anything but a rancher, but that he was a power in this savage country Ware could easily understand, watching him dominate the group without lifting his voice or altering the mask-like stillness of his face. Whatever Capen did would be well done, he conceded.

Briggs was a worried young man. He would not look directly at Capen. His eyes roved back to Alf Mullit, and as minutes passed he grew more nervous. Ware wondered if Briggs were thinking of the orderly pro-gression of deaths, in Los Alamos·political circles, think-ing that in a progression he might logically be next!

'I got so much on my hands!' Briggs protested, almost plaintively. 'Theo and the kid just going like—like smoke! Then Thornton running off with the bank-money. Now, Alf! And you, Ware! Sending in that Mex-ican you killed on the D-Bar-D without never a word about how-come, except what I could prize out of the *hombre* Carlos Smith sent in with him! I swear——'

'You would leave the cowboy's happy life, to be a sheriff!' Bar Nothing reminded him, grinning. 'But, cheer up! Maybe you'll not be elected, won't have to worry about these puzzles. You can hand 'em all over to Capen to wrangle.'

Briggs looked venomously at Bar Nothing, but said nothing. It was Ware who yawned and moved beside Rocket.

'So far as I can see,' he observed wearily, 'this is all interesting to local people, but buys a Ranger nothing.

The important thing is, we've got Alf Mullit, dead as Pontius Q. Pilate. We have got to ask who killed him and what for. You do it, Capen? Yes or no, and can you prove it?'

'No-o. No, I really didn't, as it happened,' Capen answered, with amusement in his voice. 'I can prove it.'

'You three!' Ware addressed the cowboys. 'How about you?'

The cowboy who seemed most talkative, who had spoken to Briggs of the coming election, waggled his head solemnly.

'Oh, no, Teacher! We never done no such thing. *We* never killed the lowdown son! And we can swear for one another we never. Or would it be all right if never swore —just said "dern," huh?'

'Briggs? You killed him?'

'Huuuh?' Briggs grunted, gaping. 'What on earth would *I* kill him for? Anyhow, if I done it, Quagson must've helped. He's been with me all time!'

From a small building, before which the group stood, Hannom came at a loafing gait. Ware saw him as he stepped from the door; wondered how long Hannom had stood in the gloom of that room, listening. But he ignored the stocky figure; looked at Quagson, who shrugged.

'That's a fact, Ware. I don't pretend to expert on Los Alamos affairs, political or otherwise. I don't know whether Briggs preferred Mullit alive or dead. But he certainly didn't kill him!'

Hannom had come without a look at any of them to where he could stare down at Mullit. His heavy face was expressionless. He turned to Capen, shaking his head.

'You know, King, I don't believe I ever seen Alf look better!' he drawled.

Ware's eyes met Bar Nothing's. Ware grinned faintly.

'No doubt about that, Quagson,' he said easily. 'As a matter of fact, all this talk was just a sort of stall, same as you law-sharks use in court to lead up to something. The man who killed Mullit had trouble doing it. He

shot him but Mullit's horse was fast; so Mullit ran
away. The killer chased him, but it wasn't till Mullit
fell off his buckskin that he could come up. He was
happy about it, the killer. He got off and built him a
cigarette and hunkered down by Mullit to watch him
die. He talked to Mullit; told him how he'd missed in
town, but evened up on the range. When he thought
Mullit was dead, he rode off.'

'You mean, Mullit wasn't dead?' Quagson asked,
frowning.

'No. Just playing possum. So he lived long enough
to tell who killed him. I've just waited to see if the
killer would admit it. But you seem to want to cover it
up, Hannom!'

Hannom had been facing him, from where he stood
beside Capen, reddish brows drawn down over little
blue eyes, thumbs hooked in the belt of his leggings.
He said nothing, but his hand jerked to the butt of his
low-swung Colt and it came out with smooth, practiced
jerk.

But Ware, managing the scene, had known the pre-
cise instant when Hannom would draw, if he decided to
draw at all. His own hand had been closer to a Colt than
Hannom's. He drew from the holster on his left side,
flicked the pistol to cover Hannom, and let the hammer
drop. The slug struck Hannom's gun-arm and went on
to puff dust from his shirt. His hand twitched and with
the bellow of his gun a slug whined close by Ware, who
lowered his muzzle a trifle and fired grimly at Hannom's legs.

Capen had jumped lightly two yards to the side. The
three cowboys had surged back to the doorway from
which Hannom had appeared. Quagson and Briggs had
skated away from Ware. Only Bar Nothing, by the buckskin, had not tried to get away. His gun had come out
and he looked uncertainly from Ware to Hannom. Now
he leaned and his long arm lifted and fell like a flail.
The barrel of his Colt flicked down upon Hannom's
gun-wrist and the pistol dropped from Hannom's hand

as he began to sag on the wounded leg. Ware streaked
forward to kick the pistol aside. But he was drawing his
second gun, watching the door through which the cowboys had vanished.

Hannom came down to his knees, then fell sideways
at Ware's feet. His face was white, but he glared up
with bull-dog grimness and his mouth worked snarl-
ingly. Ware stepped back, looked flashingly from point
to point, and called to the men in the shed:

'Come on out! All over now.'

Bar Nothing turned to watch the door over the buckskin. Briggs gaped at Ware and began to move closer.
Capen, inscrutable as at first, came back to Ware's side.
He called to the cowboys, also, and they filed into the
light again, looking uncertainly at Capen. Each had a
pistol in his hand.

'Was this—necessary?' Capen asked Ware.

'Maybe not necessary,' Ware told him flippantly, 'but
a lot of fun! I'm tired of two-by-four, cap-pistol imita-
tions of hard cases strutting up and down across my
toes, breathing out fire and smoke. This neighborhood
is thicker with 'em than any place I've been in my life.
A Ranger has to be long-suffering, but I was downright
sick of Hannom. *Put up those guns, you!'*

The cowboys jerked with the snarled command. But,
facing Ware's twisted Colts and Bar Nothing's negli-
gently held pistol, they reholstered their guns and
watched sullenly.

'I wondered why, if he didn't have some *good* reason,
Hannom didn't walk right up to Briggs and say that
he'd had to kill Mullit. But it looks like he had that
good reason. Didn't want it known that he'd bushwhacked Mullit. The quaint thing is, he could have
told it right out in meeting, without ever a worry. For
Mullit had at least two hangings waiting for him, in
California and up in Dallam County. They called him
"Snake" Junns.'

'Well, I'm sorry it happened this way; sorry that
Hannom didn't make an open statement. But that's

past. We'd better be patching him up. I think he's fainted. You boys put him in the bunkhouse. I'll take care of him.'

He turned toward the tamarisk hedge and whistled shrilly. Bar Nothing looked at the dead man and shook his head.

'Of course! Irvin Junns,' he said disgustedly. 'Worth five hundred in Livermore, California, three hundred in Dalhart. And I walked right by him forty times. Hell and pot liquor!'

'I couldn't place him, ether. Knew I'd seen him or heard about him, but—— Nice boys Ribaut picked for his help and sons-in-laws! Must have tangled his mind to guess which side was most dangerous, his back or his front.'

A Chinese youth in white jacket and dark trousers came trotting through the hedge, swinging a black leather bag like a doctor's. He grinned and spoke to Capen in singsong Chinese. Capen answered in the same tongue and moved off toward the bunkhouse with the house-boy at his heels.

'Wonder if that was a particular kind of whistle,' Ware drawled. 'Or if they come running with the arnica and hole-stoppers as soon as they hear any whistle on the Open A!'

He looked at Briggs, whose heavy face seemed older, more drawn than when he had first seen it.

'Let's put Junns somewhere. I don't reckon you're hell on law-quirks in this county. He can be buried right here and your justice can pass his hands over things to legalize 'em, in town.'

They carried Junns into the building closest them, a harness room, and covered him with a saddle blanket. Outside again, Ware said cheerfully:

'Your backers and helpers are certainly getting whittled down, Briggs! If Ribaut's really dead, not just hiding out, you-and-you are about the only ones behind the Briggs-for-Sheriff ticket, *no es verdad?*'

'First Ribaut,' Bar Nothing said in a graveyard voice.

'That leaves Mullit—Junns—and Briggs between Capen and the star. But Junns goes. That leaves just Briggs, with a back so wide a cross-eyed man couldn't miss it at a half-mile with a slingshot. Oh, well! It may turn out all right.'

Briggs tried to grin, but it was a mirthless lip-stretching. Quagson grunted to them, then walked away toward the house. Ware watched him go and grinned at Bar Nothing.

'He's gone to hunt Georgette,' he explained confidentially. 'Reckon they'll set the wedding day this time. Well! I could eat my part of a steer——'

Capen, coming up from the bunkhouse, gestured toward the gate beyond. The Chinese servant went on with Capen's black case.

'You gentlemen will have dinner with us. If you'll come with me, the boys will show you rooms.'

Ware hesitated, then shrugged. He thought that a meal with the bunkhouse crew and a bed among them would suit him better, but something checked his objection. He asked about Hannom.

'Short of smallpox, or another bullet, he'll survive,' Capen said calmly. 'Hannom's tough as a buffalo bull.'

'And as much a nitwit,' Ware agreed. 'Born to be hung!'

XXII. *'We're another kind'*

BAR NOTHING looked around the bedroom to which a Chinese servant led them, then shook his yellow head and grinned.

'Now, the last time I was out here, he le' me unroll my bed in the bunkhouse. Reckon he's being friendlier this time account I'm a prospect for new relation, nephew-in-law, or—just scared we'll shoot up some more of his spread if he leaves us wander around?'

Ware, busy at the washstand, reached for a towel and grunted scornfully. He dried hands and face, and as he went back to the bed to get his *chaqueta* and slip into it, he glanced around the buff plaster walls of the room, on which framed prints hung, at the bright Navajo rugs on the polished dark floor and the comfortable, massive Spanish furniture.

'He wouldn't let the likes of us track up his house if if he didn't have some good reason!'

'What do you mean, "the likes of us"?' Bar Nothing demanded belligerently. 'What's wrong with us?'

'Everything! from his side of the fence. We're the kind of men he expects to hire and order around and keep at a good distance from him. He sits up here with his paintings and his piano and his books, and when he has to he puts his head out of the window to yell at us about something to do. Same as he'd yell at one of his Chinese boys. We all look the same to Capen.'

'Yeh? About the time he yelled at me, something'd land in the middle of his yeller!' Bar Nothing drawled grimly. 'He'd have him a bellyache and a dark-brown taste——'

'And he'd think his yell, allasamee! We don't have to put up with his ways, ourselves, but we can't change his ways, because he was born with 'em. We can't live like him in his kind of country. We'd be as awkward as a tomcat walking with pill boxes on his feet. What I'm trying to find a crack in that solid skull of yours, to get into it, is just this: Capen and Georgette are one kind of people. We're another kind. They're not better, they may even be a lot worse, but they're different. Now, there's Quagson. He's their kind! He talks books and Eastern things to 'em. So—Georgette may hurrah around with us, but it's Quagson or somebody like him that she'll marry.'

'Hey, Ames! Ware!' Briggs called from the hall.

He rattled the latch and came in, to sit on the bed and sigh.

'Damnedest business!' he complained generally. 'Glad you put some buttonholes in that damn Hannom, Ware. He——'

'Makes it safer for Ben Briggs, for a spell,' Bar Nothing contributed, grinning. 'Hannom is too salty for a man no better with the hardware than you are.'

'Yeh? Well, I reckon——' Briggs began in a blustering tone, then shrugged wearily. 'He's bad, all right. I did think that Mullit was worse—better, I mean. So'd Marie. She put more stock in him uncovering about Theo than even in 'Pache Logan and Buzz Bingham. That was why she rawhided him into coming out with that skinned arm, for more looking. She——'

'No! He really came out to kill Hannom,' Ware disagreed—as if he really knew, and with such flat conviction that both Bar Nothing and Briggs stared hard at him. 'He tried to rub out Hannom in town. He and Marie knew about Hannom being there. They talked it over and Mullit slipped down to get a good, quiet shot at Hannom. But it happened that Hannom was on the same *negócios,* and either better or luckier.'

'Ahhh! You're just guessing some fool thing!'

'We went to the Ribaut house that night, to talk to Marie,' Ware told him, eyes narrowed, grinning. 'Marie and Mullit were on the porch, rigging their li'l' bush-whacking. Mullit slid off when we walked up—but not quite fast enough or quiet enough. Marie hurrahed us into leaving; said she had a headache. Hannom skylined Mullit first and winged him. Probably would have killed him if we hadn't run up. We didn't say anything about knowing all about it, because Mullit asked us not to and because I didn't see any reason to tell the town.'

'She—she never told me all that. Not all,' Briggs grunted, gaping at him. 'Why——'

'Don't trust your head too much,' Bar Nothing remarked solemnly. 'I don't aim to hurt your sensitive soul and tender feelings, Ben, but the truth is you're more pretty than smart! And Marie and Mullit and Theo—huh! They'd be ahead of the first to know it. Say, Ben; supposing, just supposing you never run for sheriff this election; who'd be elected? Capen, huh?'

Briggs nodded, looking from one to the other.

'Of course! But don't you hairpins think for a split minute I ain't going to run and get elected! I ain't worrying——'

'Then you're a heftier nitwit than I've run onto since I saw the big one, stuffed, in a drugstore window!' Ware grunted caustically. 'Your only sensible play is to be so worried nobody can make the Briggs ticket look like a used-up meal ticket?'

'He laughs last that shoots first!' Bar Nothing supplied owlishly. 'Suppose you and Capen both was out? Who'd loop it?'

'Ah, there was some talk old Clem Tooley'd back his partner, Hack Kinney. But they decided not to even try.'

'We-ll, now,' Ware meditated aloud, 'Kinney wouldn't make a bad sheriff, I would say. Seems to have good sense . . .'

'Hell with the hurrahing! I tell you, I'm running. Nobody's going to rub me out or scare me out. I'm sticking! I——'

Somewhere below them a mellow gong vibrated, rather than rang. The door opened and a Chinese head appeared in the crack.

'Comida!' the Chinese said, in accentless Spanish. 'In the dining-room, below.'

'Kind of different from our way,' Ware told Bar Nothing thoughtfully. 'Now, if he'd hammered a dishpan and yelled, "Come and git it before I th'ow it out!" we'd have felt more at home.'

He surveyed himself in the mirror above the washstand, grinning at his reflection, while Bar Nothing snarled. Ben Briggs got up from the bed, making gestures with thick hands.

'I'm going to dig to the bottom of all this business——'

'Listen!' Bar Nothing cried wearily. 'We ain't got a vote among us for this county, and I be swizzled if I'm going to let you practice out your speeches on me when I'm starved enough to eat boiled boots. Besides, Hack Kinney's already a constable, so if he has to take on sheriffing, it'll turn out all right.'

They went out and along the broad, dusky hall to the great stair. Ware looked about with open admiration. The staircase he called the others' attention to—the thickness of the great rail, its balusters carved, its newel post the figure of a helmeted *conquistador.*

'When I build me a house for that ranch I aim to own,' he proclaimed, 'I'm going to have one like this—no! two like it.'

'For the fat, tongue-tied cook?' Georgette inquired from above them. 'One to the kitchen and one to the parlor?'

She came down the stair very deliberately and Ware looked broodingly at her. Her dress was dull red, full-skirted and close-fitting of bodice, and her shining dark hair was piled high against a Spanish comb. She watched them all but Ware the most, and when she stood beside him swept skirt aside from the point of scarlet, high-heeled slippers and made a mocking courtesy. Solemnly, he bowed to her as once he had seen old Don Miguel Ronquilla bow before a dance-partner in San Antonio.

She took his arm, but smiled up at Bar Nothing, who shook his head despairingly with enormous sighing sounds.

'You're just too pretty to be let run around loose,' he told her. 'In buckskins I thought you was the loveliest sight I ever had put two eyes on. But that red frock makes you——'

'Perfect!' Ware finished for him briefly. 'So ne' mind the dictionary.'

He was looking at Quagson, who had appeared in the arched opening of the hall-end. Quagson's grim face was lightened by his smile as he stared at Georgette.

'Why—Jimmy!' she cried. 'I didn't know you were

here. I thought you'd deserted me for some Stonewall charmer.'

'I came out with Briggs,' Quagson said. 'Trailing rumors of Thornton. If I'd needed an excuse to come here, that would have served. May I—?'

'You may sit on my left. Steve, here, was ahead of you.'

They went into the dining-room and Georgette looked quickly about. Capen came silently through another door and moved to the head of the long table. Ware watched curiously, as he might have watched the play on a stage. There was something theatrical about the scene; about the way Capen stood at his chair with a statue-like Chinese behind him, and bowed gravely to them all; about Quagson seating Georgette, and Capen sitting down without a look behind him, upon the chair pushed under him by the servant. Bar Nothing and Briggs sat opposite Georgette, Quagson, and Ware. The quiet Chinese moved about sideboard and table like two ghosts.

From the wine onward, that was a memorable meal for Ware. The table itself with linen and silver and crystal was like nothing he had ever seen, but like many things he had read with half-comprehension in books come upon here and there. He was in no way made uncomfortable by the unfamiliar setting of this table, only watchful. He had a thought, too, which increased his natural self-confidence, while he followed Capen's example, and Georgette's, during the meal:

In spite of all the complicated formalities of this meal, at which Capen dominated; in spite of the story-book quality of this little 'castle' in which Capen lived in ways to get him the title of 'king,' the important man here was not Capen. It was the man whom Capen looked down upon as his inferior in every way, even though his play at courtesy toward a guest did not let that appear openly. It was Steve Ware.

Capen was like a prisoner at the bar, when the husk of all this was cut through and the truth examined. Ware thought of this while he studied the courtly figure on his right, and listened to Quagson and Georgette talking easily of books and pictures and music and people of the East and Europe. Capen was more than mere prisoner to be found guilty or not guilty. To Ware he was a criminal of particularly unpleasant type, whether he could be openly convicted or not.

It seemed ridiculous to believe that Hannom had killed Mullit for any reason of his own, separate from Capen's real reason for wanting and needing Mullit killed. It was equally ridiculous to believe that Hannom had not come back here to report to his employer that Mullit was satisfactorily dead.

But he let none of his thoughts show as he talked to Capen and Briggs and Bar Nothing, and smiled at Georgette when she divided her attention between him and Quagson. Part of his mind was busy with her as he watched the way the lawyer looked at her. It seemed very plain that what he had said to her was true; that her mocking play with the men of the country was just that—play. Quagson, with his education, his experience in another kind of world, was Georgette's kind of man.

It seemed plain, also, that Georgette knew nothing of the trouble with Hannom. Ware could almost believe that she had never known trouble of any sort! But when Capen at last asked Ware if he had any evidence in the Ribaut case she turned a little in her chair so that she watched both him and Capen.

'Not a bit of evidence,' Ware answered calmly. 'But I do have a theory that fits everything I've heard or seen: Ribaut was killed by somebody who didn't like him, or was afraid of him in politics, or wanted the money he was carrying, unless he was just roped and tied to keep him out of the election, or unless he simply took all the money he could get together and slipped off to make a new start somewhere else. He was killed—unless he was not killed—by one or more men. He knew that man or those men, unless the man or men were strangers to him.'

Capen laughed, but almost without movement of his face. His dark, bright eyes were very steady, trained on Ware's gravity. But before he could speak one of the Chinese came noiselessly up behind him and whispeerd. Capen listened without turning.

'You'll excuse me,' he said to them all. 'I have something to do. Take them into the living-room, Georgette.'

XXIII. *'Find Ribaut!'*

QUAGSON led Georgette to the grand piano in the great living-room of 'Capen Castle.' Bar Nothing and Briggs sat close about in huge, handmade Spanish chairs. But Ware was restless. He had the sensitiveness of a wild animal to atmospheres, and there was something about this room, with its green-tinted walls and furniture and furnishings combining East and West, that set his nerves on edge. It was not that the mixture of furnishing and the arrangement did not rouse admiration; he could look everywhere and see something that pleased him. He still had the feeling of a boy at a theater or museum. It was the house itself that disturbed him.

' "The House of Whispering Shadows," ' he thought. 'Well, your Mexican is a great believer in things he can't see but can feel. And damned if I'm not about ready to expect something whispering in my ear! If one of those Chinese of Capen's slides out of a corner behind me without using his feet, he'll be lucky if he gets off without a split head!'

Georgette sang something in French, to a sad little accompaniment. Her voice was husky and pleasant, but Ware prowled about the room, looking at Indian baskets, lances, tomahawks, war-bonnets, and paintings that seemed to have come from all over the world. Stopping finally at a door opening upon the patio, he looked behind him quickly. Quagson and Georgette were consulting, heads together, over sheets of music. Bar Nothing and Briggs watched. Ware stepped noiselessly into the patio and flattened himself against the wall.

Around the patio ran a tiled roof making a shallow veranda. Except where doors of lighted rooms stood open, the veranda was dusky. He went without much sound along the tiles toward the rear of the house, and before he had gone thirty feet he heard voices. Words were not distinguishable, only the low tones of men talking. He thought of Capen and the message which had taken him from the table.

Now he went more quietly than before. Whatever interested Capen interested him, with a Capen enemy dead on the Capen range at the hand of a Capen tool!

A rasping voice said something. Capen's deep, smooth voice replied. The first speaker was hard to understand even as Ware worked closer, but part of his sentence carried the names of Bingham and Logan and Monument Rock.

'That makes no difference!' Capen said in a louder tone than he had used before. 'They have been hired by Marie Ribaut to prowl and they have to prowl to justify the wage. Let them go anywhere they like on my range, Isom, so long as they don't bother the stock.'

Ware hesitated. There was something about the lift of Capen's voice to make him wonder if he had been heard. So he went on and within twenty feet found the two leaning against the wall.

'Ware?' Capen inquired. 'Taking the air?'

'Yeh,' Ware drawled. 'I'm not much on houses, even castles like this of yours, Capen. Reckon I've been outdoors too much.'

'I thought that my niece's music might hold you. She plays rather well, for a child, and her voice is good, if untrained.'

'Do'no' a thing about it. I know two tunes; one's *Dixie* and the other ain't. I heard you say something about Bingham and Logan being here. That's the two trackers Marie Ribaut sent out, huh?'

'Yes. Isom, here, found them sleuthing about my range today. I usually require outsiders to get my permission for riding over the Open A. But so much to-do has been made about the disappearance of Ribaut that I'm disposed to slacken my rules this time, this once I can understand the daughter's feelings. Apparently, she has called on most of the population to search.'

'And the Rangers!' Ware reminded him dryly. 'Ames was ready to report for an important case; and I was trailing a murderer; then we got orders to drop everything and practically serve under Marie Ribaut. I suppose Carlos Smith told you.'

'Why, Carlos said that you came into Satan Land on the track of a murderer. But—Carlos isn't precisely brilliant of mind. I wondered if you weren't doing a fairly usual thing, evading admission of your real business. As a matter of fact, I hoped so! And now that I've seen you, I hope that you're not taking this Ribaut affair as a case in which you're going to merely go through motions. I hope you will really work!'

'Well,' Ware hesitated, 'to tell you the truth, I was not a bit pleased to have the job delivered on my neck. I still don't see why the captain couldn't have let Ames handle it on his own.'

'I'm glad that he isn't handling it alone. Ames is doubtless a good man, Ware, but there are various kinds of good man. Some fit one job, some another. In a situation needing courage, I'd ask no better Ranger than our Bar Nothing. But where the detective instinct, more than usual intelligence, is required—well! If you don't mind my saying so, I'll prefer you!'

'Why, of course, I'm pretty good at figuring things out,' Ware admitted. 'Ames is more on the bulldog build. That's likely the reason Cap' Durell had me take charge. He knows I generally dig down and find the things the others miss. But, from what I've heard here and there, it's no skin off your nose whatever happened to Ribaut.'

'You're wrong! I'm very much interested. And so,

having seen at first glance of you that you're the detective type, intelligent, of education above the common run and——'

'Oh, now!' Ware protested, laughing. 'I'm not educated, not as you'd say it. Of course, I have read some books and I've done some figuring about things. But educated——'

'Let me judge that! I assure you that I don't often misjudge men. I say again that I'm glad you're on this case. But don't take it lightly, as you've been inclined to do. Find Ribaut! Dead or alive, find him. It's important to me because I'm candidate for sheriff. I believe that the county needs a man of my type and ability to straighten out certain fairly criminal neglects and abuses. Otherwise, I couldn't justfy the time and energy I'll have to divert from my own affairs. This is a matter of good citizenship, you might say.'

'I—I don't quite gather that,' Ware said in a puzzled tone. 'I mean, what it's got to do with Ribaut?'

'It's very simple! I am confident that, whatever anybody may do, I'll be elected. But in politics of the sort played in this county, one doesn't take anything for granted. If Ribaut is dead, I want to know that. If someone—smugglers, say—have kidnaped him, I want to know that. If he has merely decided to vanish, believing his race run in this country, again, I want to know. For without his support, Briggs's candidacy is punctured. I am so interested that, if you'll really work this case and settle it to my satisfaction, I'll hand you five hundred dollars out of my own pocket—and thank you sincerely, besides!'

'Well, now! That's certainly generous! All right, sir! I can promise you that I'll scratch the gravel. So will Bar Nothing, I can tell you.'

'Good! Now, I've some work to do at my desk—Isom, you do as I told you. Don't get into any arguments with Miss Ribaut's trackers. I don't want any of my men taking shots at anybody, for any reason, without my order. Hannon had no business shooting Alf Mullit.

But'—he turned back to Ware—'if he's to be believed, and I've always found him truthful, Mullit was looking for him and fired first. You can hardly blame a man for defending himself.'

'All right, King,' Isom answered, with what seemed to Ware a note of hesitation in his rasping voice. 'I'll let 'em alone.'

'Don't forget any of my orders,' Capen told him. 'All right, Ware. I'll count on you to really clear up this mystery—— Oh! You don't have to explore this business Briggs speaks of, this embezzlement of young Thornton's?'

'Not yet. I mean, I'm not interested in any local case, until the sheriff asks Austin for help. From what I heard of the Thornton business, he had it all planned and he won't be caught in the neighborhood. Briggs ought to be sending wires to block the railroad stations. What's your idea of Thornton?'

'I hardly knew him. Zyrall's bank is one of those loosely managed cow-country institutions where anything might happen. Thornton's reputation was that of a serious, hard-working boy, with an eye to the main chance. My opinion of him was sketchy. But I thought he was a little too good to be true. Apparently, he had no human feelings; lived a sort of bread-and-water life. But the country expected him to get the bank by marrying Zyrall's rather stupid, plain daughter, not by theft. But it would seem that his face, as we saw it, was only a mask. Briggs says that letters were found indicating a much more interesting life led during his trips. That's not an unusual situation, you know.'

Isom moved off into the darkness. Ware and Capen went along the veranda, but within a few steps Capen halted.

'I'll have to let Georgette entertain you. Good night.'

Ware moved on toward the door out of which he had come. He walked slowly, considering Capen and the talk which he had interrupted. For he had small doubt, now, that Capen had heard his approach and spoken of the trailers for his benefit. Isom had seemed puzzled by Capen's words.

' "House of Whispering Shadows," ' Ware said softly to himself. 'Shadows enough, anyway. Monument Rock . . . Might be a good idea for us to slide out that way tomorrow. If we run onto Bingham and Logan and put what they've found with what I suspect——'

He made a cigarette and reached into a pocket for a match, found none, and turned toward the living-room, where the piano was being played jerkily. It was Quagson on the bench, but looking up at Briggs as he touched the keys. Georgette was not with the three. Bar Nothing turned to face Ware.

'Where you been?' he asked. 'Georgette's mad, account you're so impolite you won't listen to her singing——'

'I think we've identified that Mexican you killed,' Quagson interrupted. 'In fact, I'm sure of it. On a theory of probabilities, your one-eyed man with fancy belt wouldn't have a twin named Barela, of a type to try killing strangers without real reason. So I think it was Barela. I had him in jail in Stonewall, suspected of murdering a whole family in my county. But he got away after nearly killing our jailor.'

'Know anything about his friends and his doings?'

'Not much. He was from Old Mexico, just wandering in Texas. Stayed with these people we think he murdered. The man of that family was reputed to be pretty good at getting rustled stock across the River. But that's said of so many that——'

Ware nodded as Quagson broke off with a shrug. He took out the mutilated note found behind the saddle of that little man he had fought on D-Bar-D range, and handed it to Quagson. Bar Nothing and Briggs moved to read over the lawyer's shoulder.

'You see, the two men with Barela were not Mexicans,' Ware explained. 'I couldn't swear it, but I'd be willing to. It looked to me like a couple of Anglo *buscaderos* with Barela making a li'l' gang of 'em. That letter's an answer to a letter one of my men wrote, asking about conditions in some place a lick had been struck before.'

'No doubt of it,' Quagson agreed. 'And there's something about the respectful tone of this that makes me feel that our letter-writer has a vast admiration for the addressee. Which might well indicate that the gang is an important one; that an amateur long rider would be proud to ride with it—— Oh! So you thought of that, too!'

'I even tried to fit a name to the gang,' Ware drawled. 'Trouble is, while the name fits, so might some other.'

'What else was on that dead horse that might tell something?' Bar Nothing asked.

'Northern range hull, old but good; maker's name shaved off. Fishline girth. Stirrup leathers up for a man with legs no longer than mine. Common Fish slicker. Old wool blanket. One new flannel shirt. One pair of new gray socks. Plug of chewing.'

'No burning tobacco, huh?' Bar Nothing grunted.

'Nary sign of it. Why?'

'Rip Andress is awful short. And he don't smoke. Just chews.'

XXIV. 'Somebody's listening'

QUAGSON and Briggs stared fixedly at the big man. Ware leaned to get a match from the smoking-stand beside Bar Nothing.

'Rip Andress,' Quagson repeated slowly. 'That would argue some truth to all of the rumors we've had about Black Alec Pryde's gang being in the country.'

'Ah, I don't believe it!' Briggs cried suddenly. 'Lord! We heard that tale so often—— Just because Doggy Tibb used to punch cows around Satan Land, every time something pops, somebody says it's Black Alec and

Doggy Tibb and Baldy Burr and Rip Andress on the prod. *I* never met a man that'd say he's seen Doggy in this country since he pulled out four-five year back. And there's quite a few who'd know him.'

'It's just a guess, a surmise,' Quagson said, as if thinking aloud. 'In court, you'd have to call it negative proof of a very weak sort. Because you find chewing tobacco in a man's effects, but no smoking tobacco, you say he chews; doesn't smoke.'

'Hell! I ain't electing him,' Bar Nothing declared flatly. 'All I pointed my stick at was the size of Rip and this Winchester-mate of Steve's, and the tobacco that either one of 'em would use. This letter does show that the pair with Barela are hairpins with awful nervous consciences—for awful good reasons.'

One of the Chinese who had served them at dinner came quietly in and across to Quagson.

'*La señorita*,' he said tonelessly, 'she asks that you come to speak with her. If you will come with me—'

Quagson nodded and got up. Bar Nothing scowled after him and Ware laughed. Briggs looked blankly from one to the other.

'It's like this,' Ware explained blandly. 'Capen made her entertain all of us. But what she really wanted was to talk to Quagson. You and Bar Nothing couldn't see that the way I did. So you stayed, crowding around, until she had to slip off and send for Quagson. Next time, I hope you'll look harder—and see the facts when you look.'

'Ah!' Bar Nothing snarled. 'I'm going to turn in. You and your notions!'

'I'll be up pretty soon. I'm going to get that belt of Barela's for Quagson to see.'

He went out into the patio again and through it to the hedged yard behind the great house. Their saddles were in that neat outbuilding from which Hannom had stepped. Ware saw light in the bunkhouse down the line and grinned mirthlessly at thought of Hannom there. Nobody seemed to be outside, so he opened the door of the saddle room and instinctively paused at the side of it, to listen, before going in.

The belt was easily found in an *alforja*, rolled as he had left it. He went outside, looked at the bunkhouse and all about, then recrossed the yard to the hedge, crossed the house yard to the patio entrance, and stopped short. Once more he heard voces in the darkness. But this time Georgette was one of the speakers and the other, of course, would be Quagson.

'You know I'd do just about anything, no matter how hard or dangerous, that you asked!' Quagson was saying.

'Then, you will? And never breathe a word?' Georgette asked in a husky, shaken voice. 'Ah, Jimmy! You're a darling! I knew I could depend on you. No, no! Not—now! But, thanks!'

There was the quick patter of her feet on the tiles, running lightly away. Ware stood stiffly. Quagson seemed also to stand for minutes, then he moved up the veranda toward the living-room. Ware gave him time to go in before he followed. Even then, he went very deliberately, so that Quagson had disappeared before he reached the stair.

'It's exactly what you told Bar Nothing!' he reminded himself grimly. 'So, what's to be surprised about, now that you happen to see it coming true?'

But, no matter if he admitted the truth of his predictions about Georgette and Quagson, he did not want to see the lawyer. It was in no sense of the word jealousy. He was very sure of that. It was only that——

'I wonder what it is that she wants him to do for her?' he puzzled as he climbed the stair softly. 'Something that he mustn't breathe a word about; something special—something that she wouldn't ask *me* about . . . Of course, she's known him for quite a while and I'm the same as a stranger. But——'

He shook his head frowningly and went on to the door of their room. Bar Nothing was sprawling comfortably upon the wide bed, bare feet over the end, smoking. Ware tossed him the belt and undressed while Bar Nothing looked carefully at the spots and conchas of gold and silver, and at the heavy buckle. In underwear, Ware perched cross-legged on the bed and watched.

'If Quagson ever saw this, he ought to remember it!' Bar Nothing decided, handing back the belt. 'Well?'

'How'd you like to stick here three-four days?' Ware asked, squinting against the smoke of his cigarette. 'Sort of loaf around and take it easy and see if something happens?'

'Fine! Sounds like a good notion——'

'Just what I thought! So we pull out early tomorrow. It's not altogether that we may stumble onto something. But for your own sake, we'll split the breeze. I watched you downstairs and I said to myself: "Stephen Fuller Austin Ware!" I said. "If you stand around and watch that fine, beau-ti-ful young man, with all his future partly ahead of him, go on the way he's going, you'll never be able to look you in the eye again," I said. So——'

'Hell with you! When you get to be my age and size, you'll know how to wrangle things to a frazzle-dazzle— same as me. Now, I have been watching you, and I tell you it's been a sad, sad sight! I can read you like primer print. A boy that never went out a-sweethearting. Serious boy! Plenty brains; always studying. No fun, though! So you meet up with a pretty girl and, bango! You come down like a brick house on a June bug. All the loving affection you ought've scatterated around amongst forty-'leven bundles of calico, over years and years, you unload on one. Why——how many girls you ever——'

'None!' Ware said innocently. 'But I've *spoken* to three. Not all at once, naturally. But within nine-ten years. So in spite of all the trail-covering, Mister Ames, we take our foot in our hand in the freshness of the morning, tomorrow, and we light a shuck. I promised Capen that we'd really dig into this Ribaut business.

He promised us five hundred to settle it, so he'll know what he's bucking, come election.'

Bar Nothing rolled a narrowed eye toward him. His grin disappeared. He blew out smoke with a whistling sound.

'Five—hundred!' he breathed reverently. 'Why, there's a hell-slew of *gunies* around this country that'd drag Ben Briggs clean to Timbuktu for that, and *hand* Capen the election!'

'Well, we'll pick us a direction tomorrow, and make some kind of real start; quit making motions on the case. It's one thing to have to look at the case because of the Ribaut family's pull at Austin, and something else to work for five hundred.'

He wriggled under the cover and stretched luxuriously. Bar Nothing got up and blew out the wall lamp. When he came back to bed, he was saying softly, 'Five-hundred . . .' Ware leaned a little to him.

'No talking—here!' he whispered. 'Somebody's listening outside that door.'

They slept quietly and were up early. But Briggs and Quagson were before them at the breakfast table, with Capen. Ware looked swiftly for Georgette and was disappointed not to see her. They sat close to Capen, near the head of the long table. While the Chinese brought their breakfast, Capen discussed some point of criminal law with Quagson, and it interested Ware to see that the lawyer listened respectfully to his host's statement of French procedure.

'That,' Capen concluded, 'is an essential difference between France and England and, of course, this country. . . . Well, Ware? What are your plans for the day? Briggs is going on to La Piedra. Quagson thinks he must get back to Stonewall.'

'I reckon we'll side Briggs,' Ware told him, after a moment of hesitation. 'First chance we've had to ride that road with somebody who knows the country.'

'Glad to have you!' Briggs said, with what seemed very real cordiality. 'That's a lonesome trail.'

Georgette had not appeared when they finished the meal and went out to the corrals. Ware caught Bar Nothing looking furtively toward the house, and grinned. For he had caught himself doing the same thing. They saw Quagson ride straight away across Open A range, as if the girl were not in his thoughts. Then the three of them mounted and looked down at Capen.

'*Hasta la vista*—until I see you again,' Capen said. 'Come again, any time.' "The house is your house." I hope you'll be claiming that reward quickly, Ware. Briggs, luck to you in everything but elections! Ames, we always like to see you.'

'Smooth as a bottom-card deal!' Briggs said abruptly, when they had gone a hundred yards toward the Piedra road. 'Yes, sir! Theo Ribaut was slick enough to talk a gopher into living in a tree, but alongside Capen——'

'You never did show Quagson that belt,' Bar Nothing reminded Ware. 'Slip your mind?'

Ware nodded and looked across the rolling flats to southward. Almost like a motionless pillar of smoke, a finger of stone rose there. Monument Rock . . . He had been thinking of the belt, but thinking more of the grim-faced, likable, efficient Quagson, and even more of Georgette, for whom the lawyer was to do something, never speaking of it. 'What's special about Piedra, for you?' he asked Briggs quickly, to change the subject. 'Thornton trail lead that way?'

'I do'no' where the Thornton trail points. Do'no' whichaway wasaway, like the saying goes. But I got to go somewhere! I ain't going to stay in Alamos with Marie punching at me all time. Now that Alf's rubbed out, she'll be a sight worse, too.'

'You know, I have just been thinking!' Ware drawled. 'No sense to Bar Nothing and me going to Piedra, after all. Not a bit! What we had better do is put in three-four days exploring down yonder, in between D-Bar-D south range and Three-Jag Hill.'

'I was about to say that myself,' Bar Nothing agreed, nodding solemnly. 'Seems to me that if somebody sacked

old Theo's saddle for him and toted off the buckboard
and mules, any sign we could find, it'd be off the trail,
right out in Satan Land.'

Briggs looked uncertainly ahead, then shifted in the
saddle to stare across the savage distances to the south.

'I–I could side you,' he began vaguely.

'Glad to have you!' Ware assured him promptly. 'It's
going to be rough work, *sin dudar*. Nary doubt! My
notion is, we'll stumble onto some hard cases and plenty,
like Barela's two friends. That's all right for a man like
me, built close to the ground. But you and Bar Nothing loom up like a couple of windmills. You'll get your
hair parted while I'm comfortable and safe down-cellar.
From all I've picked up, between Olin's and here, Satan
Land is full of *buscaderos*; they're thicker'n splatter.
Three of us is twice as good as two. Now——'

'But I don't see how I can, right now,' Briggs interrupted with worried head-shake. 'Nah, I reckon not.
Too many things to do; too many hens on around my
bailiwick. Wish I could, though!'

'Well, then, we'll divide the trail with you down yonder. You keep the Piedra half and when you hit town,
ask Clem Tooley if he's got that pickle-squirt noise out
of *Pinafore*.'

'*Pinafore*? I bog on that crossing——'

'Don't let your mind wrinkle. He'll play it for you
and you'll know all about it, including the place that
sounds like a rusty nail scratched on a tin roof. Be seeing you!'

'Well,' Bar Nothing drawled, looking after Briggs,
'you played that right slick, Steve. I was scared for a
minute that he was too scared to let us out of sight.
If you hadn't roused him up to be more scared of Black
Alec jumping him out here, he would have stuck
closer'n a tick to a hairless dog.'

'You could have the whole Briggs family helping, and
still be all by yourself! And you don't dare talk around
him the way I'm about to talk. It's like this: You're
brave, but——'

XXV. 'Buckboard tracks'

BAR NOTHING listened grimly as the horses walked toward Monument Rock. When he came to the snatch of talk between Georgette and Quagson, Ware hesitated briefly, then told of it.

'What's on her mind, I wouldn't even guess at. Likely, no more'n some girl-notion and, sad as it may be to you, my brave, but no detective, *campañero*, it's dead-certain something that has got nothing to do with us and our business.'

He laughed shortly, picturing Capen, recalling the thick flattery Capen had turned upon him.

'He told me how bright a boy I am. Yeh! He could see it. Intelligence . . . Detective instinct . . . Education . . . So I plead guilty; couldn't deny I'm something special. Then he offered the five hundred for settling the Ribaut case one way on another. Good thing he didn't get a chance to talk to you! Two of us as bright as Capen would make us, why, we'd set the prairie on fire!'

'I be damned! This snaky, lanky Ebb Isom, he bulged up to the house to tell the Big Auger something important about Bingham and Logan. I know him right well. He's got a face on him like—two yaller shoe buttons stuck on the sides of an axe. I wouldn't trust him behind me till hell started shipping ice! He coyoted up to unload on Capen about Marie Ribaut's trackers' being around Monument Rock and—You think Capen smelled you behind him, huh? Changed what he was saying to fit you?'

'I would bet that way. Isom bogged down when Capen began to spread the soft soap about letting 'em go anywhere they wanted to; and about understanding how Marie would naturally worry. You could hear him guggling over it. Then, when Capen thought he could choke a kid-Ranger with his compliments, everything began to smell of fish—dead fish. I couldn't tell you all this last night. Not in that house! Somebody had an ear wrapped around our door. I heard the floor give a li'l' bit in the hall. And if that was one of Capen's shadows, it was damn' solid.'

'Looky here!' Bar Nothing grunted, twisting to hook a leg around the horn comfortably and gesture with his tobacco sack. 'Our notion runs about like this, huh? Capen's running an outfit in a style nobody's cow's children can ever pay the half of. That's bad. For all the talk around Alamos is, when he hit the country from South America, with Georgette along, he didn't pack enough to weight down a chee-chee bird——'

'Clem Tooley told me something like that. He worked with Ribaut at first, to settle his feet under him.'

'Yeh! The point is, everything we see around Capen is paid for, one way or another, by what he's got in this country. We know the cow-business didn't build Capen Castle; don't keep it going. So, what does?'

'We do'no' and maybe we never will. But there's no law against our taking a good guess,' Ware said grimly. 'A lot of murders have been committed around here, and every one of 'em had a money side; somebody made money out of the murderees. Capen was around! Claims have been jumped and come up in Capen's hands. Ribaut was backing Briggs for sheriff; and he was packing a lot of money. Just because he was packing the money, he might have caught a poor gunman's eye. Just because he had Alf Mullit to tell about Capen deals——'

'Ex-act-ly! We're figuring that Capen had Ribaut wiped out, and somewhere out here'—he waved a long arm—'Ribaut and his kid and the buckboard and a span of Spanish mules are all waiting to be uncovered. Bingham and Logan are trying to uncover 'em. Ebb Isom's worried plenty about their poking and, maybe, so is Capen. You know . . . if I was Bingham and Logan, or even one of 'em, I think I'd waggle my John

B. over the hogbacks before I showed myself. Lots simpler to buy hats than to grow scalps.'

Ware nodded for answer. Capen's dark, still face was
in his mind. Did Georgette look like her father, Capen's brother? Or like her mother? He visualized the
two faces. Capen's and Georgette's. In coloring, they
were much alike, but——

'Huh?' he grunted absently. 'Fool Capen? What do
you mean? I was thinking. Reckon I didn't hear you.'

'Oh, nothing! Nothing a-tall!' Bar Nothing told him
with elaborate carelessness. 'Excuse me for busting in
on your day-dreaming about what a lovely, sweet girl
she is, and how sad and all it is she's kin to a slick
scoun'el like Capen, but you could take her off and
help her to *forget* the scarlet past—— What I am trying
to say is: Suppose you never fooled Capen, my intelligent—and educated—with a detective instinct—young
corporal? Suppose he aims to make you a notch on the
old tally stick? Same as Ribaut and Mullit, huh?'

'You're dead right! So, hereafter, *you* ride point. Capen's not worrying about you; account you're just
brave. It's my intelligence and education and detective
instinct he's afraid of. So you'll skyline yourself and
draw fire if there's any——'

He touched Rocket with a rowel and jumped him
into a lope. Far ahead, Monument Rock rose from its
jumbled shelves and ledges, a weather-carved, symmet-
rical pillar that looked as if men's hands had set it up.
Riding toward it, Ware lost his grin. If their suspicions
were correct, somewhere about the Rock was evidence
that Capen thought searchers might uncover. But, what?

'It wouldn't be on Ribaut's road, any way you can
figure,' he told Bar Nothing thoughtfully. 'We know
he got to Piedra and turned around there. Carlos Smith
claims the Ribauts stopped with him again, on the re-
turn-trip. He claims they had a mean-looking Mexican
with 'em, you remember; but Clem Tooley never saw
that Mexican. Now, the way Ribaut would have gone,
from the D-Bar-D, he'd have used Smith's road back

to the Alamos-Piedra road. The Rock would have been clear off to eastward of him.'

'But, and yet,' Capen's boogering about anybody exploring around the Rock!'

They came closer to the great pillar as the morning went. At last, Ware suggested to Bar Nothing that they separate and look for sign, either of Bingham and Logan or—a buckboard.

'And don't forget,' he warned Bar Nothing gravely, 'if you happen onto anybody that looks like shooting, rise up and yell and attract their attention. Don't let 'em shoot at me!'

Presently they were a half-mile apart, sometimes out of sight of each other. Ware studied the ground and the skyline all about. Somehow, he felt closer to the mystery of Theo Ribaut than ever before. If only this day's ride could settle it, he could move to investigate the movement of that man on the Plumb Bob bay, sighted by Smith riding northward. He thought of Verde and Sheriff Loren and kindly old Fyeback, as for some time he had not thought of them. One thing seemed certain: Dave Loren had not done anything in that case, not even so much as he had accomplished by the accident of direction.

Noon came and Bar Nothing drew toward him. They rode up to the base of the rock and studied it curiously. It was really a volcanic formation rising from the sand and caliche, low hills with basins and pot holes everywhere, knife-edged ridges running in patternless confusion up to the towering pillar. One tiny cañon with stone floor worn by countless feet led into a shallow, cool cavern. Here was a well of cold water fed by some deep spring. By sprawling at its lip they could put their faces into it. The floor was very smooth, glassy where the hand fell naturally when a drinker leaned to the water.

'Another one like this, down at Three-Jag Hill,' Bar Nothing said when they had drunk and watered the horses and come out into the sunlight again. 'Still another at Two-Day Water. Reckon they've been used a thousand years.'

'Reckon. There's a *tinaja* like this in the Hueco Mountains above El Paso, on the old Butterfield Stage Route to Crow Flat. The Pueblo Indians at Ysleta say it's been used since the sun was first turned on. Lots of killings have been done around that tank. I wouldn't be surprised if that's true about this one, too.'

Bar Nothing looked around and shrugged.

'Strike you as funny that we haven't seen a track? Not one to show that Bingham and Logan scouted around here?'

'Yeh. Maybe we'll run onto 'em, though. How about grub?'

They had a cold lunch from Ware's saddlebags, of beans and tomatoes bought at Hack Kinney's store. Afterward, they rode all around the edges of the little hills. But no tracks showed, so they separated once more and rode slowly southward. Rabbit trails and the occasional furrow of a snake were all that Ware found for three hours. Then, upon a slope closely grown with greasewood he saw a groove that stopped him short. He sat staring. Except for that yard-long depression in sand sheltered by a bush, there was no more trail. But he recognized the mark and coursed back and forth around it, searching for another sign that a narrow-wheeled vehicle had passed.

Then he rode up to the crest of the highest dune near-by and looked for Bar Nothing. When he saw the tall figure well to his left he waved his sombrero until Bar Nothing answered with flourish of his own hat and came at the lope toward him.

'Buckboard tracks,' Ware told him quietly. 'A track, anyhow. Come look and tell me what *you* think.'

Bar Nothing studied the imprint, then nodded.

'Somebody took the trouble to wipe out the trail. Missed this one spot, it being under the greasewood. It's wiped out, all right, not blown over. Old blanket-drag, likely.'

'Smith's place is over yonder, west of us,' Ware calculated. 'Trail could be pointing that way—or coming from the house there. Could be pointing southwest, toward Three-Jag Hill. It's going to be too dark to trail pretty soon. Let's look around here, then go back to the Rock and sleep and pick up again tomorrow.'

Circling produced no more tracks that they could be sure of. When it was almost dusk they turned back toward Monument Rock and built their supper fire in a sheltered hollow where the wind did not reach. When they had finished their bacon, beans, and coffee, they smothered the fire with sand and went out to sleep in an arroyo a mile away, with the horses staked close by.

There were no tracks around the water cañon next morning and they returned to the single buckboard rut after breakfast. The long day carried them south almost to the triple spikes of Three-Jag Hill, but stock trails were all that they saw. But when they came to Monument Rock before dark, the tracks of horses paralleled and crossed their own morning's trail.

'Three of 'em,' Ware said after some examination. 'Interested as get-out in us! You can almost hear 'em talk, here, where they puzzled out our trail! Look! They rode up here about the same way we did at first, coming from the direction of Capen's. They spotted our trail and—yeh! looped around after wawaing awhile and rode off the way they'd come, pretty much.'

He followed the later looping of the trail for long enough to show him that the trio had gone away toward the Open A. Bar Nothing was building their fire. Ware looked at the stony ridges above them, then left the camp to scramble upward. It was difficult climbing. One slope fell to a pocket and he must work upward over the next. There were flat surfaces that ended in deep cracks out of which puffs of air came. He thought that in time of rain, water would run down these myriad sheds into the caverns below.

Slowly, he went from one side to the other of the tumbled mass. The sun disappeared. Bar Nothing called to him. It seemed simpler to go on and down on the opposite side of the Rock than to retrace his course. He half-slid, half-ran, down a rooflike slope, and stopped at the bottom before a cave-mouth larger than any seen before, a dark opening two yards wide and half as high. He leaned and scratched a match, illumining the passage. The stone floor was filmed with dust and under the small glare of his match footprints showed, and smeary stripes as of something dragged. He stepped closer, stooping to enter, and on his knees, with a fresh match, worked along the cave floor. Five or six feet within the passage he stopped before two pairs of worn bootsoles, glimpsed as his match burned down.

'Bingham and Logan!' he grunted without hesitation.

It was difficult to draw out the bodies. One was a big man and heavy, with an Indian cast of features. The other was a man smaller, even than Ware, red-haired, beginning to be bald. But one thing they had in common: each had been shot in the back, the big man once, the other twice. Nothing was in their pockets, not so much as a sack of tobacco.

Ware found himself in dusk when he came out of the cavern. He let himself down to the flat and rounded the rocks to where Bar Nothing toasted bacon and watched their coffee tin.

'Something around here,' Ware said deliberately, 'is or was hidden. Something important enough to make it worth killing a man or six, to keep it from being found. But I haven't found it yet. You happen to know Bingham and Logan?'

'Seen 'em, yeh. Bingham's a big, dark fellow; part-Indian. Logan's a happy-go-lucky li'l' wisp of an Irisher. Why?'

'I found *them,* if I didn't find what they'd been hunting. They're up above. Shot in the back.'

He reached to take the coffee from the fire while Bar Nothing, starting a rasher of bacon toward his mouth, stared as if frozen, then continued the movement. Ware reached for bacon and beans and ate placidly.

'Up above?' Bar Nothing repeated at last. 'I be damned! Say! You reckon it was to tell Capen that, that Ebb Isom slid up to the house the night we stayed there?'

'I reckon Ebb Isom's going to get a chance to tell somebody whether or not it was!' Ware assured him grimly. 'Tomorrow!'

XXVI. *'Scalps to you!'*

WHILE they ate, they held an informal council of war. Ware reminded Bar Nothing of the three men who had stopped to look at their trail, then turned straight around to ride toward Capen's house, if not actually to Capen.

'I always look on the dark side of things,' he said grimly, staring into the fire. ' "Hope for the best, but expect the worst," and "Every silver lining has its cloud," and all that. So, figure it this way:

'Some of Capen's handymen know that around here is something outsiders mustn't find. So, when Bingham and Logan get skylined, prowling around, they get bushwhacked. The Capenites, they hide Marie's trackers up where nobody'd look for 'em in a thousand years. But they're riding along on some business or other and they spot the trail of two more inquisitive hairpins around the Rock. But those hairpins have got away—else they might have been candidates for slugs singing *"You Won't Go Home."* But just sight of the trail is enough to worry the three *gunies* and they wonder what to do. They make medicine and decide to run ask the Boss.'

'And if the Boss tells 'em to hightail back and see if that cave'll accommodate two more boarders—uh-huh!' Bar Nothing finished for him, nodding, staring appreciatively at Ware. 'Right-ho! my young corporal with what rightly Mister Capen figured was detective instinct. So, we reach up and catch hold of our ears and stretch 'em out to catch every sweet li'l' breeze that blows?'

'And more! We don't let anybody come in between us and the late Bingham and Logan. Somehow, we camp right up there until tomorrow. Then we put the two on Rocket—I can make him pack 'em—and we double up on that horse-impersonator of yours and we take out for Capen's to lay 'em on his stepstone! We'll gather in Ebb Isom and sort of hold him up by the fetlocks while we shake and see if something drops out of him!'

'How about the horses? Can we get 'em up there?'

'There's a place around yonder that looks possible. I saw a hollow or two big enough for 'em to stand in. They won't be comfortable, but they can stand it for one night.'

The crack that Ware had seen made a path upward that the horses could climb, with help from their own-ers. It was not easy in the darkness to find a deep basin with bottom smooth enough to hold the two, but pres-ently they were standing just beyond the cavern which held the two dead trailers. Ware and Bar Nothing were more comfortable, sprawled upon their blankets and using saddles for pillows.

'You know, I thought I'd found the Ribauts, at first,' Ware confessed. 'I was certainly hoping so! I'm tired of this case. I would like to close it up and get back to my man on the Plumb Bob bay. Don't suppose I ever told you that Carlos Smith admitted seeing that murderer on this range; every time we've tried to wawa about something, something else has sat down in our lap! I told Smith that I wanted a man with an Arrow Head horse and he was fresh out of Arrow Heads, but handed me a Plumb Bob. Well! Le' me finish with the Ribauts and I'll start after that killer.'

'You are a lot like an Injun,' Bar Nothing said slowly.

'Uncle Lige Fyeback always treated me like his clos-est kin! And I was walking away from his store in Verde when he was murdered. I was close enough to hear his death-yell; and I had a glimpse of his killer, but he got away. He won't get away again! I never in my life wanted to kill a man before. I've taken a lot of chances to keep from having to kill one, same as you have. But that's one cold-blooded murderer I'll treat the same as I'd treat a snake! Well, no use jawing about it.'

Bar Nothing smoked silently for a while, then:

'I'm still wondering what it was Georgette got Quagson to do for her. Funny, she wouldn't ask me or you . . .'

'That's another reason for cleaning up and getting out,' Ware drawled. 'Georgette! She can put notions in a plain cowboy's head, or a Ranger's, that are too big for his skull to hold. Chances are she never thinks about it again. But that cowboy, that Ranger, he has to bed down for a long time with the notions. Maybe for the rest of his life . . .'

'Now, I don't see that!' Bar Nothing began argumentatively. 'A man's a good man or he ain't. If he's a good man, on the upgrade, going somewhere, he's good enough for the like of——'

'Of course he's good enough! But still not right. The devil of it is, *amigo*, a long time after the Georgettes have gone along and married their Jimmy Quagsons, the Ameses and Wares are remembering 'em; likely carrying their picture in mind for a sort of model; comparing every girl they meet with that model.'

'Not me! I like the ladies, God bless 'em! I like 'em dark and light and redhead, tall and short and in-between. Too many pretty girls in the world to grieve over any one of 'em. Georgette's the prettiest I ever saw. But if she wants Quagson—I know a yaller-haired girl in Kerrville almost as pretty and with a sight better disposition——'

'Turn in, Brigham Young! Turn in! You belong over in Turkey, bossing a harem!'

Ware lay long awake, after Bar Nothing's regular breathing indicated that the big man's problems of the

heart did not interfere with his sleep. Thought of the
two dead trailers moved Ware very little. They had accepted a dangerous mission with open eyes and they
had not been alert in enemy-country. Only the manner
of their death roused natural anger in him. But on that
score he looked forward with grim pleasure to facing
Ebb Isom and trying to get from him admissions enough
to justify a murder charge.

The same question that Bar Nothing had voiced
persisted in his mind: What had Georgette so wanted
done? He remembered how her husky voice had shaken;
the note of deep relief in it when Quagson had promised his help. He asked himself how much Georgette
might guess of Capen's activities. But Capen was not
an easy man to fathom; she might actually know nothing, suspect little or nothing in spite of her nearness
to violent crimes.

Before he drowsed, he admitted to himself that he
had spoken no more than bare truth in saying that he
would carry out of Satan Land a picture against which
all other girls must be compared.

A rasping sound waked Ware and he lay motionless,
listening. The sky was graying and the smell of morning in the air. The noise came closer, and he moved
the hand which had closed instinctively upon a Colt.
Bar Nothing shifted position slightly and Ware saw
that he, too, had been roused and held his pistol. Ware
freed himself soundlessly of the blanket and rolled to
prop himself on his elbows.

Bar Nothing's Colt bellowed thunderously, the roar
of it blending with the shot of a man just risen above
a ridge of stone three yards away. The man's bullet
glanced from a shoulder of rock between them, rico-
cheted with wasplike whine past Ware's ear, and flattened against the ridge behind which the man was sink-
ing.

Bar Nothing fired again before Ware could cover the
man. Dust jumped from the target's blue shirt, then he
was out of sight. Bar Nothing came to a crouch as Ware

wriggled to his feet. They worked cautiously up to the ridge as from the flat below someone yelled an inquiry.

'Got him!' Bar Nothing grunted savagely. 'Now for his friends!'

They went as rapidly as they could scramble over the sharp ridges and Ware thought of yelling a reply to the question from the flat, a muffled 'All right!'

Horses below them were so close to the foot of the rock that it was difficult to see the riders. Ware leaned around a shoulder for clearer vision and was greeted by a shot that sent a slug within a yard of his face. He let the hammer of his Colt drop with no more than general aim, and a horse jumped out into the open, riderless, galloped for a few feet, then crashed down.

Hoofs thundered and dust rose almost in Ware's face. He shot the Colt empty without seeing a target, reholstered it and went downward. But when he came to the level, with hands bleeding, the hoofbeats were distant. He ran after them, but the pair of riders were already out of range, marked by rising dust well out on the flat.

He went back up by way of the path they had used the night before. Bar Nothing stood over the dead man, whose shirt he had opened and drawn back to show tattooing on the upper arms.

'Thought I knew him from the general looks and piece off the ear,' he said quietly. 'But the bronc' rider on one arm and the Chinese girl on the other made me certain.'

'Baldy Burr,' Ware answered, staring down at the dark, stocky lieutenant of Black Alec Pryde. 'Do'no' how many times I've wondered if I'd ever see him. He's out of Spicewood County and I've met some of his kinfolk; all dark like him, all salty. But he's the only one to actually slap the law in the eye. And there he is, lucky to cash in from a slug instead of kicking at the end of a rope. He's been overdue at a hanging for a long, long time. Twelve hundred dollars to you, for that fast center shot. Maybe more. Good thing you drilled him, or we'd be the ones laid out like cans of corned beef! That slug of his bounced off a rock and nearly set my ear afire.'

'Ah, he lifted up right in my face! I never even aimed at him. My gun just went off by itself, he scared me so bad, and happened to hit him. Well, what happened to his li'l' playmates?'

'They changed their minds about playing,' Ware drawled. 'Good judgment on their part, too. Two men could hold these rocks in the face of a young army. Let's get the *caballos* down and take a look at their trail.'

They saddled and led the horses to the flat, mounted, and rode out from the Rock for a few hundred yards. But the hoofprints showed that the friends of Baldy Burr had continued to gallop, so they turned back.

'It was Baldy and the others, looking at our trail, all right,' Ware commented, reining in where the double set of tracks could be seen close together. 'I—wonder! Are those coy and stand-offish friends of Baldy's Doggy Tibb and Rip Andress, or Black Alec and Doggy, or Rip? Howcome Baldy was climbing around the rocks? Just to see if somebody might be up there? Or——'

'Yeh! "Or——" is exactly it. How about him coming up to take a look at Bingham and Logan? To see if we'd lifted 'em out of that cave?'

'*Quién sabe?* But I think we'd better shake out another loop today . . . I would certainly admire for to know if that's two more of Black Alec's murderers out yonder and where they hole up, if we can hang to the trail.'

'Well, we can put Baldy in with Bingham and Logan, then take out after 'em. Likely they won't be expecting us to crowd 'em and they'll slow down after a spell.'

Once more they climbed to the rocks. When Baldy Burr lay in the little cavern with the men who, possibly, he had helped kill, they went back to the horses, watered them, ate the last of their food, and moved to look at the dead horse—a bay branded B-Connected-L—before taking the trail. There was nothing in the rolled slicker of interest, nor anything about the saddle to mark it, except the rig that indicated what they knew of Burr, that he was a Texas cowboy.

The men they followed had galloped for more than a mile before slowing to the trot, then halting in an arroyo for a time. But within another mile the tracks divided.

'I'll take Big Hoofs,' Ware said, scowling. 'Maybe they're just trying to forestall us, guessing that we might try this. If we don't come together on these trails, let's make the meet for Capen's—outside of the Castle, too! Remember that narrow arroyo we crossed, mile or so this way from the creek?'

'Good enough! Scalps to you! If I come up on this dilly-dallying son, he better give up quick or I'll have hair hanging on my bridle when I rack into that arroyo!'

He sent King Solomon forward, and Ware, after a look at the land's lie and the track of the big hoofs bearing left, sent Rocket ahead at the long, mile-eating hard trot. Now, he drew out his carbine and rode with it across an arm.

XXVII. *'By his own gun!'*

FOR a time, the trail was easy to follow, going so directly toward the position of Capen's that Ware wondered if time might not be saved by riding straight up to the Open A corrals and there waiting for the rider. Then it twisted abruptly eastward across the arroyo-gashed greasewood flat, and he was puzzled.

Was it possible, he asked himself, that no connection existed between the several groups of men he seemed to sense in Satan Land? Did they merely ride back and

forth, each group independent of the other, each busy
with its own particular businesses of murder and robbery and discouragement of chance-met Rangers?

'Starting at Olin's store,' he thought, 'there was Olin,
seeming to have ideas all his own; and up rode Eagan
and his gladiators with troubles, wearing the 66 brand.
Eagan practically swore that Olin's standing in with
buscaderos generally and Doggy Tibb in particular. A
friend of Doggy Tibb is probably a friend of Black Alec
Pryde and Rip Andress and Baldy Burr. Eagan was hell
on hitting a lick at Norman and the Lightning Rod
spread; called Norman a thief . . .'

He shook his head as the picture spread before his
inner eye.

'Olin and Norman didn't seem friendly, but Norman wasn't on the prod against Olin, the way Eagan
was. Norman called Eagan all that Eagan had called
him. Said that talk about Doggy Tibb being in the country is just talk. But Norman's from the northern ranges
and—so are Black Alec and Rip Andress, who always
ride with Doggy Tibb . . .'

He slowed Rocket to a walk, let his carbine down
upon his lap, and twirled tobacco into a brown paper,
then reached for a match while scanning the skyline
all around.

'The man I've trailed from Verde to Olin's, wondering if he's out of Black Alec's gang, he pops up in this
neighborhood as plain as a steeple—but nobody knows
him! Barela, bad Mexican from Across, bulges into my
life with a couple of tough Anglos. Capen's worried
about people hunting over his range and those people
die. And right where they're cached Baldy Burr comes
a-shooting! Horse, horse! Talk about spiderweb trails!'

But there was a theory which would fit all these seem-
ingly unrelated men and incidents into a single, under-
standable picture. Vaguely, Ware had seen this since he
had looked down upon Baldy Burr's face. It argued a
connection between Capen and whatever Capen's needs
of any moment might be, and Black Alec Pryde's gang

as individuals or all together. The weak point of it was, there was as yet no evidence to prove such a connection. All he could say was that the theory explained everything that had happened in Satan Land since Theo Ribaut's disappearance.

'You can even go back to Verde and come on from Uncle Lige's murder, past Olin's, to take in Eagan and Norman as well as the Pryde gang and Carlos Smith and Capen! But—prove it! That's the hell of it,' he confessed irritably.

There was some consolation in sight of those large hoofprints before him. They were solid. If he could come close to that rider, mere sight of him might furnish a link that would tie together other parts of this web. If he could be taken, ways might be found to make him talk, however tight-mouthed he might be. Ways would be found . . .

The trail led him on at the slinging trot into land more broken, where heaps of bare red-and-black rock rose from the greasewood and mesquite. It was dangerous to ride fast, where a man followed might stop in shelter of those piles of stone and watch his backtrail. But Ware was in no mood to count possible odds today. He merely intensified his caution when riding up to the rocky heights into which the trail was leading.

In mid-morning he found himself going through the arroyos and shallow cañons of a little range of stony hills. He recalled them as showing hazy, distant, from the Open A yard. The trail was not so plain in these stony watercourses and tiny cactus-studded flats. But here and there the big hoofprints showed and he pushed on, watching every ledge above and beyond him, halting at each turn of the way about a buttress of rock to listen. Then he heard the faint but unmistakable sound of water running. Around a cliff-shoulder he saw a narrow creek tumbling over boulders, and guessed that it was the same stream upon which Capen had built in the little valley miles below.

Beyond the creek was a small grassy flat, walled in by

low cliffs. Ware slipped to the ground and hitched Rocket to a greasewood. Then he hung his sombrero on the saddle horn and inched forward with carbine at the ready, to study the creek from behind a great rock.

His man had gone up or down the creek. The sheer face of the cliff opposite this arroyo was unscalable. Looking upstream to where the water seemed to flow from narrow cracks in the rock, Ware dismissed that direction. Downstream lay Capen Castle and a road passable to riders. He looked at the curve of the cliffs that fenced the tiny meadow. His man had crossed here, ridden the flat to that end of the grassy level, then taken to the creek again. He might be just around the curve, or might have gone steadily on as he had ridden all morning.

Ware stood and looked uncertainly at Rocket, then went out afoot, to cross the creek on rocks that served as stepping-stones and run across the grass to the shelter of the cliffs. He worked quickly along the feet of these until he came to the creek-edge. The water was nowhere a foot deep and he waded cautiously, testing each foothold before setting his weight down, until he had worked downstream a hundred yards and more, between steep walls.

Then the cañon widened again. Another, much larger meadow had been gouged out of the cliffs. Huge boulders made a sort of terrace back of the flat, against the cliff. Among them, hardly to be seen at a glance, a stone house had been built. It was no more than a single room, dirt-roofed, blank-walled at the end Ware could see, with only a narrow door for opening at the front. Beyond it a rough log corral hugged the cliff. A buckskin horse and a tall iron-gray, hobbled and side-lined, grazed between house and corral. There was no other sign of life anywhere.

Ware decided that this was one of the Open A line-camps. It might very well be deserted at this time of day, though the hobbled horses seemed to indicate that men were not very far away. He wondered if the man he followed had merely passed without halt. Neither buckskin nor gray showed any sign of having been ridden as recently as the big-hoofed horse trailed here. He stared fixedly at the dark rectangle of the open door. It was not reasonable to believe that a man awake would stay in that dark cell, when outside the bright sunshine tempered October chill. But such men as used these trails might think of other things than comfort!

Slowly, he grinned. Between him and that door was a boulder, perhaps forty yards from the house, a little nearer his position. If he sprinted toward it, he would be a target until he made the shelter. But unless a man sat inside, looking straight at him, he might cover half the distance before being seen. He drew a long breath, shifted his feet, then jumped into the open and raced toward the boulder.

He was throwing himself to the ground when the shot came. He heard the hollow thud of the bullet in the ground behind him. Then he pushed the carbine around the boulder and aimed without exposing more than hand and arm in the general direction of the door. Another shot and a third drove lead into the ground close to him. He was about to squeeze the trigger when an oddity about those shots checked him. They were not coming from the house!

Ware hugged the boulder more closely, drawing up his legs and keeping elbows closer to his sides. A fourth shot and a fifth dug up earth so near him that he felt the ground vibrate.

'Somebody,' he remarked thoughtfully aloud, 'has got up in the rocks above the house . . . was up there. Must have been turned the other way or, close as he's coming, he'd have stitched five new buttonholes in my clothes . . .

He ventured to move his head for a one-eyed look at the cabin. There was still no sign of life. The horses grazed calmly, as if shots were familiar sounds. On the

cliff, so far as his limited view let him see, there was no
movement, no projecting rifle. He shifted to the other
side of the boulder and studied the face of the cliff.
There were spots that might be no more than natural
shadows or discolorations, but seemed to form a diag-
onal line across the cliff up to a long streak perhaps fifty
feet above the meadow, fifteen or twenty feet below the
cliff-top.

Ware thrust out his hand and waggled it, then jerked
it back. Three fast shots came, lead ringing on the boulder and glancing off. He peered out cautiously, and this
time saw smoke drifting up from the shelflike streak.

'So that's where he's holed up!' he drawled. 'And if
my guess is any good, shooting a pistol, not a long
gun . . .'

He twisted about, carbine a little raised, then dropped
sideways to the ground beside the boulder, aiming at
the shelf as soon as he was exposed, squeezing the trigger
and jerking down the lever, firing a second shot with
no more than general aim at his target, intent on hammering the cliff rather than coming very close.

The unseen marksman had the first shot, and the
slug came so close that as he concentrated savagely upon
correcting his aim, it seemed to Ware that the lead
ruffled his hair, but he saw the shelf over the front sight,
now. He could drive his own bullets accurately at the
line of it. There was no reply, and he drew a knee up
under him while he waited after his third aimed shot
to see movement.

He scrambled to his feet and ran toward the stone
cabin. Again the pistol sounded on the shelf, but he
was exposed for only ten feet of his run. The bullets
were not so close this time. Safe in the shelter, he reloaded the carbine and looked about him. If the man
had no more shelter than a ledge would give, his position seemed desperate against the fire of a gun below.
Ricocheting lead would glance across the shelf to shred
him. If there were no road to the ledge except by those

rude steps on the cliff-face, he must surrender or die.

Ware moved back to the corner of the house, carbine lifted. Without exposing himself, he yelled:

'Come on down from there! This is the Rangers! Come on down before I set your breeches afire!'

'Come on up and get me, you want me so bad!' a high, rasping voice answered furiously. 'I know who you are! Hadn't been for my horse getting killed, I'd have rubbed you out the other day! You——'

'Goodness me!' Ware drawled, listening to the profane tirade. 'So that's my short tobacco-chewer; Barela's friend!'

He looked at the roof; looked at the boulders against and in which the cabin had been nested. Then he went back and began his cautious scramble to a position where, unseen, he could aim at the shelf. By staring hard, he could now make out the crack from which the little man fired. Deliberately, he sent a slug just above it. Two quick shots answered, but their aiming proved that his position was unknown; the lead rang on the cabin wall well to the left. He fired again, but there was no reply; and again and again without drawing an answer.

He squatted comfortably, frowning up at the ledge. There might be plenty of ammunition up there, but he doubted it. Probably, since the little man had no long gun, he had just what shells had been in pistol and belt—and he had been firing fast and frequently. Unless that were a regular lookout-point, regularly used, a cache of shells seemed improbable.

'Hey!' Ware called. 'You might as well roll up the twine, before we roll it for you! I'm going to start bouncing 'em in on you; and my big friend up above you, he's going to drop a few valentines on your lap. Give it up! and when they come to hang you, I'll beg 'em to use a soft rope! Come on, now!'

Out of the crack the pistol threw three slugs, but no more accurately than before. Ware began to shoot with cold precision, tryng to fire so that his bullets must glance across the shelf. He blew through the barrel when the carbine was empty, reloaded, and yelled again, as to a companion:

'All right, now, Ames! Come on down on the rope! I'll dust him when he moves!'

On the shelf the pistol sounded, but no bullet struck below Ware, nor did he see sign of one splashing the rock above the ledge. He watched curiously, then fired twice more. No reply was drawn. He swore suddenly, impatiently, and began to move through the boulders, ready for a quick snapshot upward, to crouch almost at the base of the cliff.

Now he could see the crude 'steps' by which the shelf was gained; mere widening of natural knobs and ledges. He inched closer to them, carbine at his shoulder, covering the shelf, until he stood by the lowest foothold. Now he could see the end of the ledge; now, by moving slightly, the narrow shelf with its rim protecting the man; now—the sole of a boot, heel upward, as if the wearer lay upon his face.

He stepped soundlessly upon the first hold, covering the boot; waited. The second step was harder to take and he made a small noise. But the boot was motionless. He made the third small shelf in a catlike jump and both feet of the man above were visible. He leaned against the cliff for a steady aim.

'Don't move! I'm coming up!' he called.

Neither sound no movement answered his command. He went on to the ledge and stood over the prone figure that sprawled with the muzzle of a long-barreled pistol in its mouth, its skull shattered.

'By his own gun,' Ware said grimly. 'He was a wolf!'

XXVIII. 'Bury it'

WARE looked quickly about the ledge. There were splashes of lead everywhere and no sign of any ammunition. He knelt beside the small man, to draw the pistol gently back. Even in death, the short-chinned, freckled face was as vicious as a side-winder's, the light eyes glaring out from under a bristle of red hair.

'Rip Andress,' Ware said, nodding. 'Worst of all Black Alec's gang. Worse, even, than Doggy Tibb. Lots worse than Baldy Burr. Durell called him a homicidal maniac; he loved to kill . . .'

He looked at the long Colt, and a spin of the cylinder showed that Rip Andress had used his last bullet upon himself. The loops of his shell belt were empty. A glancing slug had broken his right arm; he had used his left for the final suicidal shot. Other ricocheting bullets had wounded him in body and legs. And a bandage on the right thigh told of that other fight on D-Bar-D range, when Barela had died and Rip and his companion had run away.

Methodically, Ware searched the little man's pockets. The plug of chewing tobacco that he had expected, he found. A push-button knife with long blade, razor-sharp, he dropped into his own pocket. Two twenty-dollar gold pieces and some silver, both Mexican and United States, were in the trousers watch-pocket. But the tubular cartridge belt held Rip's real hoard, more than seven hundred dollars in notes of a dozen banks.

Ware went down to the flat again. It needed no more than a glance at the hobbled horses to prove that neither was the one he had followed here from Monument Rock. Study of the ground at the downstream edge of the meadow showed what he had already suspected, that

179

Rip Andress had not been the man on the big-hoofed horse. He went back to the cabin and looked for sign.

'Big Hoofs rode up and yelled.' Maybe Rip was already upstairs,' he muttered. 'Anyway, Big Hoofs didn't stop long. What would he naturally say to Rip? Probably that there'd been trouble at the Rock; might be strangers coming along; but he had to hit the grit. So Rip was watching, but not sharp enough, as I came to the ball . . . Big Hoofs must have been in plenty of hurry, else he'd have heard us snapping caps and come back . . .'

He stepped inside the cabin for quick examination by the light of matches. But the piles of blankets on rough bunks had nothing to tell. He came out again, and now he moved faster than before, back to where Rocket stood patiently. Mounted, he rode back to the cabin and found the cold beef and biscuit and beans which Rip or one of the others had cooked. He packed enough food in an *alforja* to supply himself and Bar Nothing, though he began to think that he would not see his trail-mate until dark at the earliest. It seemed to him that when the two men had split beyond Monument Rock, each had a definite goal.

The creek was his trail for three or four miles. Here and there along it were little flats, some stony, some grassy, like that which held the cabin. Occasionally, on the soft bare spots, he saw the hoofprint he knew. That man had gone steadily—and fast, where it was possible —toward the open range.

'By Gemini!' Ware grunted at last, puzzling the reason for this course that the man had taken, longer than a direct line across the open from Monument Rock. 'I begin to believe that I'm after a smart and careful hairpin, yes, sir! Maybe he did hear us unraveling the powder, but wouldn't turn back.'

His thought was that a cautious man, riding away from a pair of men able to kill or capture Baldy Burr of the famous Alec Pryde gang, might have worried about his back-trail. Such a man might very well have arranged to have pursuers forced though a narrow, guarded passage like this creek!

The hills ended, though the creek continued northward across rugged land to where Capen had put it to work. It was mid-afternoon when Ware checked Rocket among bare ridges and slopes for a look at the Open A home range.

His man had gone on, breaking into a lope. Here and there between him and the northern crests that hid the House of Whispering Shadows, cattle grazed, most of them close to the creek. Ware studied the landscape almost inch by inch through the glasses before leaving the shelter of the rocks.

He had been very careful to leave no more trail than was unavoidable. Now, he kept to the stoniest arroyos, and turned and twisted, until after two hours he could look behind him with satisfaction. An Apache might track him, he decided, but not rapidly! He went straight ahead, until the hills were seven or eight miles behind him ,to slide down into that deep arroyo no more than a mile from the buildings of the ranch.

Here he stripped the saddle from Rocket and spread the Navajo blanket to dry, and with the glasses perched upon a shelf just under the arroyo-rim to keep watch upon all the surrounding country, now lighted by the last sunshine. He saw three riders about the corrals, before darkness came, but even the powerful lenses did not identify them. He could only be certain that none was a woman.

He thought a great deal about Georgette, as he waited with Indian-like patience. There could be no doubt, now, that what Clem Tooley had said of Capen was true: the Open A was a hideout for criminals. When in a Capen line-camp Rip Andress was found recovering from wounds; when a man riding past that camp had been associated with Baldy Burr——

It was plain that some of the mysterious disappearances of Black Alec Pryde's raiders, after a murderous blow in other regions, could be explained by their use of the

Open A and Satan Land generally, for haven. The Open A would offer more than mere hide-out: in the bunk-house were such as Hannom and Ebb Isom, recruits when Black Alec needed more men.

'And that poor girl sitting in the middle of the damnedest spread of human wolves you could find between Sonora and Milk River!' Ware reflected. 'So——'

But what he could do for her, he had no idea. She had flared up in defense of Capen. Could he make her believe, now, that she must leave the Open A, leave this neighborhood, before Capen's downfall caught her? She was dependent upon her uncle for everything, so far as he knew. Where could she go; and what could she do?

He had to remind himself that Quagson appeared very willing to solve that problem. But the lawyer's pleasant, grim face somehow failed to please Ware in this connection. Besides, he had no assurance at all that Capen Castle was about to crash; only the barest hope that it could be crashed.

Capen's power extended a long way, in plain sight of anyone who looked. It might very well go much further, up to the courts. Ware had been well-drilled by the pessimistic Captain Durell in the rules of evidence and the law of probability in trails. He considered what he had against Capen, and could not be enthusiastic. Capen might be suspected of ordering Theo Ribaut's murder —but where was the body to prove that any murder had been committed? Even if it could be found, what proof was there that Capen was guilty?

As for the two dead trailers, Ebb Isom might be so worked on as to confess a part in murdering them and implicate Capen as ordering them murdered. But that was only a hope. A clever lawyer, a cow-country jury, a denial by Capen, and the case would go through the window. But it was the best handle he had found for snatching at Capen; so he was grimly determined to use it and hope to make his grip good. But Georgette stayed in his mind. He told himself irritably that he wished he had never seen her!

'If a man could only work his cases without coming to know the people,' he thought savagely, 'he'd be a sight better off! A Ranger has got no business owning feelings. First thing he knows, he's making excuses for the murderers he's chasing, or thinking about a rustler's hungry family—— Ah, hell!'

He wished that Bar Nothing would ride into the arroyo and give him something else to think about. But dark came and still there was no sign of the big man and his screwtail horse. So Ware ate more biscuit and beef, resaddled Rocket, and mounted. Again there was no moonlight, so he rode slowly and cautiously down into the valley and stopped near a motte of cottonwoods well behind the line of corrals and outbuildings.

He could see lights vaguely, around the bunkhouse and the great bulk of the *casa grande;* and there were voices carrying faintly to him. While he sat Rocket, listening, horses came at the trot toward the corrals from somewhere on his left. He rode into the cottonwoods and waited. The horses went on into the yard and he heard no more of them.

After a few minutes, he swung down and hung his sombrero on the saddle horn. With carbine across his arm he crossed to the back wall of the bunkhouse and moved along it until he could see the yellow square of a lighted window at the end. Nobody was in sight around the yard beyond, so he ventured to go up to the window and look in.

Hannom lay on an iron-framed cot, smoking, holding a newspaper. Two of the cowboys who had stood by at the time of Hannom's shooting were sitting on the floor, looking at a man of whom Ware could see no more than feet and legs.

'Hell of a couple of wolves you turned out to be!' Hannom said in a disgusted tone. 'That's what I still say.'

The half-seen man suddenly came forward with a snarl. He was a lemon-colored Mexican whose jaw had been twisted by kick or fall so that one eye was almost closed. He waggled a finger at the stolid Hannom.

'You do so lots better, hah?' he cried. 'I git tired to listen! I git sick! He is *un diablito*—and who know? You! Big talk! Little do! You! In town, w'at? He hit you; beg you for *combate*. You no care *combate!* Here, he leave you have gun out, w'at? He make *cigarro*—scratch him—pull gun—bang! Hannom git sick, Yah!'

'If I wasn't tied to this damn' mattress I'd move that face of yours back over,' Hannom told him grimly. 'Soon's I'm half-up, Squints, I'll wrap you plumb around a windmill.'

The Mexican made a contemptuous sound, half-sniff, half-snarl. The cowboys looked from one to the other, grinning.

'Ebb, he no care stop for *combate*,' the Mexican growled. 'He shoot one time up at them Ranger. Ranger shoot down. Kill them *caballo*. Ebb no care more. He go. I go. You wait. You tell Ebb he *no bueno!*'

'What'd him and Carlos Smith go up to the Castle for?' Hannom asked, apparently of the sitting cowboys.

'Do'no',' one answered indifferently. 'Packing a tow sack between 'em. Something for King. What was it King sent Ebb to Carlos about, Mig'?'

'King tell you. Ebb tell you,' Mig' replied, grinning.

Ware moved back from the window. He knew now that it had been Mig' and Ebb Isom with Baldy Burr, but that seemed of no immediate importance. Isom had doubtless continued upon his errand after the shooting at the Rock, while Mig' had come back to report to Capen. Which meant that Capen knew of the discovery of Bingham and Logan; knew that he and Bar Nothing were the finders. For Mig' had made it plain that he, at least, had been recognized. Meanwhile, Carlos Smith and Ebb Isom were in the Castle with Capen; they had brought something important.

'Must have been important,' Ware thought, 'if Isom was sent to Smith to get it, and he went on after it, even when Baldy was killed or looped by us, to his knowledge; and we'd found Bingham and Logan.'

He looked about; moved to look toward the cotton-

woods where Rocket stood. Bar Nothing had trailed
Ebb Isom, then. So, unless he had lost or quit the trail,
he should be somewhere near. But there was no sound
to tell of Bar Nothing's presence; nor, he thought, was
there likely to be. Bar Nothing was as efficient as himself; as able to move fast and noiselessly.

He looked at the tamarisk hedge. If he could get close
enough to learn what Carlos Smith had brought to
Capen, that might very well explain something of interest! The talk went on in the bunkhouse. The yard
seemed empty. He crossed in a run and flattened himself against the hedge to listen, then moved up the feath-
ery line of salt cedar to the opening into the house-yard.

Within ten feet of him a man cleared his throat, then
laughed softly. Before he spoke, Ware had identified
Carlos Smith. He had never heard another gasping
laugh just like the D-Bar-D man's; he had disliked it
too much to forget it.

'Bury it?' Smith asked. 'Shove it down with the
rest——'

'Quiet!' Capen commanded sharply. 'Isom, you go to
the bunkhouse. Just see that Hannom and the others
stay there for a while. Carlos and I are enough, here;
and the three of us are quite enough to know of—my
private arrangements.'

'Bueno,' Isom said curtly. 'They won't prowl none.'

Ware stepped silently back and hugged the hedge.
Isom passed him and Ware saw the tall figure go into
the bunkhouse door. Then he moved to the opening
in the hedge again. Two shapes darker than the darkness, Capen and Smith were going toward what seemed
to be a tiny room built out from the house, plastered
like the other walls, with tile roof like the main house
eaves.

Ware ventured into the yard and closer to them,
keeping to the shaggy hedge. He heard a lock click and
a dull jangle as of chains moved.

'I still think it'd been all right at the Rock,' Smith
said.

'Yes. Isom thought those two were all right, in the cave on the Rock,' Capen snarled. 'Don't think! Don't even try it!'

XXIX. *'That kid-Ranger!'*

WHEN they had entered the little room, Ware moved along the hedge until he could see the door, set on the face opposite the arched entrance of the house-patio. There was a light showing in the crack of the half-open door, and inside were shuffling sounds and that clanking as of metal jarred. He slipped across to look in at what seemed to be a shelter for garden tools. Spades and long-handled shovels, picks and mattocks, hung in a neat rack along one wall that he could see. But Capen's back blocked view of the rest of the little room.

'Swing it around! Swing it around, man! We haven't all night!' Capen ordered. 'There are things to do as important as getting that burned iron out of sight. Bingham and Logan were bad enough, but Ware and Ames are twenty times as dangerous! You have got to help Isom and Squinting Mig', too. I won't have any more in the affair than necessary. Bingham and Logan and Burr have to be brought here——'

'Uh-uh! Uh-uh!' Smith cried instantly. 'Not for me!'

'Do you want that scrawny, cowardly neck of yours in a noose? Those three have to disappear, so completely that when Ware and Ames tell their story they'll be laughed at! If more Rangers come in—and Marie Ribaut is quite able to get more—and I'm charged with their removal, anything may come to light. Including your part in adding shadows to the House Where Shadows Whisper! Never forget that.'

'I never rubbed out ary one!' Smith snarled at him, to accompaniment of a steady, rasping sound.

'All parties to a conspiracy are equally guilty, under the law. You profited. You had back your mortgage—large pay for making a team of mules disappear over the River and burning a buckboard and reciting some lies ready-written for you. Go on down! Take this mattock. The lantern is at the foot of the steps. Bury the sack under the loose planks. And hurry! You and Isom and Mig' have a ride to make, yet. You will bring in those three, so carefully that nobody sees you anywhere. If you have to fight like cornered rats with Ames and Ware, you will fight like cornered rats! Hurry! This is one time you don't play coward; one time that all of you do precisely what you're told.'

Hoofbeats thudded beyond the hedge. Ware ran back to the hedge, reaching it only before Capen came out of the room and trotted to the opening in the hedge. The horses came on up to that opening. Capen stepped through and Ware caught the mumble of voices, Capen's lifted in a high, furious oath.

He watched the door of the room from which Carlos Smith might appear; edged closer to the talkers. One voice was rasping, authoritative:

'—Shot to pieces up on the lookout. Two horses'd been through, one with a clumping hoof you could track to hell! We come straight on——'

'What's it, King?' Isom called from the bunkhouse. 'Trouble?'

'Let's see what he can figure in this,' Capen said. 'Mig' came in before dark. He'd passed the lookout and spoken to him, he said; warned him that he might be trailed——'

They went toward the bunkhouse. Still the door of that room that masked some sort of cellar stood ajar. Apparently, Smith was still at his work below. Ware considered flashingly and chanced running across to that door. He could hear no sound, but a glance within showed a set of heavy shelves swung out into the room, exposing a trap and wooden steps leading downward. There was a padlock hanging open in a hasp on the

door. Ware slipped it off and raced back to the opening in the hedge.

Two horses, breathing heavily, stood with trailing
reins just beyond him. Near the bunkhouse door, silhouetted against the lighted rectangle of it, the group
of men stood talking. Mig's broken English was plain,
protesting that Rip Andress was alive and on guard
when he passed.

'If I could just open up on that bunch!' Ware
thought. 'If only I could open up, I'd save I do'no' how
many hangmen overdue jobs!'

He divided his watch between the open door and the
talking men. So he was not caught when the light in
that room vanished, but slid softly back into shelter
of the salt cedar. He heard the door close and the growl
of Smith about the lock. Then the D-Bar-D man passed
him and went into the outer yard.

Ware took up his watch again. He stared at the two
horses. Who were the men, so close to Rip Andress,
who had ridden them? The first, natural thought was
that Black Alec Pryde and Doggy Tibb had shared the
line-camp with Rip, had been out on some errand of
their own while Baldy Burr was with Isom and squinting Mig' at the Rock. But this was only a guess. Those
two might be no more than lesser lights of the fratern-
ity, highliners joined for the time with Andress and
Burr.

He could think of no way to be sure, now. If the two
were really the Southwest's most notorious *buscaderos*,
the Ribaut case, Capen, all else could wait while he
tried to take them! Not a Ranger or other peace officer
in Texas but would drop any other case to make that
attempt.

Another horse came suddenly into the yard, moving
at staggering walk, to stop beside the group and abruptly crumple. Its rider got clear, but stood swaying, to
talk in grunts. Then all of them whirled and came
toward Ware, snarling, talking fast.

'Go on in! We've got to do some fast, sure thinking!'

Capen snapped. 'Then riding—perhaps shooting! Damn it! I haven't come this far to be stopped. Not by two Rangers and the like of Eagan! Come on! You, too, Carlos; don't try to hang back or you will certainly find yourself hanging another way. Stop moaning, Norman! Rip had been living on borrowed time for years. We've all played it hard and dangerous; give us just average luck this time, and we'll live to laugh and play it that way again!'

'That kid-Ranger!' a husky voice mumbled. 'I could've wiped him out at Olin's. And he killed the kid. I'll settle that if it's the last thing I do. I——'

'Stop moaning!' Capen said again, angrily. 'One would think that you trained him for the ministry, instead of the long rope! He's dead, so he's dead. And we have to move fast to save our own skins, man!'

They passed on into the patio and Ware stood, beating his hand against his leg, thinking furiously, assembling what he had learned so quickly, arranging all in as clear pattern as he could.

Norman had brought bad news to a man who knew him well—desperately bad news. That was very plain. Norman had his place in Capen's organization and Eagan—evidently Eagan had struck some sort of blow at Norman such as he had threatened that day in Olin's store. But it was a stroke that threatened Capen, too. Norman and Rip Andress were closely connected, by what had been said and the way it had been said. Father and son, Ware guessed. Which tied together his suspicions of Norman and the Pryde gang, formed at Olin's on the day that seemed so long ago.

But these facts were more interesting than important, tonight. He and Bar Nothing were on Capen's list of condemned, just as Theo Ribaut and Alf Mullit had been. That was not important, either. Eagan was to be counter-struck, by Capen's statement, and that was important! For Eagan's place in this puzzle was not yet plain to Ware. The only thing that seemed plausible was a place as Nemesis on Norman's trail, which must be Capen's trail also. Eagan, in spite of the unpleasant way of him, must really be on the Law's side.

'And he must've hit Norman one hell of a lick!' Ware thought suddenly. 'For he just about killed that horse making it here with the news.'

He looked through the hedge, past the horses, at the bunkhouse. The door was unblocked. The men not with Capen at his conference were either in the long room there, or prowling out of sight about the yard. Ware risked scratching a match and holding it in cupped hand for a quick look at the horses.

One was a buckskin like that animal seen hobbled at the line-camp. The other was a heavy bay. Ware stiffened with his glimpse of white upon a foreleg, stepped closer, and flicked another match upon his thumbnail. He leaned to look at the shoulder, stared incredulously, then snapped out the match.

'*Por dios*! *Por dios*!' he breathed savagely, whirling to face the house. 'Plumb Bob!'

Then he relaxed and coldly began to consider what he must do. Five, perhaps six, men were in the house, without counting the Chinese servants. In the bunkhouse were three men who could be counted as fighters, if not more, leaving Hannom off the tally. Capen's conference might be brief; might send Carlos Smith, Isom, and Squinting Mig' off to Monument Rock to bring in here the bodies of Bingham, Logan, and Baldy Burr, as Capen had planned before Norman's arrival. But that plan might be changed, now; the nine or ten men at Capen's disposal might be scattered on other errands, or go in a body somewhere—as to face Eagan.

Ware would have given a year's pay, in that moment, for sight of Bar Nothng! But he was coldly determined on one point: standing alone as he did, still the man on that Plumb Bob horse, murderer of Lige Fyeback, would not get away again.

'If I could bulge through the door on 'em,' he reflected, 'throw down on the bunch and corral 'em all,

I could probably hold off the bunkhouse crowd . . . Bar Nothing's bound to be around somewhere. What's under the house?'

Carlos Smith had brought the iron from the burned buckboard of Theo Ribaut. There was no other sensible explanation. It had been hidden somewhere but Capen had wanted it here, with—with the bodies of Ribaut and the boy! For if he had been afraid to leave the buckboard remnants buried on his range, surely he would be more careful to have those murdered ones under his eye!

Ware took a quick step toward the tool room, then stopped. While he had a look at that cellar, the men might come out. He went back to the horses, felt for a rope on the buckskin, unstrapped it, and cut lengths from it. The weary animals made no move of protest when he improvised rope hobbles for them. He grinned without humor at thought of men coming out fast, scooping up reins and swinging into the saddles to gallop off—on those close-hobbled horses.

The shelving in the tool room was held by a hidden latch so that it seemed as solid as the wall. But he hunted and fumbled until he found it in a corner and drew out the shelves upon their pivot. The stairs were steep, descending into a yard-wide tunnel timbered like a mine-stope. He found the lantern Carlos Smith had used and by its light went along the passage for twenty feet.

There was a room four or five yards square, walled with field stone, floored with wide, heavy planks, absolutely empty. The passage continued out of it. Ware swung the lantern to look at the thick dust of the floor and the smudges of footprints everywhere. A sprinkle of fresh dirt was in one corner, and when he lifted a plank there he found newly dug soil beneath.

He dropped the plank and stood erect, looking at the loose flooring. The boards seemed to be nailed nowhere, only laid flat upon the earth.

'The House of Whispering Shadows!' he thought. 'If what I suspect is right, there's plenty under here to furnish shadows!'

He moved on to the continuation of the passage. This part of it was only ten feet long and ended in another stair that, at the head, was blocked by a well-fitted door that had bolt, but no latch, only a bit of thin cable of twisted wire with a knob, dangling from a hole in the facing. Ware hesitated before that door, which must open into the house. But he went back to the other stair, blowing out the lantern in the cellar and hang- ing it on its nail.

There was no sound to alarm him as he listened at the top of the stair. But he came up noiselessly, carbine ahead of him, to listen again at the door. Then he pushed the shelving back and was turning when a shot sounded outside, then from two other points a second and a third explosion. A long, savage yell rose, appar- ently from front and back of the great house.

XXX. *'Listen to reason'*

THAT shrill, high yell in which many voices blended seemed to end in a stentorian bellow.

'Capen! Come on out of that! And come a-reaching!'

Ware pulled shut the door of the tool room and stood uncertainly, carbine up, looking left and right. A sud- den ragged volley beyond the hedge, from somewhere about the bunkhouse, jerked his face that way. He trotted to the hedge, pulled away branches of tamarisk until he could peer through.

The bunkhouse was dark, now, except for the stab- bing flames of shots from door and windows. Over to Ware's left, to the side of the bunkhouse, the flash of shots showed a line of men. Then to the right the darkness was spotted with fire. Still that great voice commanded Capen to come out.

Ware swore softly. If this were Eagan's spread, come to assault the House of Whispering Shadows, it was not for a Ranger to do anything but command them and see that what they did was performed in a legal manner. But, remembering Eagan's savage hatchet face, he thought that halting the 66 attack would not be easy, even if he could find Eagan in the darkness. Meanwhile, there was his man of the Plumb Bob horse——

Hoofs pounded down the hedge as he hesitated. There was a great thud in the yard beyond him and a man swore furiously. Ware whirled from the hedge as a second thudding of hoofs and crash of branches came simultaneously with a yell from the ground:

'Damn' horse fell! Come on!'

Ware ran down the hedge, squatted, shaped a figure against the plaster of the house.

'Stand still!' he snarled. 'Grab your ears!'

The dark shape moved convulsively. Flame spurted from it and Ware squeezed trigger, threw down the lever, fired again. His eyes were dazzled by the shot and he shook his head viciously. But retained vision of the flame persisted. He heard more shots beyond him and fired blindly with eyes shut, twice again. But now there was so much shooting in the outer yard that it was hard to distinguish between shots close to him and those at a little distance.

His eyes cleared and he glared toward the huddled shape vaguely silhouetted against the wall. It seemed to move, but when he snarled there was no answer. He worked toward it, hearing heavy breathing of man or horse, and his Winchester punched something soft, unresisting. He put out a hand and touched a flannel-clad arm.

'You!' he growled, punching harder with the carbine.

There was no response, and he squatted beside the man to make quick examination by touch. He could detect no heart-beat and, sure of this, he ignored the fallen horse and crawled to the opening in the hedge where, he thought, the second hobbled horse had fallen with its rider.

The horse still stood there, but the man was not to be located by looking around. Still the bunkhouse was being hammered by attackers on right and left and almost in front of Ware. He turned back to the house. There was no firing in front, nowhere except at the bunkhouse. No yelling, either.

He thought abruptly of Georgette, perhaps trapped in there with men slipping from room to room, cocked guns ready to fire at the slightest movement before them. Then a shadow rose on his right, a mere blob of darkness against the wall of the tool room. It disappeared as he stared.

Capen, trying to escape? Certainly, he thought, the two men whose horses he had hobbled had run out of the house with the first alarm, trying to get away from the fight. They had come out of the patio and Capen might have been at their heels.

He ran to the tool room and let the carbine down softly, while he drew a Colt. The door was shut, but through it he heard the rasping sound of the shelves pivoting. He pushed the latch down, then flung the door back. In the darkness someone gasped.

Ware lunged in, leaning, flailing blindly with pistol barrel. He felt the steel crunch upon flesh. Then slipping, tumbling noises told of a limp body crumpling on the stair. He followed quickly and at the stair-foot found a huddled man, hardly breathing. There was no sound in the passage ahead of him and he ventured to light a match. The tiny flame showed the dark face of Carlos Smith, beginning to be blood-streaked.

Ware snapped out the match and went on softly to the central room of the cellar. The shots outside came so faintly into the passage that they seemed hardly to be shots. Louder was an odd swishing noise, though that, to, was almost a whispering in the darkness before him. He flattened his back against the wall, Colt up.

'Whispering shadows!' he thought. 'Hell, I'm no child!'

The sound came nearer and suddenly he identified it, with such a sense of relief that he knew how tense he had been! It was someone walking across the planks of the floor, making no noise except as trousers-legs brushed. Ware moved very slightly, turning, balancing on one foot so that his right leg was out, barring the passage to the tool room.

The swish of the trousers came on deliberately. He thought that he could hear soft, even breathing. Then against his leg was pressure and he jerked his foot toward him hookwise. The tripped one fell forward with loud slap of palms on planks and a heavy, jangling thud as of something heavy dropped. Ware pounced like a cat and poked the muzzle of his pistol into the back of his prisoner, while with left hand he caught a man's shoulder.

'Easy!' he advised. 'If this .44 goes off——'

The man breathed gaspingly, but did not move. Ware put out his foot and sat spraddling upon him, while he drew a match from his hatband and scratched it on the floor.

'Ah!' he drawled. 'Sort of expected it, Capen.'

'If you'll permit me—to get up,' Capen said pantingly, 'I would like to—tell you about it!'

'Tell me about Georgette, first! Is she still upstairs?'

'She's in town—poor child! Fortunately! If you'll let me up, Ware——'

Ware let the match drop and in the darkness reached under Capen to get from a belt-holster the Colt he had guessed to be there. He slipped it into his own empty scabbard and stood crouching, shifting his grip to Capen's shirt collar.

'All right! Up we come. And if you happen to entertain any notions about making a break, better remember that this has been your bad day. Hold still!'

He reached behind him to his sash and got the light handcuffs from their pouch. A touch on Capen's wrist and one cuff clicked. Capen jerked and swore and seemed about to turn. Ware prodded him with the pistol.

'Other wrist! Behind you! There!'

'There's no sense to this!' Capen told him with a calmness that Ware gave tribute to. 'In the first place, no matter what you may think, you can't prove a thing against me. In the second place—what do you make in the Rangers?'

'A decent living. So, save your breath, Capen. Something tells me that you haven't got a lot more breath ahead of you.'

'Nonsense! I'm temporarily worried, by this murdering gang of Eagan's. Any man in my circumstances might be—must be! But that's all. Suppose you take me into Los Alamos and make any charges you like; what, then? I simply make bond, my able attorney goes to work and even if a grand jury indicts, we laugh the prosecution out of court! That's one way of operating. But I prefer another—principally because of poor little Georgette. I think you appreciate this feeling; she's very fond of you and I believe that you're fond of her. So— suppose you take these silly things off me and listen to reason!'

From the yard carried faintly a prolonged yell. Distant as it seemed, Ware recognized his own name. Again it came:

'Steve! Oh-h, Steve Ware! Ware!'

'Quick!' Capen snapped. 'Here's my proposition: Forget all this that you didn't want to do, in the first place; and what you may have heard or discovered. Report to your commander that the case can't be settled, but that you suspect Ribaut to have decamped. I'll hand you five thousand dollars in cash. You go back to your company. Then resign. Come back here and join me. I'll make you quarter-owner of the Open A. Then, there's Georgette . . .'

'You—son! You'd cut anybody's throat to save your skin, now, wouldn't you! But it's no buy today. You're going to hang, Capen! For Ribaut and his kid! For Bingham and Logan! Your smart lawyer won't get you out of this noose. *Because I will produce the bodies!* Oh-h, Bar Nothing! Ames!'

'Where you, boy?' Bar Nothing answered. 'Down a well?'

'Move!' Ware snarled at Capen. 'Straight ahead, slow!'

He pushed Capen with hand and pistol. They moved a slow step forward, then another. Ware called again to Bar Nothing. Then under his hand Capen collapsed and Ware stepped back, almost letting the hammer of his Colt go. Capen huddled on the floor and did not move when Ware prodded him with a toe. Bar Nothing's feet sounded on the stair.

'Come on down!' Ware called tensely. 'Watch out for Carlos Smith at the end of the stairs. Lantern there. Light it and let's get a look at this.'

'What the devil are you doing down here? How'd you stumble onto this? Boy——'

Ware had scratched another match. He hardly heard Bar Nothing's comments. Capen was prone, head twisted so that his side-face showed. He seemed to be grinning sardonically. Ware stooped more. He was bending from side to side, in the light of another match, when Bar Nothing came down the passage with the lantern, saw Capen, and swore softly.

'You kill him?' he grunted. 'Carlos is still breathing.'

'No. I was herding him to the stair and he dropped like—like heart-failure. But that son never owned a heart! He's cuffed . . .'

Bar Nothing put down the lantern and squatted for rough but effective examination. He shook his head at the end of it.

'Well, he's cashed his last chip, anyhow. He never shot himself, or knifed himself. Reckon it was poison? But how could he swallow anything when his hands was behind him? Hell!'

'He did something to beat the rope. Now, what's up

above? What happened? I've been so busy since I hit here——'

'I rode right up into the middle of it. I trailed my man till he killed his tracks, then I scouted back and forth and finally give up the job and headed for the arroyo. Found Rocket in the cottonwoods. About that time it sounded like Lee had took back his surrender from Grant, up here. So I ghosted up and run into Clem Tooley and Hack Kinney and Ben Briggs and some more, flipping blue whistlers into the bunkhouse where Hannom and three-four more was cracking caps at 'em.'

'I thought it was Eagan and the Hooks crowd!'

'Was! Eagan wiped out Ten Sleep Norman's Lightning Rod thieves in two licks, one at the Little Bend store of Olin's—they weighted down a cottonwood with Olin *I* wouldn't be surprised—and finshed up at the headquarters. Norman bust through somehow, but a weak-kneed boy they caught spewed his insides. Enough to make it good and sure what Eagan already figured: Capen and Norman and Black Alec's highliners, they was all in together. So Eagan brought his fire-eaters right on, picked up Tooley and some Piedra lead-slingers, and—oh, yeh! they let Briggs come along!'

'Good enough! I know the rest,' Ware checked him. 'Is it all over now? Bunkhouse bunch give up?'

'Same as so many locoed wolves! It was the Alamo, all over. Do'no's that Eagan bunch really wanted prisoners. They have got right tired of the way things have been happening. They seemed to kind of figure that Satan Land needed fumigating—and they used black powder smoke to fumigate. What'd you have on Capen?'

'Murder! Murders! Somewhere under your feet the Ribauts are buried, or I'll buy you a fifty-dollar hat. Lord knows who else or what else. Carlos Smith is the one who can tell things, if I didn't crack his skull clear in two.'

XXXI. *'Who killed Thornton?'*

Bar Nothing lifted the lantern and held it high, to stare curiously along the passage, shaking his head. Ware went back to look at Carlos Smith. The dark-faced man still sprawled where he had first fallen, but his breathing was stronger and he made small groaning sounds. As Ware looked down at him in the faint light that came from the lantern, he heard footsteps above.

'Ames?' Clem Tooley called huskily. 'You find Ware?'

'This is Ware. Come on down. I—have got Capen and Carlos Smith down here. Watch the trap door. Better light that lantern on the shelf up there.'

He waited until the light showed overhead. Bar Nothing was exploring the rest of the cellar, so Ware went back to Capen, took off the handcuffs, and came back to put them on Carlos Smith. Clem Tooley wheezed down to him.

'Glory be!' he panted. 'The House of Whispering Shadows ought to have some new shadows to whisper, after this! And he had this young mine underneath, huh? I sort of suspected it, a goodish while back, from gossip among the Mexicans. So you've got Capen's dog . . . Where's his master? Eagan said he couldn't find him, though they searched every room and dropped Norman in the very beginning, along with two-three of the Chinese who elected to fight.'

Carlos Smith stirred and groaned. Ware caught his shoulder and shook violently.

'My head!' Smith mumbled. 'Somebody hit me——'

'Worry about your neck, not your head!' Ware snarled at him. 'Come on! This is our prize murderer, Tooley.

Let's get him up where we can take good care of him. There's a hangknot waiting for him and he mustn't die on us here.'

He caught Clem Tooley's shrewd eye, and after an instant of hard staring the fat man nodded very slightly and stood back. Ware half-pushed, half-lifted the staggering Smith until he stood in the tool room. Smith blinked stupidly around. Then, outside, some cowboy yelled and another answered, and Smith's face jerked. Comprehension came into the murky eyes; stark fear.

'*Amor de dios*!' he muttered. 'Listen, Ware! You got to gi' me a chance. That devil, Capen, he shoved me into some deals. But I never would go no farther'n I could help. I never done much. He's the one you want. Hell! I never even more'n suspicioned the most of his doings. He wouldn't trust me, account he was certain I had my limits. You got to gi' me a chance, Ware! Le' me clear out before that hanging crew of Eagan's sees me. If you don't, it'll be the same as you murdering me—that never was in more'n a li'l' bunch of one-horse deals. You——'

'Coming up!' Clem Tooley announced. 'We found something interesting; and'—he broke off until he had climbed the stair painfully and moved so that he looked straight at Smith—'and we knew where to find a lot more things, interesting to lots of people in this country. Par-ticu-larly interesting to Marie Ribaut! Carlos! Carlos! The first time I ever set eyes on your scoundrel father, I could see your finish! Yes, sir! I knew that you'd rise high before you died—away high, with nothing but air under you . . .'

'I—I never——' Smith began desperately, gulping 'I—'

'Capen's testimony is all we need,' Ware said coldly. 'He couldn't deny his signed confession if he wanted to, and if we don't try him for covering Smith, here, he will go into court to swear that Smith murdered the Ribauts and came to him expecting a big reward. As Capen said to me, Ribaut's disappearance was the worst thing for him! But Smith had done it with some nitwit idea that Capen *wanted* Ribaut wiped out——'

'That's a damn' lie and I can prove it!' Smith yelled. 'Hannom and Ebb Isom and Squinting Mig' killed Ribaut and the kid. Capen had Theo and Alf Mullit on the list a long time. He had 'em watched. When Theo come by my place to see about the mortgage and hint around it was worth a thousand to rub out Capen, all I done was——'

'Send word to Capen,' Tooley finished for him. 'Yeh.'

'Not quite,' Ware objected. 'He sent Ribaut's mules over the River and burned the buckboard and buried the iron. But he dug it up again and brought it here tonight. It's under the boards, down-cellar. Then he got worried about Bingham and Logan prowling around Monument Rock. So he shot 'em in the back——'

'That was Ebb Isom and Squinting Mig' again! Yeh, I packed the iron here. But it was account Capen sent orders to! You can't hang no murders on me! I never was mixed in none!'

'No-o?' Clem Tooley drawled. 'Who killed Thornton, the cashier, out here?'

'Capen! That was one he done with his own hand. All we done was catch him in town and make him open up the safe in the bank. Black Alec and Doggy Tibb and Ebb Isom worked that. All I done was watch the horses. Then we brought him out here and—and Capen shot him down in the cellar. He's down there, now, with the Ribauts—and old Druscovich the prospector that Capen robbed—and Martinez that used to be Capen's partner in smuggling! I——'

'Reckon some good man, like Hack Kinney, would take him to Piedra and keep him safe?' Ware asked Tooley, who nodded.

'I'll bring Hack. Meanwhile, here's what Capen aimed to skip with—and there's some bonds from the bank, with money.'

He pushed a pair of leather saddle bags with his foot.

Bar Nothing came up and stood with hat over a blue
eye, to look at the shaking Carlos as at some strange,
unpleasant animal. The three were silent until Clem
Tooley put his head in the door and grunted.

'Here's Hack. He knows enough. He'll split the breeze
with him. If Eagan's boys smelled him, the lot of us
couldn't stop a necktie party. Take him, Hack. Keep
him in my room until we get back. Let nobody see him.
And while you've got him there, kind of hold your nose
some and let him write down the story of his life—and
Capen's. And, Carlos! In case you're tempted to sort of
skim over anything, you think about how shadows may
quit whispering and start yelling! And you think about
me coming back, Carlos, and how it won't be that flute
of mine, you've made so many comical remarks about,
that I'll point at you. It's maybe the deadly weapon
you've said, but I have got some a sight deadlier. Be
you sure you remember that!'

Hack Kinney disappeared into the darkness with the
prisoner. Ware drew a long breath and looked at Bar
Nothing and Tooley.

'I reckon we'd better hunt up Eagan and sort of get
our notions sorted out? I dropped a man down the
line—his horse had thrown him because I thought to
hobble it——'

'Doggy Tibb,' Clem Tooley said placidly. 'I take it
you noticed the brand on that bay he was riding—
Plumb Bob. And I reckon nobody can deny that it was
you, Ames, that dropped Black Alec beyond the hedge.
You hobbled his horse, too, Ware? I sort of made out
a tumbling by the salt cedar. Then Ames, here, he yelled
at somebody running, then cut him in two. I had a look
awhile back and it was Black Alec.'

'Huh?' Bar Nothing cried. 'Baldy Burr at the Rock—
Black Alec and Doggy here——'

'And Rip Andress blew his own head off up the creek
when I had him cornered,' Ware summed up. 'Which
winds up the famous Pryde Gang. And you're the only
one due a reward, Bar Nothing. Baldy was the only one

with a dead-or-alive price on him. But it's still a new July Fourth for the country. Clem Tooley, if ever you locals let things get to a head like this again——'

'I think we won't. In fact, we had been taking slow steps for quite awhile, to smash this head. We had a sort of loose association, Ware, before you dropped in on us. Eagan and some others between his range and Piedra; good friends of mine. We didn't work as fast as you and Ames have done, but we made headway. I admit that I wasn't certain I wanted you around; a Ranger sort of meant law-courts and we needed something faster, surer. If you haven't got a lot of bugs in a house, you can go around cleaning 'em up a few at a time. But when the house is eaten up with 'em, you might better burn all and make a quick riddance.'

'So when Gall Yager brought you a word from Eagan, the day I was in Piedra, you hurrahed me about Eagan losing a sorrel.'

'You mean, I didn't fool you?' Clem Tooley cried. 'Then I lose five dollars to Hack Kinney. He bet me I hadn't fooled you a speck. Well, well! Live and learn. Gall Yager recognized Doggy Tibb right after Gall took on with Eagan. Seems he knew Baldy Burr and Doggy, both, over around Spicewood, once. Eagan sent him to me with the news. I was to check on Alec Pryde being hooked to Capen. Well, well! You're smarter, even, than I figured!'

They passed men moving and talking in the darkness, or under the light of lanterns about the bunkhouse. Eagan they found in the big living-room, that looked now as if a tornado had swept through it. The hatchet-faced 66 owner grinned ferociously at Ware, who looked past him at Burt.

'Well!' Eagan grunted. 'Seems like you and me was on the same trail, after all, Ranger! Reckon either one of us'd have cleaned up the mess, the way we was heading. I'm glad you got in Capen's way when he was trying to split the breeze, though.'

'You couldn't say that fairer,' Ware assured him, with

answering grin. 'You had part of the puzzle and I had dug up part of it here, tonight, before you drove up and hitched. But I'm free to say that I never was happier to see visitors than I was when you rounded up the ranch. Now what do we do? Tooley says all your pigs are pork.'

'You're damn' right!' Burt Eagan said blusteringly. 'We have cut a swath from Olin's across to the Lightning Rod and now here. If as much as two of them long-ropers got clear——'

'You mustn't blame Burt for talking loud,' Eagan said solemnly. 'We-all just pulled back and Burt, he done it all.'

'Where's Briggs?'

'Well, if somebody ain't said "Boo!" kind of loud, and somebody else was in between Ben and clear country when it was said, he ought to be outside. What you want *him* for?'

'Need him. He's acting sheriff, if you do have to say "God help us!" in the same breath. Up in a cave on Monument Rock Bar Nothing has got a cache—two trackers from Alamos that Capen had murdered, along with Baldy Burr, who's a voucher for twelve hundred. Briggs has got to handle that. On his way back, he can stop at the line-camp up-creek and find Rip Andress. And down-cellar the floor needs digging up. Ribaut and his kid; young Thornton the cashier that was supposed to have skipped; couple more. They have got to be looked at, just for the record.'

'I'll take care of all that,' Briggs said from the door behind them. 'Deputize some of your bunch, Tooley, for the digging and the trip to the Rock and back. Old Tom Gold can take a look at everything and hold inquests right on the job and settle it up. Reckon there's nothing that'll ever get to court, now. Nobody to charge! Lucky we had one justice of the peace along.'

Ware moved to sprawl in one of the great chairs. Bar Nothing looked about the big room, stared at the piano, and shook his head. Ware saw and understood. He, too, was thinking of the night when Georgette had sat there singing her little French songs. He wondered what she would do when news carried to Los Alamos of this battle and its outcome. Doubtless, she was Capen's heiress. But if the bank, and men despoiled by Capen's thieves, brought suits for recovery of their losses, there might well be little to inherit.

'Huh?' he grunted, turning to Tooley. 'Oh! Georgette's in Alamos; been there for days, according to Capen. No! No, I'm not going to Alamos. Piedra will do me for the time being.'

Bar Nothing disappeared, to come back complaining but bearing a quart of whiskey and beef and bread. He and Ware and Tooley and cowboys coming and going ate and drank. Eagan and Burt had gone with Briggs.

Ware half-listened to the talk around him, as time passed. Presently he dozed. Bar Nothing shook him awake and he stretched and yawned.

'We're about ready to go,' Bar Nothing told him. 'Everything's clear down-cellar; inquested and covered up. Briggs is gone.'

XXXII. *'Forget her!'*

FROM the crest of a low ridge, Ware turned in the saddle to look back upon the little valley with its mottes of trees and the orderly group of buildings about the massive 'Castle.' He could see riders coming away from the place, the drag-end of the straggling procession of 66 riders and Clem Tooley's friends from La Piedra.

'Nothing like it in this end of Texas,' he said slowly.

'You could add a heartfelt *grácias* to that,' Clem Tooley drawled grimly. 'He had plenty of notions about making a show place, but we can worry along with less prettiness and less snaky deadliness of his kind. Nothing about him like other people. Even that poison ring he wore—and used at the last—yeh! That was how he died so fast on you, when he saw the game was all over and he'd not only lost, but owed more than he could pay. I've read about such dago tricks, but that was the first one I ever saw. Little poison needle in the ring . . .'

'And somebody will live there—over a murderer's graveyard,' Bar Nothing remarked cheerfully. 'Looky!'

From a dozen points about the buildings, smoke began to rise. The riders coming from the house yelled and waved their hats. Ware scowled and began to turn Rocket, then checked himself. After all, if the Eagan crew had fired the sinister House of Whispering Shadows, they could hardly be blamed; and there was little hope of checking the blazes, even if every man would try. Clem Tooley swore softly.

'Now, they hadn't a bit of business doing that! But— let her burn! Maybe that's best. Some little man will come along and make the Open A an honest cow-ranch; nothing like that, because the range wouldn't support half of it. But a fair-sized house for a little spread . . .'

They rode on through the day without much talk, cutting into the Alamos-Piedra road and turning south. Dark had come when they saw the lights of La Piedra ahead. Hack Kinney was in the store. He talked generally with the 66 men, but after they had got meals of a sort and made camp on the edge of the *plazita,* and the four of them were alone, he jerked his head toward the ceiling.

'Our author has been awful busy all day. I stuck with him till just before you-all come in. He's good and shackled, but if he's heard the hellabaloo and knows it's the 66 around him, I bet he'd stay right there if I hitched him with thread. Seems like the more that scoun'el thinks, the spookier he gets!'

'We'll send him over to Alamos when Eagan's gone,' Ware said indifferently. 'It's no business of ours to convict him of anything. Our job was just to settle what happened to Ribaut and who made it happen. We've done that.'

'And you cleaned up Fyeback's murder,' Bar Nothing reminded him. 'That ought to make you feel awful good, Steve.'

'Yeh. It really does. I'm not much of a killer, but I reckon I wouldn't ever have been quite satisfied if somebody else had looped Doggy Tibb for that sneaking murder!'

He laughed abruptly, harshly.

'I just happened to think: Capen's estate owes us five hundred for settling the Ribaut case.'

'Yeh,' Bar Nothing agreed, watching him. 'But I reckon there won't be much estate, with the buildings burned and all the money he had in the saddlebags still not enough to cover the Alamos bank loss. *I* have been wondering about what Georgette's going to do.'

'I'm going to borrow blanket-room from you,' Ware said curtly to Tooley. 'Now that I've got time for it, I'm tired!'

But he lay long awake, beside Bar Nothing in a room of Tooley's quarters. What *would* Georgette do? Doubtless, marry Quagson—and be fortunate that so good a man was at hand. He thought of that, then inwardly laughed at himself.

'And what would a Ranger, even a Ranger captain, have to offer a girl like that, you nitwit?' he thought.

They were up with the first light. Eagan and the 66 men rode away. Small ranchers gathered for the war from about Piedra went home. Ware perched on Tooley's veranda, Hack Kinney and Piedra's blacksmith came up, spurred for riding. They took Carlos Smith from the inner room where he had been shackled for his work of authorship and mounted him with hands cuffed to the saddle fork, then swung up. Ware lifted a hand in response to their brief good-bye and watched them ride toward Los Alamos. They carried two curt telegrams he had written the night before, one to Captain Durell, the other to Sheriff David Loren of Verde

County. The only departures from the matter-of-fact Ware had allowed himself, in explaining to Loren the identity and the fate of Lige Fyeback's murderer, were in address and signature. He had sent the wire—collect— to Sheriff *Goliath* Loren, and signed it *David* Stephen Fuller Austin Ware.

La Piedra drowsed in bright sunlight. Ware took one of Clem Tooley's black cigarettes and lighted it. Two small boys came along the street and stopped to look up at him, very round of eyes and rigid of body. Then Clem Tooley appeared upon the stair, wheezing, carrying rolled newspapers and envelopes.

'Doddern Hack Kinney,' he panted. 'Stuck the mail in a corner. Never mentioned it. Two for you, sent over from Alamos on a happen-chance, I reckon. Hope yours are better than mine. I get a doddern sight more bills and circulars than I do greenbacks.'

'Thanks,' Ware grunted, without interest.

He took the envelopes, but continued to stare across the low buildings opposite, at the green ribbon of *bosque* through which the wide, shallow River twisted like a great yellow snake. Clem Tooley rustled his papers in the great chair, muttered over them, at last dropped all to the floor.

'Our friend Bar Nothing drew three letters,' he said. 'You could smell any of 'em for fifty yards against a wind. One had a big violet wax heart on the back— that was the one from Kerrville. He opened 'em all at the same time and when I came up he was reading all of 'em at once. A great Bar Nothing!'

'Yeh, he probably owns the right system. Scatters his fond feelings around among so many that, when he loses one or two, the jolt's not so bad.'

'No . . . One girl could never jolt him the way it would a boy with your disposition,' Tooley said quietly. 'Oh, it's no secret, Steve. Not to me. You've got a fine poker face and, doubtless, most people can't read your mind through it. But fat old Clem Tooley is a long way from being most people.'

Ware stared sourly at him without answering.

'I can guess how you feel,' Tooley went on slowly. 'Bar Nothing spoke of the way you and Georgette clawed at each other; and I've seen a thing or two on my own. Now, you're sticking in Piedra to keep from seeing her. Because you're wondering what you'd say to her if you did meet her.'

'Why, I killed her uncle! Eagan would have hit his lick if I hadn't been there; Capen would have had to skip, but only for the time being, likely. Clever, nervy as he was, if I hadn't been down-cellar to trip him, he and Carlos would be off somewhere now, rigging a defense against the law. I happened to be the only one of our side who knew certain things.'

'Right! It would have been a sort of blind blow if you hadn't known and been down there.'

'So I'm the one who really snubbed him. Now, she may not have thought a lot of him. But still he was her uncle; her blood. No matter how many kinds of cold-blooded killer he was, a girl——'

He shrugged and lifted one of the letters from his lap. The envelope was blank as to return address, but he knew Durell's writing. The half-sheet of paper had but one line upon it: 'Expected report by wire before this.'

He laughed and read the message aloud.

'Well, he'll feel better when Hack gets my wire off. And who else? Verde . . . Must be from Dave Loren. Probably a hurrah about my trailing. Well, he'll have crow for dinner when he gets my wire!'

He took out the folded sheets, wondering a little at the number of them, read the first paragraph with deepening frown, then re-read:

Dear Mister Steve: I canot write so famillar now as once acount of Lige Fyebacks will has been found and tally made of his proppirtie he left to you acount of he didden have kinnfolkes. Like the morgidje on Chick Graves G-Bar and other outfitts and bank stock and monnie and the store and thinges. Now Friend Mister Steve I hoap you will not looke down on olde friends acount you are riche——

He shook his head bewilderedly and held out the letter.

'Here! Read this, will you? I—I don't trust my eyes!'

'Why,' Tooley told him, after a minute or two of deliberate reading, 'it's plain enough—even in the Loren tongue! Evidently Fyeback thought a lot of you. He had no kin, so he made you his heir, except for a few small bequests to friends. Made you executor without bond—hmm! that'll save a few dollars . . . I'd take it that you're a rich young man, Steve!'

'The G-Bar,' Ware said softly. 'The G-Bar . . . From the time I was a button-cowboy, I thought of that outfit as absolutely what a cow-spread ought to be. Nothing I've seen since has changed my opinion! Old Chick built it up; left it to young Chick all clear. But Chick never was a manager, a cowman. He's lost it. I'll buy his remnant from him, instead of foreclosing . . . I—I——'

He sat staring blindly at the *bosque* for minutes. Without facing Tooley, he said:

'Last night, I asked myself what even a captain in the Rangers could offer a girl who'd been used to everything she wanted or could want. Now——'

'I wish I could say something to help.' Tooley groaned. 'I do that, Steve! I know what you're thinking now. But—suppose you hoolihaned her into marrying you and going off to live on the G-Bar. You youngsters think that running to a preacher is all there is to marriage. But there's years and years after that. Time to think about all kinds of things. Time for her to remember that her uncle's name is that of the scaliest, slimiest kind of snake. And how you killed him—for, as you said, you did practically kill him. And how she's married to you and you know she's a Capen—Steve, if you were my own son, I'd have to say: "Forget it! Forget her!"'

'Forget?' Ware said harshly. 'You could tell me not to do it. But it's no use telling me to forget. That's one of the things I can't do. No matter where I go, or what I do.'

He got up and went to the far end of the veranda, rolling a cigarette, lighting it blindly, looking out over the yellow range beyond Piedra. There was nothing to keep him here. He would get Bar Nothing and head for Los Alamos; resign from there; go back to Verde——

He turned, to see Georgette's bare, dark head lifting to the veranda level. She looked at him, then at Tooley. He drew a long breath. Sight of her stopped him short. What would she say? Something about her white, set face told him that she knew. He made himself go toward her.

'I heard all about it, on the road from Stonewall,' she said evenly. 'One of the Lightning Rod boys who got away met me. He was hunting a climate better suited to his clothes, he said. But he stopped to give me the general outline——'

'But, doubtless, you didn't hear it exactly the way it was,' Tooley interrupted quickly. 'If you'll let me sort of fill in——'

'Bar Nothing just filled in the outline. I think I know all that I need to know, now.'

'I'm sorry!' Ware said miserably. 'Sorry for you, that is. If there'd been any way to do it, to save you trouble, or knowing, I'd have been glad, Georgette.'

'Don't be sorry for me! You don't know certain things. Only Jimmy Quagson and I know—now. Capen knew. So did Black Alec Rawles. I only came to know on the night you were at the house. I saw Black Alec going into the library with Capen and I listened at a crack in a linen closet that is—was—against the library wall. For I'd suspected a good deal, for months. I wanted to know what business Capen had with a man like Black Alec. I

heard them talking and after a while I slipped away and
sent for Jimmy Quagson. He took me to Stonewall and
helped me. Then I came back, and if you hadn't blasted
that horrible place, I would have done it just as thoroughly! I would have ended Capen.'

She looked at Wáre; lifted her chin.

'Do you know who I am? Don't say "Georgette Capen," for that isn't so. Thank God! it never has been
so! I am Adrienne Marron. When I was a baby, my
father and Pierre Lebeaux were partners in a Louisiana
firm, buying cotton. Lebeaux embezzled the money of
the partnership and thousands upon thousands of
clients' money. My father was ruined. He committed
suicide, though no fault was ever attached to him. My
mother died. Lebeaux was arrested. Black Alec was in
the same jail. They killed a jailer and got away. Lebeaux
hated my father's people. He kidnaped me to hurt them.
He changed his name to Capen and—you know his record here. Jimmy and I got the Louisiana end through
a college-mate of his in Baton Rouge, by wire.'

They stared at her, Ware frowning uncertainly. She
lifted a shoulder, let it sag, moved to the chair beside
Tooley.

'Black Alec seems to have recognized his old jail-mate
on the street in San Antonio some time back. He used
the Open A for a hiding-place after that. But they must
have worked together, too. I—I heard all about the Ribauts. Black Alec was demanding a larger share of their
loot. He threatened Capen with exposure to the Louisiana authorities.'

Tooley got up, nodding like a genial Buddha, flute in
hand.

'That's certainly fine! Well, I have got things to do
inside. I'm still after that run in *Pinafore*, Steve.'

He played the run with eyes half-closed, lowered the
flute, and stared as at something strange.

'Why—why, it came right! Just goes to show, Steve,
how if you hang and you rattle, things do come right!'

Ware looked down at the girl, when Tooley had waddled out of sight.

'Quagson is my notion of a fine man,' he said slowly.

'Few better,' she agreed. 'I'm very fond of him. He's even fonder of me. So'—she looked up at him—'it would be a shame to hurt him, unless you're really serious in your intentions . . .'

'Serious! I——'

'I can't cook and I'm certainly not fat'—she looked down at her slimness very admiringly—'and I can't think of any other qualifications I own on that list you have. Except—oh, except that I don't know of any other man in all the world——'

'You *diablito*!' Ware said very softly, from the arm of the chair, to the dark head against him. 'You knew I was just whistling past the graveyard; and that you just had to crook your finger . . . You knew it, and I knew it!'

'Hoped it, anyway! And, now, if you don't mind, I'll cry—just to prove it!'

Eugene Cunningham grew up a Texan in Dallas and Fort Worth. He enlisted in the U.S. Navy in 1914 serving in the Mexican campaign and then the Great War until his discharge in 1919. He found work as a newspaper and magazine correspondent and toured Central America. He married Mary Emilstein in 1921 and they had two daughters, Mary Carolyn and Jean, and a son, Cleve. Although Cunningham's early fiction was preoccupied with the U.S. Navy and Central America, by the mid 1920s he came to be widely loved and recognized for his authentic Western stories which were showcased in *The Frontier* and *Lariat Story Magazine*. In fact, many of the serials he wrote for *Lariat* were later expanded to book-lengths when he joined the Houghton Mifflin stable of Western writers which included such luminaries as William MacLeod Raine and Eugene Manlove Rhodes. His history of gunfighters—which he titled *Triggernometry*—has never been out of print and remains a staple book on the subject. Often his novels involve Texas Rangers as protagonists and among his most successful series of fictional adventures, yet to be collected into book form, are his tales of Ware's Kid and Bar-Nuthin' Red Ames, and ex-Ranger Shoutin' Shelley Raines. Among his most notable books are *Diamond River Man*, a re-telling of Billy the Kid's part in the Lincoln County War, *Red Range* (which in its Pocket Books edition sold over a million copies), and his final novel, *Riding Gun*. Western historian W.H. Hutchinson once described Cunningham as "as fine a lapidary as ever polished an action Western for the market place." At his best he wrote of a terrain in which he had grown up and in which he had lived much of his life, and it provides his fiction with a vital center that has often proven elusive to authors who tried to write Western fiction without that life experience behind them. Yet, as Joseph Henry Jackson wrote of him, "everywhere he went, he looked at life in terms of action, drama, romance, and danger. When you get a man who knows what men are like, what makes a story and how to write it, then you have the ideal writer in the Western field. Cunningham is precisely that."